PRAISE FOR *THE BREADMAKER'S CARNIVAL*

'It is impossible to describe this novel in a few words. Read it and marvel, and give thanks that such a novel can come out of Australia.' —Dorothy Hewett

ndsay's first novel [*The Breadmaker's Carnival*] is a first-class, rounded book … an irreligious, ribald and rollicking tale. owsers beware! Read this and you might suffer a surfeit of smiling.' —Neil James, *Sydney Morning Herald*

rare bird among first novels — a mature adult entertainment ened by verbal wit, bawdy narration and a profound sense of the b. rre codes that unify small communities. Lindsay has contrived what few of his contemporaries can bring off — funny sex scenes.' —Michael Sharkey, *The Australian*

'Like the goods cooked at La Tarantula, the bakery at the centre of the town's madness, *The Breadmaker's Carnival* is fresh and irresistible — Must-Read of the Month.' —*Elle*

'Drips off the page like honey from a spoon … A stunning debut. Few writers can use language with Lindsay's redolence and precision.' —Christopher Bantick, *The Canberra Times*

'A rumbustious, Rabelaisian extravaganza … which resonates powerfully, both symbolically and satirically, with modern Australian concerns … the reader can only glory in Lindsay's intoxicating way with words.' —Katherine England, *Australian Book Review*

'*The Breadmaker's Carnival* is a gorgeously theatrical experience, a feast for the eyes and an assured debut for Lindsay.' —Thuy On, *The Age*

'A surreal soap opera. The collective sexual tension and confusion builds a critical mass … The result is an orgy of saturnalian ferocity … startling, extraordinarily disquieting.' —*Publishers Weekly US*

THE SLAPPING MAN

ANDREW LINDSAY

ALLEN&UNWIN

First published in 2003

This project has been assisted by the Commonwealth
Government through the Australia Council, its art
funding and advisory board.

Allen & Unwin
83 Alexander Street
Crows Nest NSW 2065
Australia
Phone: (61 2) 8425 0100
Fax: (61 2) 9906 2218
Email: info@allenandunwin.com
Web: www.allenandunwin.com

National Library of Australia
Cataloguing-in-Publication entry:

Lindsay, Andrew, 1955–.
    The slapping man.

    ISBN 1 74114 032 3.

    I. Title.

A823.3

Set in 12/14.5 pt Bembo by Asset Typesetting Pty Ltd
Printed by Griffin Press, South Australia

10 9 8 7 6 5 4 3 2 1

5078448

For anyone who ever felt like a slapping man ...

PART ONE:

WELCOME TO SALVATION

HIS CROWNING MOMENT

His jawbone is a relic that confirms his unique stature. When he was born that mighty jaw had been the first thing to emerge, and the midwife wondered if this was not some terrible misfit now crowning in the vulva. She'd once delivered a head with no body, and feared she was about to repeat the experience. Cursing herself for this morbid speculation she grabbed him then and pulled him free of his mother. To the midwife's relief Ernie had his legs and hips; his torso was quite functional, if somewhat shrivelled, as if his jawbone had consumed the nutrients intended for the entire corpus. The midwife thought he looked like a gummy shark as he flapped and floundered on the table.

His little eyes staring out like two small caves set above a massive cliff of bone. Most newborn babes are ugly, but the little tyke of Ernie seemed to have set a new precedent, and the midwife hoped there would not be many more pop out looking like him.

Some people said his mother had copulated with a pit bull terrier and this was the secret truth of Ernie's striking physiognomy.

Irene never cared for the story about herself and the dog. She knew the world was full of disgusting people, and the stories that spread about her purported canine cavortings only confirmed her worst intimations. Some nights Irene and Ernie's dad, The Burner, clambered through the family trees, searching for a jawbone that might serve as a precedent for their prodigal boy, but they always came back from their searches empty-handed. There were big noses, big front teeth, huge appetites for the perverse, but there was nothing like that jawbone of their boy. The lad was a one-off, freakish, if not a freak.

There were those who took a less charitable view than The Burner and Irene. They said the lad was a freak when he was born, lived a freakish life, and died a freakish death.

Irene found it difficult to breastfeed her child: the power of his jaw meant that at times he seemed about to bite her nipple off, and given the strength of his mandible, she could not pull the nipple from his mouth. Watching with a curious mix of intrigue and abhorrence as she tried to pull him from the teat, her breast distending to an unusual length. Relieved he never bit her nipples off, while never doubting he had the strength to do so. Unable to dissuade him from grinding stones between his jaws, she briefly tried to muzzle him when he played in the garden, before abandoning the muzzle. It made him seem too doggy. Resigning herself to the grey gravelled stools he passed.

One night Irene and The Burner were sitting by the fire. Irene was breastfeeding little Ernie, staring at the flames, losing herself in the glowing coals, only half aware of the intense pressure her babe exerted on her nipple. Glad he refrained from chewing the already chafy skin. She could hear The Burner snoring quietly, closed her eyes, and wondered if she too were about to doze. Unsure whether she was delighted or ashamed to discover what she could only term a sexual pleasure then, as her bub sucked her dug. Blushing with confusion as she wondered if she was committing some gross act or discovering a novel aspect of motherhood. Deciding to postpone her moral investigations, she gave herself to pleasure then, and her confusion only heightened the power of the orgasm that slowly overtook her. When she opened her eyes she was appalled to find The Burner staring at her, eyes wide, mouth open. Relieved when the man smiled shyly, before they both started laughing. The sound of the baby crying did nothing to lessen the easy intimacy inspired by the unprecedented situation.

'Is that one of the secret codes of motherhood?'

'If it is, it's one that's been well kept. Are you jealous?'

No one, not Ernie, nor his parents, ever suspected his jaw might be so strong that in later life it would be the foundation stone of his prosperity and survival. Though Irene had been intrigued to see her child fall flat on his face, when he first tried to walk, and land on that jaw, which supported him like an ungainly fulcrum. He did not cry out, did not register any pain. It seemed that he felt none. Irene was surprised, but did not glean any intimation of a possible vocation. The Slapping Man was among them, but his time had not yet come, and so he remained unrecognised. How could his mother recognise a gift for which there is no precedent? A child sits at a piano and plays with a virtuosity beyond its years — easy then to say, 'This child is gifted!' But if the child has a gift that is unique, who's to blame if they fail to recognise it?

When he was young he was sure he was deformed. There

was too much jaw, and not enough of the rest of his face to accommodate the remaining features. It made him shy, and when in public he always hoped to see someone who was at least as ugly as he was. Wanting some consolation. The more his mother tried to bolster his confidence the uglier he felt. Convinced he was the ugliest of an ugly lot.

It was a shock to see him with the prow of that jawbone sticking out. It was no child's jaw; it was as if his jawbone had been born adult and was waiting for the rest of his body to catch up.

Was he really a bad omen? He'd heard it said his face was that of a man who'd bring a curse onto the town. There were some who believed it would be best to have him killed before the curse could form, others claimed that killing him would be the sure thing to bring the curse to life. And so he found himself oddly tolerated, if not loved or quite accepted. There were some who were kind to him, though when people spoke to him their vision locked onto the bony mandible, unable or unwilling to look him in the eye.

Irene grew exasperated by her child's conviction that he was ugly. She only hit him once, though that single slap was enough to confirm, in his own mind, that he was on an irredeemable path, and his ungainliness would remain an incontestable fact of whatever life was to be his. Irene hadn't meant to hit him, had lost her temper and slapped him on the jaw. She didn't think she'd hit him all that hard, and was surprised to notice the next day that she'd sustained deep bruises on her palm.

When he grew older that stunning jaw gave Ernie's face an extraordinary definition. People expected him to be headstrong, or at least decisive. His jaw suggested that he was a natural leader. They grew angry when he disappointed them in this regard.

How could a man with such a decisive jaw be so timid and indecisive? He was suspected of playing dumb, hiding his real abilities, when the truth was simpler: the essence of his gift had not revealed itself to him, and so he blundered on like all the rest, his confusions and his certainties blended in a porridge he called his life. He wondered sometimes if his primary gift was for making other people angry.

Ernie never grew to be a tall man. His jaw usurping the vital stuff his other bones had needed, exalting its own stature at the expense of his clavicles, thorax, thighbones and the like. Though his male member had not suffered, as if it alone could provide a necessary balance to that mighty jaw, and so he jutted out on the horizontal and vertical planes, and achieved a curious equilibrium.

KNOWLEDGE POINT

Ernie had not wanted to know the cruder details of his conception, his mother's need to tell him greater than his need to listen. Yet once she had begun he did not want to silence her. She had been drinking, and it fuelled what seemed to him an alarming honesty.

'Your father and I were standing by the bay, he was teasing me about my bottom and gave it a little slap. He must have noticed my ambivalence, because he gave me a second slap, much firmer. I was surprised by the sound it made, and the way it made my blood go round in circles. A delicious moment then, neither of us talking, just looking at each other, feeling some barrier between us had dropped away. More than the slaps I think it was that intimacy which made us so dreadfully aroused.

KNOWLEDGE POINT

'We'd been bathing naked, not far from Knowledge Point, the little cove untouched by currents. The pebble beach. You know the one, we've been there on your birthday. Your father was standing with his back to the water, I had a lovely view over his shoulder, and was thinking I'd rename it Carnal Knowledge Point. It made me laugh, and your father asked me what's funny. When I told him, he said I was a filthy little slut; I didn't mind at all, and said if that were true he'd better slap my arse again. He obliged. It made a lovely cracking sound. We were embracing, with the pebbles underfoot, they hurt a little bit, yet I didn't mind that either.

'I slapped him back this time, and felt his hipbone bump against me. I hit him harder than I meant, and didn't get that lovely cracking sound, though I liked the feeling as he bumped against my pubic bone; I tried again, and got it right that time. The lovely buffet on my bone; my hand was stinging, so was his arse, I'm sure, that one slap sounding like a shot. The pair of us feeling a dreadful agitation. I could feel his heart and mine both throbbing as we held each other, and the quickened sounds of breathing, though we were trying to stay calm. And it wasn't just my heart that I felt throbbing as the blood pulsed in my body. The pair of us wrestling with some small confusion, and I could feel him nudging.

'Not wanting to make a move, just holding each other. Listening to the water slapping on the rocks, again and again that slappy sound. Thinking this was how the water made love to the rocks, your father like a rock, that stubbornness in him. It made me want to slap his arse again, and I did, and I got him in me and slapped again, loving the buffet and the audacity. He slapped me back, the funny dance we made like clockwork, taking turns, the slapping of the waves merging with the slaps we now exchanged, as if we'd never needed rings, the slaps could consecrate our vows. A perfect moment, a harmony provoked by the discords of our slapping. Don't mind me talking, son, I never knew the manner of my birth or my conception, and felt a need to know. Perhaps it's bred in me a fault for saying things best left unsaid. I'm not ashamed of the pleasure we took in making you. It was no chore, be sure of that.

'Each time I slapped your father's arse I pushed his cork a little deeper; his answering slaps achieved the same result. I started thinking of the way a musket would be rammed to pack the powder tight, it made me laugh again, I spanked the man so hard we both came standing up. Our arses red, hands hurting, bodies panting, and the slow fading of our thumpy hearts. The sweaty peace then as we held each other, listening to the gentle slapping of that water. Become aware of the sharp pains in our feet — the bruising in our soles lasted for weeks, we both had trouble walking. And sitting down.'

In later years Ernie wondered if his course was set that day, if he was always destined to become The Slapping Man, true to the circumstance of his conception. Stunned by the unblinking honesty of his mother. Yet gratified, too, though he could never look on Knowledge Point without feeling embarrassed, seeing his parents slapping on a beach as they enjoyed a point of knowledge so eminently carnal.

Wondering if his mother violated him with an excessive truth. Taking advantage, and overwhelming him. Where was the line between too much truth and not enough? Was too much truth another form of lying, or was truth a primary virtue, regardless of the consequence of knowledge?

WELCOME TO SALVATION

When people said, 'Welcome to Salvation' there was always an irony implicit in the greeting. The town famous for disasters, pestilence, flood, drought, bushfires, to say nothing of the dangerous proclivities of the inhabitants. Only the locals could suggest that the town was unfit for human habitation. To outsiders they'd defend their town quite fiercely. And only they could use the preferred nickname of the place, its fatal alias, their 'Ruination'.

The town had been founded in the wake of disaster, when the *Good Hope* ran onto the rocks during a terrible storm, falling foul of the treacherous waters of the bay as it rushed that narrow opening known as The Birth Canal. When the tides are changing the sandbars move around, and the currents drag any boat caught in their grip onto the rocks.

THE SLAPPING MAN

The *Good Hope* had been en route to the goldfields, and most of the ship's company perished, taken by the current the locals call The Octopus. Once it has you in its grip death is certain, for it pulls down into the depths, channelling through a maze of rocky caverns before returning to the surface by the reefs off Knowledge Point.

A few survivors were washed ashore or had successfully navigated one of the few lifeboats that did not sink from over-crowding. Calling dry land Salvation. They were stuck on a remote spur of land, hooking into a murderous stretch of coast-line. A bad start to any place, when the first act of settlement is the founding of the cemetery. Before they'd built a pub, a school, a house, even a barn. Burying the bodies that washed ashore, stripping their pockets of anything of use — a pocketknife, a rusted watch, a comb — such was their destitution. Rifling luggage for shaving mirrors and razors, the first inhabitants of Salvation got out in the Sunday best of the newly dead.

The ancestors ate too much of the wild salvia growing by the shores. The salvia made them wild in their thinking, an effect of the overdose of the herb. That's when the trouble began, right back then. Degenerating from Salvation to Wildbush in the first days of the town's life.

The next boat they saw was also a wreck. No survivors. The sinking of that boat triggered a profound despond. Realising only then the truth of their predicament — they weren't just stranded, they were beyond reach. The boat had carried a cargo of matches, and the phosphorous glowed at night on the bay. Crests of white water sparkling with blue. A man's body had been found glowing bluely on the sand. Did a voice really mutter, 'He looks good enough to eat'?

So many stories had spread about the founding mothers and fathers they'd merged into a terrible mix of fact and fable, and become part of the legend of the place. It seemed better this way, as the true stories are, as a rule, much more horrid than the fabrications. The first sausages in Salvation were, it's said, made from the flesh and gizzards of that drowned man, seasoned with wild salvia and little else. More sea sausage followed. The eaten were called many names, among them The String Of Sausages. Known commonly as SOS.

People still eat sausage, but it's a strange town where the simplest sights have the capacity to plunge one into a sullen remorse and maudlin rumination. Walking past the butcher's, seeing a string of sausages in the window, averting the eyes while the stomach juices churn. Thinking about sausage, and the destitution that can lead to cannibalism. And all the while a great doubt lingered: what were the limits of proper human conduct? Had the first inhabitants acted with propriety and keen morality, they would have perished. Some said it would have been better thus, that the entire history of the town was retribution for the crimes committed by those first settlers. A compelling point of view, which for some became an article of faith.

But others pondered further; if the first inhabitants of Salvation had broken all the rules, even if in desperation, then were any of them bound by any moral code?

It was a difficult life in a difficult town, when even a string of sausages could set off such a series of meditations and reflections on local history. Though history's never been their strong point, studded as it is with calamity, misgivings and remorse.

The first houses turned their backs on the bay, without a single window from which to glimpse the water. Not wanting to be reminded of the tragedy on which the town was founded. And yet they were reminded, every time they heard the slapping of the waves.

Many houses had been built by the muddy swamps, and were slowly sinking in the ooze, lacking any solid foundation. Or was the water rising, and in time the entire township would sink beneath the surface.

Some said a fascination with disaster drew people to the town.

The most beautiful sunsets in Salvation always followed days of the most foul weather. After the winds and torrents, and the usual disasters they provoked, the wind would stop and the water grow calm. An eerie green light would settle over the town in the late evening, the sky turning purple as the green grew faint and mottled; the waters of the bay reflecting these green and purple lights.

Anyone who saw those twilit skies on a good day fell in love with the town at once, knowing right then that they could never leave.

It was a young town, not confident in its identity. It's easy to put on airs when there's a plump cushion of history to sit upon. A lack of history breeds a terrible insecurity. Wanting to be the biggest town, or the most industrious, wanting anything that will make them feel unique. Anything to contradict the certainty that they are of some brood whose defining trait is its inferiority to all others. Becoming hot-tempered and cranky, too quick to give offence, or take it. To say nothing of the usual rumours of inbreeding that haunt such places. The greater the sense of inferiority, the more preposterous the claims made for the town. That there were no dangerous currents in the waters, when everybody knew the risk of drowning. That the first settlers had abandoned all ideas of private property, living in communal bliss after founding their utopia, when the truth was they were all as poor as beggars and the common aspiration was to accumulate a private pile of goods and chattels. Others boasted that you never heard a bad word said against anyone, when foul-mouthed gossip had replaced the need for intelligent conversation.

Insults are still among the commonest forms of expressing tenderness and affection. 'Come here, you fucking bitch!' might mean 'Would you care to join me, my dear?' A common reply to this delicate enquiry would be 'Say that again, you fucking prick, and I'll bite your balls off!' Meaning 'Why thank you, I'd be delighted!'

The name of the town kept changing. Salvation, Wildbush and Redemption tripping over one another's heels in quick succession, slowly leading us to Ruination, to say nothing of Humility and Consternation. The town's postal service had stopped trying to cope and revelled in a glory of misfunction, apathy and spreedom. For all that, letters were still delivered. The number 2 was enough to reach Salvation, though as the names of streets and the numbers of houses were always changing it was a difficult situation, and a postie's hell on earth.

The number 2 hung over the town's psyche. Everyone felt they were runners-up in life's race. The town of the second best, the also-rans. It was a terrible fate, to grow up in such a place. Defeat and despair were so prevalent they'd assumed the proportions of a local art form. The temper of the town ever present in that ancient greeting, which no one ever called a euphemism: Welcome to Ruination!

A PUB IS BORN

The Bluebottle, Prawn and Oyster was the town's odd coat of arms. A fitting emblem. The bluebottle bobs in the ocean at the mercy of the elements. The prawn scavenges leftovers from the sea floor. A raw prawn is a fool, and so is anyone who comes to live here. Discovering the oyster beds had liberated the first settlers from their diet of human sausage. The oyster is defenceless when taken from its rock; one always longs to find a pearl, though seldom does, and then the pearl is usually tiny and malformed. The town's secrets were locked away like the tender oyster in its shell. It was The Slapping Man who finally prised that oyster open.

The Bluebottle, Prawn and Oyster was also the name of the first hotel, established by the banks of the bay. It had been submerged by rising waters, dismantled and rebuilt a little further up the hill, a bayside pub of charm and beauty. They served good prawns and oysters, and those who swam off the beer garden were likely to be stung by bluebottles, so it was an apt name, and always had been.

John Gobblelard was the publican, and had assumed the role of de facto mayor. The pub was the epicentre of local life. His brother Les frying up fish and chips and boiling periwinkles in the kitchen. The Gobblelards had always been Salvation's first family, descended from a survivor of the wreck of the *Good Hope*.

The captain of the *Good Hope* died of alcoholic poisoning within the first month of the voyage, being unable to restrain himself in his personal ambition to drink the major portion of the ship's supply of rum. The more he drank the more bloated he became, his face and body quite distended from the ravages of his drinking binge. It was a pity that a cask of poisoned fish led to the demise of the first mate, second mate, navigator, in fact most of the crew. The most senior surviving crewman was the cook, Artemis Gobblelard, and so he took control of the ship. Glad enough to get out of the kitchen, scarcely believing that he did not need to peel another potato for the duration of the voyage. Unfortunately, he was better at navigating his way through a three-course meal than navigating the vessel, and the passengers quickly renamed the boat the *Hopeless*. The fact that so many of the crew had perished from eating fish was one of the reasons why the survivors initially abstained from eating seafood when they finally reached dry land.

Cook Gobblelard promoted himself to the rank of captain, though he was unwilling to give up his existing title of cook, and so became Captain Cook Gobblelard. Needless to say he survived the shipwreck and was the founder of the glutinous Gobblelard clan.

Captain Cook Artemis Gobblelard kept a barrel of rum under lock and key in his quarters. When the *Good Hope* ran onto the rocks in The Birth Canal, pounded by waves which seemed to come from all directions, Artemis had the good sense to abandon his post and run to his quarters. He could hear the boat's timbers crack and split, knew that his survival depended on acting quickly and selfishly, and that only the luck of the Gobblelards could save him. Rolling the barrel out of his room, levering it over the side then jumping into the foaming water, clinging to his keg of rum. Sure that God meant to spare him, and glad he'd had the foresight to drink half the contents so that it didn't sink and instead became an excellent lifebuoy. Artemis and his keg propelled by waves and currents, defying the strong grip of The Octopus. Never quite sure if it was a miracle or an indication of his genius when, after hours in the dark, he finally made it to the shore. He'd spent his hours of immersion humming and singing in an attempt to keep his spirits warm and to block out the horrid cries and pleas of the desperate and the drowning.

He was rolling the keg through knee-high surf when a wave caught him full force on the arse, he lost his balance, banged his head on the keg and staggered out of the water to collapse on the sand. When he came to, the first thing he saw was the keg, beached on the shoreline, and Artemis knew he was the happiest man alive. Rolling the keg up the beach in the predawn light, then sitting on it, after first availing himself of a liberal dose to warm his innards and fortify himself for the trials ahead. Watching as the wreckage of the boat washed ashore, along with other survivors, too stunned and shocked and glad they had survived to grieve right then.

Artemis was glad he had his knife strapped to his waist in its leather sheath, as people noticed him sitting on the keg. In the dawn light he looked like some chief sitting on his throne. As each new plaintiff came begging for a spot of rum, Captain Cook Artemis Gobblelard felt more potent and more kingly, asking the beggars, 'What have you got? Don't think I'll give my rum away! What's yours is mine if you want to warm your gizzards on the only rum to survive the wreck of the *Good Hope*!'

A PUB IS BORN

The man was a natural entrepreneur. Artemis quickly amassed a mound of possessions at a rate of exchange that was utterly favourable. The foundations of the Gobblelard clan were laid right then, and Artemis proved he was more than a match for anyone who cared to try and wrest the keg from his possession, or sneak upon him in the dark. Sleeping fitfully, back propped against the keg.

'Any bastard who tries to do me can rest assured they'll never sample rum again in their short life!'

Artemis was as good as his word, and denied rum to anyone who tried to sneak upon him or overpower him. He forbade anyone to approach within a radius of fifty yards in any direction, without his express permission, and even then only one at a time. There were pathetic scenes as people he'd barred from the rum grovelled in the distance. Artemis loved these moments, they seemed some recompense for the horrors of the wreck and the ensuing dismay as the survivors realised they were stranded. He also knew the advantages of developing a reputation for ruthlessness. The morning after the wreck a man had been washed ashore wrapped in the stingers of a bluebottle. The agony on his face so clear to see that drowning must have been a relief to the poor man. Artemis took credit for the death.

'The bastard tried to best me in the dark and steal my rum! Well, he isn't thirsty now.'

Later on he rolled the keg up the bank, to the site of what would become the first Bluebottle, Prawn and Oyster. The bluebottle had become his talisman.

Artemis was quite inventive and resourceful. For all his ruthlessness he was also enthusiastic, and visionary in his way. True, he put his own interests before all others, but he was not immune to seeing avenues of mutual advantage. Thus, when metal barrels and pipes started to appear around the shoreline, he used his rum to good advantage, ensuring that they fell into his hands. In similar vein, when some sacks of potatoes were found wedged between the rocks, Artemis used his personal charm, and the rum, coupled with threats of violence, to ensure that not only did he have enough potatoes to eat but he also had a stock of seed potatoes and a monopoly on the skins of the potatoes. People thought he'd lost his wits. What they did not know was that Artemis had foraged and bartered the materials to construct a crude still. The rough shed built to house it was the true progenitor of The Bluebottle, Prawn and Oyster, that bayside pub of charm and beauty. Once Artemis produced his first batch, and none died when they drank it, the future of the Gobblelard clan was secure.

The first wife of Artemis Gobblelard died in mysterious circumstances within a week of the wedding. It wasn't really a wedding, just a decision to share their bedding. His second wife was a more formidable candidate, the union prospered, and a small tribe of Gobblelards ripened in her womb. The first matriarch of Ruination, Henrietta was also the town's first barmaid. She preferred to call herself a nurse, which she had been. Jokingly calling the makeshift shack that housed the still The Dispensary, as she dispensed with all formality, making lewd jokes as the customers nursed their drinks, which she also dispensed. It didn't take long for the drinkers to dispense with the rule of polite conduct — brawls and loud arguments were de rigueur.

As the timbers of the *Good Hope* washed ashore, and other driftwood was accumulated, the Dispensary was dispensed with and The Bluebottle, Prawn and Oyster started to take form. The pub was a kind of history of the town, as rooms were added through need or prosperity, outbuildings became part of the main structure, verandahs stretched immodestly from what had been a pauper's hutch, and the unwieldy yet functional structure slowly evolved. When parts of the building became too derelict, their timbers rotted, there'd be another round of shouting and hammering in the yard, as the place grew, was renovated, demolished and rebuilt. A living palace of dereliction and unreason, The Bluebottle, Prawn and Oyster.

IN HIS ELEMENT

The history of the town was so littered with corpses and calumny that people did their best to shut it out of their minds. It was only during the annual remembrance of the first shipwreck that the inhabitants forced themselves to dwell on the disturbing foundations on which the town had been built. At any other time it was considered a gross breach of manners to press for details of anything connected to the past. Not only were people squeamish about discussing family history, it was even considered rude to ask people what they'd had for lunch, as if the town could only function in the present.

The habit of fasting for six days before each year's remembrance of the wreck was born of a simple fact: as the anniversary approached it became impossible to avoid the horrid visage of the town's poor history. Overwhelmed by so much unwanted knowledge, people lost their appetites, and their bellies shrank. As if for that one week a spirit of propriety briefly reigned, before itself being devoured by the usual rabble of daily life.

The six-day fast had evolved into a strict custom. To be seen eating, whether in public or in private, was to give gross offence to the entire population of the living and the dead. It was one of the few strictures imposed on the residents, and the only social convention that was universally upheld. When absolutely necessary one might nibble at a sausage, but that was all, and only in emergencies.

It was hard for the townsfolk to make peace with the fact that the survivors of the *Good Hope* had only survived by eating corpse meat. Everybody understood the desperation, suspecting they would do the same if the choice was imminent death by hunger. Easy to be repulsed by their actions when you had a belly full of fish from The Bluebottle, Prawn and Oyster. Quite another thing to be possessed by the delirium of hunger, and so convince yourself that the spirits of the dead now urged you on, preferring some small chance to be remembered rather than be forgotten for all time. The slow reading of the lists of all those who had been eaten was one feature of the annual Shipwreck Feast. It didn't necessarily improve one's appetite for the coming meal.

John Gobblelard swore he lived on beer and nothing else during that week, and he was not alone in that stern vocation. The hunger and alcohol fuelled a terrible depression, and to know you were of a dynasty founded on a diet of human meat only heightened the sense of guilt and remorse. No wonder people said to every stranger, 'Welcome to Ruination.'

The recalcitrant mob sitting on the beach, the beer making them weepy as they watched the re-enactment, some old boat going under. The ones who manned the boat leaping off, usually some murderers or other villains who were granted liberty if they made it to the shore. The Octopus always took a few.

Because the entire town was terrified by its history it was considered extreme bad luck to look over your shoulder. 'Over your shoulder, blood runs colder' was a common saying. A favourite prank of the cheeky was to call out to people from behind, and so trick them into looking back. The only way to fend off the bad luck was if your entire body followed suit, compelling you to walk back in the direction from which you'd come. As a boy Ernie had spent whole afternoons walking up the same small stretch of ground as drunken fishermen stood fore and aft, calling his name, trying to set a new record for the number of times he could be tricked into turning round.

To protect themselves from this common prank people cultivated an extreme rigidity in the neck and shoulders. It led to the adoption of a curious gait and posture that became a defining trait of the town's inhabitants: over time, as people walked with head and neck thrust out, the muscles stiffened and became locked in that position.

Neck pains, headaches and chronic spasms in the lumbar region were common ailments. It also meant that when sleeping, people usually required several pillows. One enterprising woman had manufactured a pillow of uncommon thickness and made her fortune. New arrivals were counselled to buy one as it would induce the requisite local posture in the shortest possible time. It meant you had to sleep on your back, in which pose the body is most inclined to dream. The dreams of the populace were, naturally enough, nightmarish. The effort of suppressing all thoughts of the past ensured that when asleep these troublesome thoughts had full rein of the sleeper's consciousness.

Insomnia was not just common, it was seen by many as a blessing, and three cups of strong black coffee was a typical bedtime drink. The lack of sleep made people cranky and unpredictable, yet this was preferred to the nightly parade of horrors their sleep ensnared. It may have been one reason why arguments and fighting were other common features of the town.

'No friendship without fighting!' was another local saying. Men picked fights with their closest companions to demonstrate their affection. There were recorded cases of bosom buddies killing each other through excessive expressions of such affection, and the phrase 'friend-death' had been coined to justify it.

Some children felt unwanted unless they were regularly beaten, and birthdays were often celebrated with a sound thrashing in public. If the children bit or scratched, people applauded, glad to see a happy family going at it.

No wonder then that in time The Slapping Man became a local icon. Nor that his willing labours were later seen to be a turning point in the poor fortunes of the town. While Ernie often felt out of his depth, as The Slapping Man he was clearly in his element.

THE VIRGIN WALL

The back wall of The Bluebottle, Prawn and Oyster was called The Virgin Wall. Built with virgin pine from the local forest. So many of the town's inhabitants had lost their virginity with their backs against that wall, or else studying it at close range. Les Gobblelard lost his cherry there and joked it should be called The Cherry Orchard, so much of the local fruit had been picked beside that virgin pine.

John Gobblelard had named The Virgin Wall himself, when the first stories of plucked cherries had begun to circulate, and it had been a masterstroke. The Virgin Wall exerted a fascination, as if it might be possessed of magical properties. The back bar filling up with thirsty customers, hoping that by leaning against the inside of The Virgin Wall they might find a partner willing to take the wall's true measure out the back. On a busy night you could feel the humping and vibrations as the couples went hard at it. It had a predictable effect on the amount of drinking inside, and after a few whiskies, beers or stouts the rate of eye contact seemed to escalate, the accidental bumpings into soft flesh against the bar, the keys dropped on the wooden floor, the answering bumps of feet and knees; and all the while John Gobblelard, lord of his domain, bellowing above the din, 'Drink Your Fill! We're not closing till the kegs are empty! What's that I hear? The Virgin Wall is singing! Don't Be Lonely, Don't Be Sad, Drink Your Fill And Then Be Had!' The Virgin Wall creaking with the ruction, stupid drunkards pounding with their fists, as if they might provoke The Virgin Wall to greater dereliction.

The sight of his customers quaffing booze filled John Gobblelard with delight. So did the sight of all the money in the till, its constant ringing, as if it was the biggest mouth in The Bluebottle, Prawn and Oyster. Its capacity unmatched by any of the mob. As every coin dropped into that mouth John Gobblelard felt he too had ingested another drop, slowly filling him, though like his till his appetite was boundless and his capacity without limit.

There were some problems with The Virgin Wall, although in the usual state of inebriation of those who laboured there, these problems weren't always apparent. The Virgin Wall had few secrets. Some people had even tried drilling holes so they could watch from the inside, a stupid scheme that didn't work: invariably if anything could be seen at all, it was just a piece of shirt or coat that obscured the view while firing the imagination. Some reputations had been made, and others shattered, as the not-so-secret life of The Virgin Wall spread its small tongues around the town. Just ask Jean Flinch. Not her real name, of course. She always flinched when people tried to kiss her on the lips. And so she became Flinch. Like any town there was always the danger that you might get to know each other far too well.

Jean Flinch had not let anybody kiss her on the lips since the death of Beau, her first love. She wasn't sure whether the lack of labial kissing had soured her, or the sourness had come from the dismay and grief she felt when Beau died. She wished they'd never found his body. Washed overboard by a freak wave, working on one of John Gobblelard's fishing boats. Sucked off by The Octopus, his body eaten by sea lice. They found his corpse on the rocks.

Jean loved Beau's lips. His lips were full where her own were rather thin. She thought his bottom lip a marvel, it was so plump. They could kiss for hours, she loved nothing more than the sensation as she sucked his plump lower lip into her mouth. It had a strange effect on Beau. When she sucked his lip into her mouth it immobilised him, making him feel so complete he lost all volition. Happy to remain in this simple rapture for hours, a curious habit of their lovemaking. His lips so often swollen from their kissing that they grew larger, which only made them more attractive to young Jean. Some days he swore they were too tender for kissing, and on those days Jean found a tenderness and sensitivity she hadn't known was hers. Running her tongue so delicately across those swollen, bruisy lips of Beau. He was not always sure if he was being kissed or could only feel the air upon his lips, provoked by the movement of her tongue and breathing. Lulling him utterly, and then the cunning bitch would drive her tongue right down his throat, her tongue was large and seemed to fill him. The first time he had gagged and she had muttered 'Sorry', but he'd insisted she try again.

Beau was stunned to find he'd mastered an art he didn't know existed, succeeding in holding her tongue in his throat, achieving a total relaxation of the glottis, and a subtlety of movement with his throat muscles. Gripping her tongue gently, not letting go. When he did this Jean felt a confusion of arousal that was truly blissful. It made her shudder with pleasure, and she shuddered all the more when she felt Beau shudder too. Marvelling that they could achieve such an extreme of stimulation while remaining fully clothed. When Beau needed to breathe he'd relax his throat just enough to bring some air in through his nose, then like a snorkel diver he'd go back down into himself, holding his air, tightening his throat and gripping her tongue once more. Drawing her tongue ever further out of her throat, sucking her into him.

It required a state of total relaxation and trust on both their parts, and it might have been Jean's undoing. Feeling drawn out of herself, giving herself fully to her young man. She liked this kissing more than the other kinds of sex she had explored. She liked it when she felt him entering, and yet she liked it even more when she slowly poked her tongue into his mouth and felt him suck her tongue down to his neck. Her tongue was her penis, and she was entering him. The giddy sighs she heard him utter, and the giddy thrills this brought.

She'd had to go and see his body at the morgue. Not wanting to, and yet unable to stay away. Telling herself if nothing else it would help with her grieving, the clear finality as she gazed upon the corpse. Pondering a difficult dilemma: should she kiss him on the lips? Would it help her make peace with his death? She did not kiss him on the lips. She had not thought he'd be so badly eaten, the sea lice had been unsparing and unconcerned that his body would be immune to any form of cosmetic restitution, post-mortem. The sea lice had eaten his lips. It wasn't just the lips they'd eaten, but it was the missing lips Jean noticed most. It was the reason why, when anyone tried to kiss her on the lips, she could do nothing but flinch. And so became Jean Flinch.

She felt that something else had been devoured by the sea lice when they ate her Beau. Having given herself utterly to her

young man, she felt sure she'd never have the strength to give
herself so utterly again. The only time she'd let a man kiss her
on the lips she'd been appalled to find that as his tongue slipped
into her mouth she could only think of sea lice. To her shame
and embarrassment she screamed and ran away, not daring to set
foot outside the house for a week, not knowing how she'd face
the man if she saw him again. Deciding then that she'd refrain
from kissing in the future, relieved to find that in this way she
could still find some satisfactions in her body.

'THINGS ALWAYS TURN OUT BADLY'

Ernie's father had never recovered from being bitten by a monkey. It had been Ernie's idea to visit the travelling circus, their small top erected behind The House of Pearls, ruffled by bay winds. The Burner had enjoyed goading the monkey. Ernie was surprised by his father's glee as The Burner baited the caged animal. A strange hatred.

'You filthy animal!'

The animal scratching its member, before becoming fascinated by the swelling of its arse. The Burner dropped his umbrella and bent to pick it up. Ernie thought later, He should never have turned his back. The monkey reaching through the bars, grabbing his father's coat, pulling the man to him. Fastening his strong jaws onto The Burner's head. There was a predictable commotion and the monkey had been shot before a startled crowd.

Ernie felt sorry for the monkey.

Something in his father's spirit had not revived, the shock of the encounter too great, perhaps. Ernie's mother had little sympathy for the wounded man. She took the monkey's side, feeling The Burner had provoked the creature. They did not speak for six months after the event. Irene made a show of demanding the monkey be buried in The Boneyard, and went to the funeral with flowers to place on its grave.

It was a sad, makeshift affair — no one knew the protocols for simian interment. Ernie was surprised to see how many people came to pay their last respects to that poor monkey. It was a distraction from the daily tedium, a free ticket to an unscheduled performance.

Ernie wept at the sight of the little red fez with golden tassels. The name Ruby embroidered in golden thread. The fez and a tiny red satin suit folded on the coffin.

The owner of the circus, the circus hands and performers turned out en masse. The Burner, bristling with shame and guilt and indignation, kept coughing during the eulogy, and being hissed at by the monkey's mourners.

The Boneman ran the cemetery, and was looking fidgety — he'd devoted his life to collecting the bones of living creatures, he'd wanted that monkey's skeleton and wasn't happy. The Boneman had fingered Ernie's jaw after the ceremony and winked as he muttered, 'Promise me this treasure if I survive you!' He had a collection of bones in his crude shack, of bird and beast, and some that looked distinctly human. Random collarbones and thigh bones that had washed up, unconnected and unknown. Ernie wasn't sure he wanted to feature in that collection.

At Irene's request Doctor Vronsky, the town's only Counsellor of Grief, was on hand in case the wake got out of control, which it did. The monkey's handler was inconsolable.

Doctor Vronsky prescribed neat whisky, and was relieved when the man finally collapsed.

The Burner's wound slowly healed, though his poisoned blood remained sluggish. He started spending more time indoors than out, often leaving the house only for the family's weekly fishing trip.

The monkey's bite confirmed something he'd always known. Life could not be trusted, or if it could, then it could only be trusted to fulfil one's most dire expectations.

Ernie wondered what lesson he might draw from the dwindling of his father following the monkey's bite, and had reduced it to this: that perhaps one was never safe, even when engaged in such simple pursuits as going to the circus. In later life he often felt perplexed by the fact that the most innocent undertakings so often harboured a hidden capacity for unintended villainy.

Ernie's father was afraid of mice and rats, and had earned his nickname from his habit of setting fire to an outdoor dunny, a barn, and sundry other structures, in his efforts to be rid of infestations of the beasts. One of these fires had destroyed an historic grove of trees that had once sheltered the first settlers. The flames raging out of control for three days. Thankfully there was no loss of life, though Ernie's dad had never lived down the shame of it. He had also been landed with a bill of damages that kept the family perpetually poor. It confirmed what had become his credo: 'Things Always Turn Out Badly!'

The Burner started trapping wild dogs, foxes and other furry creatures. He wanted their pelts, having set on the idea of restoring the family's fortunes by making fur coats and fur trousers. Strutting around town, the first man to take to the streets in a pair of fur pants in all weather. Fur coats and long pants in winter, fur shorts and singlets in the hotter months. He insisted that it gave excellent insulation against both hot and cold, and was perfect for the rainy climate of the town, being waterproof as well.

A fat neighbour claimed it was a ridiculous fashion, and most unsuited to the climate. The fat man was known as Skinny Roger, not because he was fat, but because of the reputed leanness of his penis.

Skinny Roger chose the hottest day of summer to demonstrate how preposterous was The Burner's claim that fur was suited to all weather. He was acting on a personal mandate, as it had been Ernie's mother, Irene, who had given him his unwanted nickname. It was generally conceded that Irene was in a position to assess the slim facts of the matter, as she had lived with Skinny Roger for six months, and there were plans to marry, before she moved two houses down the street and jilted him for Ernie's dad.

Skinny Roger hated his nickname, but such things spread as quickly as a dose of clap, and are as hard to shake. He had even circulated pictures of what he claimed was his own fat organ, but when Irene saw a copy she said, 'That organ might be fat, but it isn't Skinny!' No voice rose to contradict her.

On a good day in one of Salvation's many pubs Skinny would find himself invited yet again to compare his own fine specimen with the pictures he had circulated, would decline the offer and replace it with an invitation to step outside for a wee bare knuckle. Cursing his stupidity for ever circulating the wretched braggart's image of a fatter victual than he had.

It was Skinny Roger who first called Ernie's dad The Burner. He also started a rumour that The Burner's coats were infested with fleas, which was true. He hoped to strike another blow by walking around the town's perimeter clad in The Burner's feral furs, ending up at The Perseverance, a pub which stood at the top of the highest hill in Salvation, and therefore had the lowest prices. The publican could afford this enticement — a man needed three drinks just to get his breath back after that hike.

The Perseverance was so-called as a tribute to seven nuns who'd been on board the *Good Hope*.

To their alarm they were presented with a dilemma that lay outside their formal training. There were so few women survivors that the small community was faced with extinction. There was a growing body of opinion that the women should abandon their vows of chastity and assist in the difficult task of populating the barren ground which was now home. The nuns had undertaken a vigil, praying for guidance on the hill. A shark had washed onto the beach with a salmon in its mouth. When the shark's belly was slit open, seven sharklings were found huddled inside. This news was relayed to the nuns, in the midst of their vigil. It was taken as a sign. Principle was one thing, survival was another. They'd copulate and breed. It was better for life to persevere than die on the rock of principle.

On the hottest day of a month-long heatwave, the temperature in excess of forty degrees, Skinny Roger set off on his monstrous walk, wearing one of The Burner's dog-skin coats. To further prove his point he had decided he'd not stop to drink until he reached The Perseverance. The hill up to this fine locale was steep indeed, and Skinny Roger was exhausted. It was a painful thing to see him shrivelling and stumbling at the end, but he rebuffed all attempts to help him or persuade him to abandon his stupid plan. He collapsed halfway up the hill and died a painful death, the combination of heatstroke, dehydration, exhaustion and overheating of his vital organs leading to a kind of meltdown that coupled with a heart attack.

Skinny, being a big man, had required a special coat, and The Burner had been happy to oblige, thinking the publicity might be a boon — though as Skinny was scratching constantly at fleas, in this respect he may have erred. The Burner had needed four dog hides to make a coat that barely reached the fat man's hips. It's odd the way that people have so little respect for the dead. At the wake, held at The Perseverance, people joked about a Skinny Roger wrapped in a giant four skin. It seemed to suit the vulgar temper of the town.

Skinny Roger's death puzzled Ernie's dad. While he remained convinced of his personal truism, 'Things Always Turn Out Badly', for once he had to say he wasn't sure. He finally dismissed Skinny's demise as the exception that proved the rule.

HER TRANQUILLITY

Jean loved swimming in the bay, her broad shoulders bursting through the water, her brain and body throbbing. Feeling a joy that often eluded her on dry land. Her tranquillity merging with a sensation of vitality she often only knew while making love. One reason why, she knew, she found herself so often plunging into yet another carnal exploit. As if at such times she achieved a vitality she wished she could possess at all times.

Jean couldn't understand why so many people were frightened of the water and denied themselves one of the keenest pleasures of the town. Jean's delight in swimming was seen by many as just another of the girl's strange aberrations. Yet Jean knew that it was easy to avoid the dangerous currents, if you knew where to swim. Finding a liberty and peace, even a serenity, as she swam out from Knowledge Point, loving the strength she knew was hers.

Her mother had died when she was six and Jean's father had placed her in a convent. He did not think highly of the place but it seemed the best he could do. He'd been surprised one day to find her standing at the front door, in street clothes, carrying a small suitcase and a bag of fish and chips. She'd just been told to leave. When he asked, 'What did they get you on?', she replied, 'Excessive independence of mind and spirit.' He had no idea how to respond, but as they ate their fish and chips washed down with beer he felt a thrill of pride that he had such a daughter. She moved out of home six weeks later, into a small place near the bay she called her sanctuary. When she was low on money her father gave her some, and when she was truly desperate she ended up scraping fish for John Gobblelard, like so many others.

At the convent swimming had been banned, yet Jean had often snuck down to the bay at night, slipping out of her clothes, convinced that her personal divinity willed it thus. Saying her own small prayer of thanks before diving in, breaststroking through the kelp beds then settling into a firmer stroke and rhythm. In her own mind God was a keen swimmer.

She'd been swimming naked beneath a yellow moon when she'd first seen Beau, the young man cleaning and mending nets on the beach not far from where she'd left her clothes. She stayed in the water, hoping he would leave, yet he was intent on his work, calm and unhurried. Jean was shivering with cold when she finally decided to risk the young man's gaze, hoping the night would clothe her. After his initial shock at seeing her emerge from the water, Beau had the grace not to stare as she towelled herself dry and quickly dressed, shivering all the while. She watched him slyly as he rested briefly from his work, lit a cigarette and stared out at the bay.

He offered her a cigarette, which she declined. They exchanged few words, yet her shivers seemed eloquent enough.

He gathered twigs and driftwood and made a small fire on the pebbly beach. Jean, glad of this warmth, rubbing her arms and legs to spread the heat along her body. Shaking her wet hair like a dog, inadvertently covering Beau in a fine spray. They laughed then, their laughter somehow sealing a complicity and familiarity. They exchanged names.

'You look younger in your convent clothes than you did when you were naked.'

When Beau asked, without looking up from his work, 'Do your parents know you're out?', Jean laughed, and their eyes met, a simplicity in the contact which seemed free of any desire for ownership or dominion.

'My mother's dead, my father's either drunk or sleeping. If they find my bed is empty at the convent, I'll be dead meat in the morning.'

'Do you believe in God?'

'Only when I'm swimming. And you?'

He was about to answer when a fish broke the surface of the water, landed with a splash and disappeared. They'd both stayed silent then, lost in their reveries.

The fire burnt low. Beau's work completed, Jean brushed the sand from her feet before slipping on her socks and shoes. Her feet felt cramped within the leather. She waved once as she left. Turning back to survey the bay, the moon obscured by clouds, she could just make out the form of Beau scattering the remnant coals before covering them with sand and pebbles. The last sight she had of Beau that night was of the young man pissing on the buried coals, extinguishing the fire.

It was not the last of their nocturnal meetings by the bay. She'd slipped back to her empty bed one night to find a small committee waiting to escort her to the main office for a brief interrogation. When they asked her, 'Do you believe in God?', she answered, 'Only when I'm swimming.' She knew it was less than half the truth, yet was happy to see the consternation appearing on the faces of her questioners. She spent the night locked in a small room with a narrow bed and in the morning packed her things. Both glad and sad that she was leaving. Wondering how her father would respond when she got home, she was amazed to hear him say, 'I never thought you'd stay so long.'

LAST MAN

Les Gobblelard was the last person to see Beau alive.

Beau had been his closest friend, and Les often felt that he, not Beau, should have been the one washed overboard. They'd been hauling in craypots; Beau had shouldered him out of the way and Les had lost grip of the rope, sprawling backwards as a freak wave hit the boat, and Beau was gone. The boat had circled back, yet there was no sign of Beau. Les never recovered from the shock, and became withdrawn, happy from then to take shelter in the kitchen, preferring to spend his life in there, only setting foot inside the pub when necessary. Convinced the bar was full of disapproving glances, that Beau's death had been his fault, and the death of Les would have been more welcome.

Wondering if his real name was Less, because his life was worth less than Beau's.

Les was stunned by his own cowardice, feeling he had failed in some fundamental task at the moment of crisis. Where he'd needed a calm head he had panicked, and to his unending shame had thrown Beau a lifeline that was not tied to the boat. Now even the sight of a rope filled Les with consternation. Never daring to set out in the boats again. Even staring at the bay made him seasick.

Glad he had a small room at the back of the pub with no sight of the water, sleeping with cloth stuffed in his ears to try and block the sound of constant surging that ruined his sleep. Hearing Beau calling his name, and then no sound but the motor of the boat, the muted cries of frantic men, and the surging waters.

Jean was shocked by Beau's death. It filled her with a terrible sense of her own mortality. If her young man could be taken in his prime, before he'd had the chance to live, how could she know with certainty that she'd not be dead within the week? The prospect filled her with alarm, and she abandoned herself to an impossible ploy, trying to live each day as fully as she could. Never sleeping for more than a few hours, as if she might stuff a single day with the intensity of a week, and a week with the business of a month. After such a week she'd be exhausted, and sleep for days, wandering the house drunk with fatigue. Rousing herself, feeling betrayed by a body that demanded sleep when she wanted action, vitality, incident and purpose.

Seeing in her mind's eye the sweet life she might have known with Beau.

Dwelling on this idyll with such intensity it seemed to gain reality for her; when she made food she always cooked for two, and made a point of eating both meals rather than be confronted by his absence yet again as the uneaten morsels defied her fantasies. Doing the dishes for them both, turning down the bed, preparing for another blissful night in the arms of her young man. Yet the reality always confounded her illusions, and the wide arms of the empty bed appalled her. She didn't want to go to bed alone, would busy herself sweeping a floor she'd already swept, and when that failed to placate the dread of feeling bereft and stranded she'd take a walk down to the bay, knowing it would not be long before she headed to the pub for a single nightcap, which became two, then three. After the third drink she felt a relaxation open in her, and a crazy glee, as if she had become another, or else perhaps had found a way back to herself. She'd meet the gazes then of those who took her fancy, lowering her eyes while smiling to herself, accepting the offers of fresh drinks, until in a drunken haze she'd feel the vital urging of her body willing her to cast aside her grief and doubt and find her way back to The Virgin Wall.

She never took men home, never let them into her bed. Clenching her teeth as she came, wanting it to hurt as she fucked and was fucked, wanting that little bit of annihilation, though not too much, just enough to feel some minor agony had been inflicted and, if she scratched or bit, she felt the ledger was kept even.

She had a reputation for wildness, an excessive vigour, and the risk of deep bruising and scratches that broke the skin only made her more attractive to some men.

A young woman whose first love died, she embarked on a sexual spree propelled by grief and desire. A spiritual child who had lost her sense of the sacred, wondering if she could refind it through sexual contact: was this not a divine exaltation?

Finding herself caught between the immediate exhilaration she found when making love to some stranger, and the disgust that invariably caught up with her not long after. Some nights she'd go and find another man by The Virgin Wall, convinced that she might finally dispel her grief and self-disgust if she had an orgasm of sufficient intensity, as if it might clear her mental slates and leave her free to start again. Though she never succeeded in this, only adding to her sense of self-disgust and disappointment with each new conquest. Using her body as a tool, asking herself at times if in going through so many other men she was really on a quest to find Beau, or at least some part of him: as if she could reconstruct Beau by taking parts of all the other men she'd known — a hipbone here, a certain nuance in the eye there — trying to salvage the young man who'd become perfect in her mind with the passage of time. Though none of them had his lips, and the thought of kissing was still enough to make her gag.

It was a pity that in Jean's mind Beau slowly became a perfect man, as if her imagination and memory were conspiring to create a man the like of which the town had never seen — a man who was handsome, articulate, had a sense of humour, was never prone to fits of remorse, vanity or blind stupidity.

And so Jean slowly perfected Beau in her mind's eye, hoping she might find some counterweight to the outright revulsion she had felt when she'd last laid eyes on him.

SOMETHING FISHY

Ernie's parents had drowned in a boating accident. Out fishing on a Sunday, a ritual they enacted in all weather. After the roasted meats the three of them — Ernie, The Burner and Irene — would haul their metal dinghy down to the bay on a clumsy trolley with squeaky wheels. Puffing as they hauled the inexact machine, there was always a rank smell that came with them. Their furs were damp with sweat and salt water, and stank, to say nothing of the rotting worms and prawns that lodged in the seam of the keel, no matter how diligently they scrubbed.

To Ernie's mortification, a crowd always gathered to watch this comic family labour. The family fishing trip had become a regular part of the Sunday entertainment for those who strolled and lingered by the bay. Standing at a distance, laughing at the family as they lumbered down the steps to the sandy beach and dragged the dinghy into shallow waters.

The three spent hours sitting in the boat, casting handlines for bream and leatherjacket. Eating the catch when they got home after dark, feeding on homemade chips and bread if the catch was poor.

'Better for the soul than going to church,' Ernie's father would announce before they nibbled at the fish. 'Look what they did to that poor man. Nailed to a cross! Things always turn out badly. How's the bream?' Setting to it then, washing their throats with beer, always a stack of sliced bread handy in case they started choking on the bones.

The Burner was not blessed with excessive common sense, a trait he shared with Ernie. His stockpiles of feral furs attracted hordes of rats. Given his fear of the creatures, he should have chosen some other metier in his attempt to salvage the family's fortunes. Instead he waited until the infestation was complete, dispatched Ernie to clear the pelts out, then burnt the barn or shed or other place of infestation.

On the day his parents died Ernie had been shifting The Burner's furs out of a shed before the next round of burning, and was running late. His parents lugged the boat without him, and rowed the little boat offshore. Keeping one eye on the fish and another on the shore, waiting to catch sight of Ernie.

It was a grey day in late autumn. The water cold, the shoreline empty and no other boats in sight. Irene had hooked a large bream; in their excitement she and The Burner became tangled in the lines and tipped the boat.

Ernie sometimes wondered whether he had a gift for lateness. Often late for meals, and a late arrival in his parents' lives — on the day they died they were in their mid-sixties, while he was still in his late teens. The Burner and Irene were not equal to the frigid waters. Their muscles froze as they discovered an unpleasant truth: the old dinghy could no longer float when it capsized. It filled with water and sank. The fur coats were no substitute for life jackets and, soaked with water, weighed them down like furry anchors.

Ernie arrived in time to see, in the distance, the boat going under, and the frantic motions of his ma and pa grappling with each other. He stood, spellbound, on the shore as the hypothermia and the fur coats completed what his parents' panic had begun. And so it was that Ernie, late as he was, arrived just in time to see the final exhalation of his parents who'd been on time but were themselves now late.

Ernie heard his father screaming but had trouble hearing all the words. Only the last word reached him clearly, though he could guess the rest. 'Theeaawwwaaayurrooooww badly.' How could he argue with that? His father's truism proved right at the very end, and Ernie found a morsel of peace in that.

Standing on the shoreline, trying to speak, waving his arms, pointing at the water. Those who let their eyes travel to where he pointed saw nothing but the bay.

'My ma and da have drowned! We ate the fish, now the fish are eating them!'

Yet no one understood the boy, or proffered aid. Ernie had no idea what to do, and so did nothing. Standing, staring at the water where he'd last seen his parents. Perhaps they'd wash ashore? There were no boats within sight, and the Sunday promenaders had all gone home. And still Ernie stood there, as if he expected that at any moment The Burner and Irene would resurface, the whole display some vaunted Sunday prank. Standing, waiting, finally become aware that he was utterly alone. Disconsolate.

STILL LIFE WITH OCTOPUS AND GROPER

Ernie felt quite lost. He wandered up to The Bluebottle, Prawn and Oyster, he wasn't sure what else to do, and suspected there was nothing to be done. John Gobblelard was not good at consolation, and after hearing Ernie's tale he muttered, 'Yes, yes, I'm sure, things always turn out badly.' There was an awkward pause before he came to his senses and poured the boy a drink. 'Welcome to the world, boy. It's a horrid place. To think our common destiny is to be orphaned! Our mothers and fathers, they all die and we are left alone. What's to become of us? It's a maudlin thing, thank God for drink, and the ease with which one sleeps or else just passes out when you've stretched your gullet far enough. The ones who sleep the soundest are those who've got the longest necks!'

There were few rules and regulations in the town. There was certainly no minimum age for drinking. It was suggested that if you could see over the bar you were old enough to drink, though the truth was simpler: the only requirement was that you could attract John Gobblelard's attention. He was keen-eyed, and if you needed to stand on a box to get your nose over the bar and put your hand up, a small box could be found. There'd never been a case where service was refused. The sight of ten-year-old drunkards was not the prettiest in Salvation, though if anything the dereliction of their elders was more profound. The youngsters were not adept at holding liquor, but as John Gobblelard pointed out, 'You have to start somewhere!' A town of strange virtues, though its virtues were not unique.

Neither was death by drowning. In a good year up to half the town's deaths occurred in the bay. It was considered a form of natural death. People seemed fond of falling out of boats, or swimming in shallow waters only to find themselves caught in the tentacles of The Octopus. The current had a reputation for unpredictability, toddlers under the careful eyes of mum and dad had been seized by The Octopus and their bodies never found.

There were those who swore The Octopus was blessed with a mind of its own. It was rumoured that it claimed only the guilty and the wicked, and was one of the few forces for good in the town. Stories abounded, such as the one about the man who'd stolen his mother's teeth and whose bathers washed up on the shore, the teeth still in a pocket. Those with guilty consciences avoided swimming, though this was tricky. If a group of friends went for a dip, and one or two declined, the refusal was enough to plant a seed of doubt: were they thieves, frauds, adulterers? Of course so many people were, but that didn't alter the delicate nature of the thing. Some women seemed to be in a state of perpetual menstruation and would not even put an ankle in the water. Or was this just prudence?

STILL LIFE WITH OCTOPUS AND GROPER

There were those who said the town's real name was Disaster — it seemed to be their native habitat.

John Gobblelard claimed the men and women who fished off the sandbars were driven by a death wish, that the sandbars and The Octopus were in league, so often did those sandbars collapse as the tidal currents changed direction, the fishermen and women washed off with them. Less charitable souls pointed out that the publican had three fishing boats working those same waters, though John insisted this was a public service, and that the fish were always freshest at The Bluebottle, Prawn and Oyster. He also claimed that the sweetest fish were found beyond the sandbars. He mentioned this to Ernie as the lad supped his drink. Ernie didn't like to contradict the man, and nodded his head as he answered, 'Yes, yes, the sweetest fish called Death Itself.'

John was sure the boy had understood him perfectly, and felt a glimmer of respect for his young companion. Feeling an almost parental obligation to underscore some bit of wisdom.

'Ernie, this world is full of strangeness, but I'll tell you the strangest thing. The sweetest fish are those who eat the dead. Only last night I had a groper fillet of a delicacy a man could only dream about. You know the boy who died last week? The groper was caught off that same reef. They found a small ring in its belly, with a moonstone; the uncle swore it was the ring from his nephew's finger.

'The fishermen asked the uncle if he'd like some fillets, but he declined. Said it made him queasy! I heard them drinking at the bar, and they were happy with my offer of a bottle of whisky in return for three large fillets. You've never seen a fish that size — mind you, the boy was nine years old and quite a size himself. For a small hogshead of porter they've agreed to mount the groper's head; I'm having it installed in the back bar. They're going to make a little sign, and that bar will be The Moonfish Bar. It's a pretty thing, don't you think?'

Ernie had slowly paled as he listened to John Gobblelard ladling out his story.

'Not feeling well, Ernie? You've gone the colour of those fillets. Would you like a portion to bring your colour back? A glass of porter?'

John Gobblelard was a pasty, flaccid man. Ernie thought he looked like an uncooked fillet of fish. It made the prospect of eating some of Gobblelard's groper no more appealing. Imagining that one day the publican would find himself filleted and fried, enough to feed as many people as throttled the back bar on a busy night. He didn't know why but the thought of the thirsty mob settling their stomachs with a fillet of fried publican made him laugh.

'What's funny, Ernie?'

'I was thinking you'd make a handy size of fillets yourself. Enough to feed a crowd.'

John Gobblelard stopped wiping out the beer glass in his hands with a greasy cloth.

'You're a funny boy, Ernie, a funny boy.' He began to laugh. When he stopped laughing he began to wipe the glass again, and by the time he had finished the clean glass was streaked with grease. Setting it down he gave Ernie an odd look and Ernie said, 'It's true, you look a little like a groper.'

The publican moved away from Ernie then, though a few minutes later he came back with a large glass of porter.

'I think you need to flush your gills, lad, and swill away that maudlin humour. It's been a sad day, I think the shock has made you lose your senses.'

Ernie had no reply, and so he quietly sipped his porter, trying hard not to think about his parents. He'd thought that he would cry, but all he felt was numb. He drained his glass and stepped outside. The day was done. There was a lovely dance of evening lights upon the waters of the bay. He could just make out the form of a man bashing an octopus against the pier, softening up the flesh. The slapping sounds reaching him as he stood on the front steps of The Bluebottle, Prawn and Oyster. Having no idea what he might do, he simply stood and watched the blues and golds fade into indigo, the water turning the colour of an octopus's ink.

Ernie was surprised to find his hunger returning. He didn't want to go home. Not in the dark, and on his own. Perhaps he'd have a feed of fish after all. He'd just steer clear of groper. The raucous sounds that filled his ears as he set foot back in the pub were a pleasing music. He'd eat his fill, glad at least he had this plan.

John Gobblelard was surprised to see the lad, and even more surprised to feel a certain gladness in himself. Crooking a fat finger at Ernie, who slowly made his way through the crowd to the bar. John Gobblelard wasn't sure that Ernie had all his senses, but something in the lad's demeanour had aroused a paternal instinct.

'Go tell Les to fix you a good feed. If you want there's a bed for you tonight. It's no surprise if you're not wanting to go home. Tell Les I'm telling him to feed you well.'

Ernie nodded, and wished he hadn't told John he looked like a groper fillet.

If anything John Gobblelard was more like an octopus than a groper. He had secured a virtual monopoly on all fish caught in the waters of the bay, something he'd achieved through sheer force of personality, mixed with a bit of what he called 'native cunning'. He never set foot in the treacherous waters of the bay, knowing all too well the powers of The Octopus. If a business associate or rival mysteriously disappeared, he'd calmly shift his weight from left to right while his eyes performed the opposite manoeuvre, before leaning forward and saying gravely, 'Must have decided to go swimming.' It was funny how many people who'd fallen out with John Gobblelard became keen swimmers shortly after their disagreement.

'I told that stupid bastard, "Do you want to take a swim?" People won't listen. Would you like a glass of porter?'

He had the biggest hotel in town, in the best position, claimed he had the greatest sexual appetite, and had the highest opinion of himself. Les was convinced his elder brother was possessed of nothing short of genius.

John Gobblelard's pride and joy was a necklace made of shark teeth. He'd needed a hammer to knock them from the jaw of a shark the fishing boats had caught. Surprised to find how difficult they were to extract, and in the process he'd broken more than he had salvaged. When he wore the necklace he felt powerful, and somewhat sharky. His eyes seemed to brighten, and his stomach muscles contracted, feeling he was a man of uncommon vigour. He sometimes strutted around his bedroom wearing nothing but those shark teeth and a pair of cashmere underpants that had belonged to his grandfather. They were too big for his father, Gunter, yet they fit John like a glove, and from the moment he'd first worn them he knew why his grandfather rarely took them off. So soft and easy on the loins. They were a little moth-eaten, and he always washed those drawers by hand to ensure they'd not be ruined prematurely. They'd been woven from the fleece of a prize cashmere buck, using only the hair of the goat's beard. His grandfather had waited for fifteen years before he had enough wool to make his drawers.

They gave John a sense of continuity, and a sense of potency that married well with his shark-tooth necklace. He also liked the way they grew musty and funky smelling after a week's wearing; he liked that smell so much he didn't always wash them at week's end, preferring to keep them on as long as he could, and it was only the sight of brownish stains among the wool that convinced him the time had come to wash them. He used a soap made from lavender flowers, the underpants the only garment he washed with this fragrant soap. If he caught a whiff of lavender in the air he thought about his undies, his hand would drop to his crutch, he'd give himself a friendly fondle, and marvel once again at the abilities and foresight of his grandfather. Loving the feel of the soft wool against his flesh, enjoying the glimmer of arousal as he rubbed the thin wool against his member. With his shark-tooth necklace to complete his fundamental wardrobe, he fancied himself as a man of exquisite potency.

SEAFOOD

Ernie was gorging himself on seafood. A plate piled with periwinkles, oysters, prawns, half a lobster, and abalone he didn't really enjoy eating, though the knowledge it was a delicacy made him determined to chew through it. There were creatures he'd never heard of, hermit crabs rumoured to be on the point of extinction, blue seahorses that turned pink in the boiling water. Not a lot of meat, though the gizzards tasted sweet when sucked out of the carapace. Les had taken good care of him.

When Ernie finished eating he felt a thrill at having navigated such a huge meal. He also felt ill. Perhaps he'd just eaten too much, all that rich food curdling his guts. Or was it the thought of that poor seahorse, sucked out and swallowed? Trying hard not to think about his parents, preferring to keep his thoughts on his queasy belly. Wondering if he was about to stagger out to the pier and feed the fish with their half-digested companions. Deciding he'd take a wobbly walk down to the bay, hoping he was not about to launch his entrails.

Watching the small waves slapping the pier did nothing to settle the queasy movement of his gizzards. Feeling his life had shifted just like those shifty waters, his parents swallowed by the big mouth of the bay. Wishing he could feel something more than the numbness which seemed pervasive. Sure he should be feeling some remorse, yet the unexpected nature of his parents' demise had caught him unprepared, like the men and women who were taken when the sandbars collapsed. Floundering for some tangible support, only to find himself bobbing in circumstances so unfamiliar he could not begin to comprehend his new reality. Tapping his jaw as if that way he might arouse some proper bone of feeling. He could see a small seahorse bobbing in the water; it made him feel guilty, and he mumbled, 'I've just eaten your brother!' The thought all he needed to feel his guts contract, and the inevitable propulsion.

Felt better for it. Remembering then a story his father had once told, from what The Burner called 'history's entrails'. A man had eaten his son, the head served on a separate platter. The man had been a general, and his son a traitor. The recollection produced an encore of his meal, and he felt truly purged then. Staring out into the bay, half hoping to find his parents still sitting in the little boat. Having no idea what else to do, he decided to wobble back to The Bluebottle, Prawn and Oyster. Needing to rinse his mouth.

Ernie was an ungainly looking lad, with his large jaw, runty body and skinny legs that seemed too weak to support even the meagre frame he had. The sight of the little drunken laddie touched the publican's good humour. He towered over the boy, and with ease hauled him by the collar of his shirt and stood him on the bar. The effortless power John Gobblelard enjoyed right then filled him with gladness, and inspired the closest thing he'd ever known to affection for another human being. Humming to himself as he poured the lad a pannikin of ale. Ernie had no capacity for drink, and the unsteadier he got on his feet the more the publican warmed to him. Later that night, to Ernie's surprise, he found his back pushed hard against The Virgin Wall, could hear voices, laughter, the distant clink of boats. Heard the slapping of a pigeon's wings, and for a moment thought it was the sound of someone clapping.

And so he lost his parents and his virginity in one day. That's how he met Jean Flinch.

THE JAW MONSTER

When Ernie finally stumbled home that night he was afraid to walk inside. Unwilling or unable to face the empty house. Sitting on the back steps until he began to shiver with cold. Finally opening the back door, half expecting to hear the sounds of his mother snoring in her bed, and the whistled breathing of his father's sleep. He didn't dare light a lamp, already scared of the shadows he knew would hover in ghostly formations around the walls. Walking through the dark and empty hallway to his small bed, he climbed in, keeping his clothes on for the security they could bring. Unable to sleep, sure at times he heard the sounds of his parents' quiet whispers in the garden, in their room. Telling himself it was a foolishness, yet that did nothing to quell his trepidation, and the odd shame he felt, knowing he'd eaten,

got drunk, and been had against The Virgin Wall, instead of —
what? He didn't know, but was sure there was some other, more
proper set of actions he should have taken, which would have
shown his dead parents some last respect. Now he felt haunted
by their absence, and the overwhelming dismay that wrapped
him like the damp blankets of his bed.

He was scared. He knew he was ugly, and with his mother
dead there was no one to bolster him, nor protect him. Fearing
and expecting the worst, feeling that somehow he was a crime
against humanity, his jaw sticking out, monstrous, they said.
Lowering their voices when he appeared, though he knew some
called him The Jaw Monster. Certain that he'd be beaten, those
who called him monster rearing out of the darkness with sticks
and clubs to bash him. Lying awake, wondering what lay before
him now that he was truly alone in the world. Would he join the
ones who scavenged through the market, looking for scraps of
food, or anything of value? Might he get work at the fish-
scraping yards? Would John and Les let him work at the pub?

The Burner may have had an aptitude for depression but he
was no good at making money. Irene had cleaned fish six days
a week while Ernie's dad sat at home or went into the country
hunting his feral pelts, all the while hoping he'd yet convince
the townsfolk of the virtues of fur garments that were flea-
bitten. The family could manage week to week but there was
never anything left over. Eating wild pig stew and fox soup,
hoping they'd catch a decent haul of fish on a Sunday afternoon. Ernie had inherited a tiny house with a vegetable garden
that quickly went to seed. The house was in bad repair, with a
leaky roof, bad plumbing and a chimney that smoked the house
out when in use, to say nothing of the sinking foundations and
the wood rot in the beams.

He couldn't sleep in the house now that his parents were
dead. The house felt spooky for their absence, filling him with
a sense of destitution and abandonment. He moved his bed into

the small shed at the back of the garden, and tried not to think about his defunct parents. The shed had a roof that didn't leak, and he was glad enough for that.

Not only had he inherited the mouldering house, he had also inherited a barn full of festering feral furs, infested with rats and fleas. He was wondering what to do with all those pelts. He'd heard about canoes and boats made from the skins of animals stretched around a wooden frame, but in the wake of his parents' drowning was disinclined to pursue this course. Convinced that to paddle out into the wide mouth of the bay would be to invite a terrible emulation. What could he do with a barn full of rat-eaten pelts? He felt there was no choice but to burn them. He'd be known as The Burner's Boy, Small Flame. It seemed such a waste. Surely they'd be good for blankets, dog coats, or head warmers for the bald? He wondered whether a local ascetic order might not make use of them for hairshirts. They'd provide a suitable irritation, and for no extra charge he could leave the fleas on. Surely a most exalted penance?

Yet he was not convinced this was the answer. He was glad the barn was in a field on the edge of town, and so at least he was spared the risk of the house being overrun by rats.

Young fool that he was, Ernie kept putting off his decision about the pelts and the rat-infested barn, hoping some clear path of action would present itself. The rats were much more decisive. They bred, they ripped the pelts which made such perfect nests, and on his infrequent visits to the site Ernie was impressed by what seemed to be a fever of domesticity. He felt jealous, seeing the rats breed and cater to the dynasties they were spawning in the barn. To a novice orphan this seemed a virtue. He indulged in stupid fantasies, seeing himself as one of those young rats, smothered and mothered in the cosy nest, and didn't have the heart to kill the beasts.

As he delayed and dithered, the rats kept breeding. Ernie no longer dared set foot inside the barn. It was enough to stand in the field listening to their squeaking industry and the sounds their feet made as they scuttled. It seemed there was some vast congress of rats now in progress, as some rats left the building and other rats arrived. He baulked at the prospect of taking so many lives, seeing the great mound of corpses were he to poison them. Cursing his father for leaving such an awkward legacy, then cursing himself for his selfish curses. Not wanting to be responsible for such an epic slaughter, while knowing it was inevitable.

It wasn't long before the infestation became a problem for the farmers growing wheat and hops in the neighbouring fields. Ernie felt unequal to such abuse, and when they threatened to burn the barn themselves if he'd not do it, he quickly accepted their offer. This caught them off guard, being the one response they'd not expected.

It was a shrewd reply, the infestation thus became a common problem. Over a cup of tea they ruled out setting dogs on the place, there were just too many rats. Poisons were attractive, but the fermenting mounds of corpses and ensuing risk of disease was not.

The Burner's practice of burning barns was the only answer. Ernie could foresee one problem, given the extent of infestation: if they burnt the barn, the rats would pour into the surrounding fields, which would only compound the problem facing the neighbouring farms. Ernie surprised the farmers and himself with what seemed a most intelligent plan. Why not burn a ring of fire around the barn, at a distance of ten or fifteen metres? The rats would have no means of escape as they fled the blazing barn. Their cremation was thus certain, as was the destruction of the infested pelts and the fleas; in short it seemed an answer so perfect Ernie won a hitherto unknown degree of respect for his intellect and acumen. He'd not suspected he might be clever.

He was forced to revise this opinion when at last they burnt the rats. They had cleared a firebreak, then doused the long dry grass surrounding the barn with kerosene. They stacked bundles of old newspaper underneath the barn, and they too were well doused with kerosene. It was going to be some blaze.

Ernie lit the paper stacks then scurried back across the firebreak, stopping only to light the ring of kero. It was a pretty sight, to see the slow line of flame moving through the grass around the barn and linking up to form a burning circle.

The barn went up quickly enough, provoking a terrible evacuation that exceeded their worst imaginings. The stench was rotten, those putrid furs, to say nothing of the rats and their terrible cries. Ernie never quite forgot those sounds, so that even after years the sound of a squeaky chair was all it took to fill him with a terrible dismay and the feeling he was about to throw up. That foul smoke in the lungs, and the sight of a flood of rodents pouring from the barn, under the door, out of windows, only to find themselves surrounded by the ring of fire. Some rodents managed to run right through the fire circle, their pelts blazing, travelling at surprising speeds into the fields of wheat and hops, there to expire, but not before igniting the dry stalks of the crops and grasses. This was a problem they had not foreseen. They'd come armed with water buckets and damp sacks, in case of spot fires, but had not reckoned on spot fires caused this way.

The number of rats who penetrated the burning ring was, if taken on a purely statistical basis, quite insignificant, no more than half of one per cent. Yet even twenty or thirty spot fires started in this way were more than they could deal with, as they chased the burning rats who ran at the speed of death, or at least aspired to that velocity before they stopped, dead in their tracks, leaving in their wake new paths of flames and cinders.

Ernie and the farmers did their best to catch the flaming escapees. Yet some of the fires beyond their puny firebreak were already grown quite large; in fact the damn infernal thing was out of control, and in a panic they too now fled, not wishing to emulate the destiny they'd conferred upon the blazing rats.

Their own poor shrieks and cries now married with those that carried from the barn.

It was a fiasco. The neighbouring crops were burnt, one of the houses was saved by the fire brigade but a champion bull and two thoroughbred stallions were not so lucky. Compared to this, his father's exploits seemed the work of an amateur. Ernie became known as The Inferno. He was his father's son. Ernie tried to apologise to the neighbours and they started throwing rocks, telling him if he ever came near again they'd kill him. He knew that day he had been well and truly pelted. Convinced of the truth in his father's poor motto, wondering why he'd ever doubted the obvious. Things Always Turn Out Badly.

His parents' house was in such poor repair the irate farmers did not want it, but the small amount of cash and valued goods his parents left were taken from him.

Falling asleep at night, the rustling leaves above the shed sounding like rats' feet on the roof.

He'd been forced to parade through town with a dead rat on a string around his neck, blubbering and weeping the whole time. It was a grand joke, that was clear from the laughter as he passed by, though he'd been stunned and glad when Jean Flinch burst out from the mob, ripped the rat from him and tossed it back into the squealing crowd.

Given the nature of his formative experience, it's no surprise that Ernie proved himself adept as The Slapping Man, feeling he'd been boxed around the ears by life itself from an early age.

PART TWO:

A SPAT-OUT FROG

AMBERGRIS

Ernie's father was famous for being the most depressive man in Ruination. It was said that during protracted droughts The Burner was able to gather storm clouds overhead, such was the intensity of his depression. Something of this temperament he had bequeathed to Ernie. Perhaps the sudden demise of his parents had destabilised the lad. Or had his jaw so dominated his development there wasn't enough of his vital juices left to feed his skin? He felt as if his skin was just too thin.

He was so unstable he was unemployable. For some reason he could not fathom, people were put out if he suddenly burst into tears. No sooner would he start to blubber than he'd risk sending some other fragile soul into a splutter, before long there'd be a furtive band of them weeping in a corner.

John Gobblelard had fixed Ernie up with a job as a counter-hand, but even that had been beyond him. Not only was his skin too thin, the distance between his tongue and brain seemed to be too short. He felt there was never quite the time he needed to censor his thoughts, and so he blurted out the inadmissable. Things others claimed were best left unsaid.

'We're all stranded on a ball of spinning mud and water, and none of us has the first idea of what we're doing!'

And then he'd start his blubbering again. The guiltier he felt for blurting out his apprehensions, the more thin-skinned he felt, and thus more liable to keep on blubbering and blurting.

Standing at the counter as women tried some new perfume, he couldn't stop himself from saying, 'Made with bits of a poor dead whale! Who killed the whale? Funny that people want to have sex with us because we've got that dead whale smell on our skins, the smell gets on the nerves of a man's bone, that's why women wear it!'

The owner of the shop didn't think it funny at all, and Ernie conceded, as the owner punched him in the storeroom, that he had no aptitude for such work.

'What on earth possessed you? Telling them the smell of a dead whale makes a man want to stick his bone inside a woman? You think that's any way to sell perfume? It's not dead whale, you fool, it's a secretion! Why can't you talk about the smell of jasmine, and the essence of tender petals crushed for oil?'

The look in Ernie's eyes told the man it was no use, the lad was on the brink of tears as he contemplated flower petals being crushed for oil. He'd been about to thump the lad again, but now lost heart, feeling himself oddly defeated.

'You're not fit for this world, boy, I doubt you'll see the year out. You've got thumb prints on your jugular. Did they use forceps at your birth?'

Ernie had no idea how to reply, and simply stood there trying to control the involuntary movement of his lower lip.

Edging slowly towards the back door, hoping to make his exit. He didn't dare ask if he'd be paid for his morning's work, and having made it to the door he turned the handle and fled. As an adolescent you'd have to say he was an awkward child, and a late bloomer.

Without knowing why, he found himself walking to The House of Pearls. It had been the brainchild of Hans Magnus, one of the few successful businessmen in town. Hans had made his fortune cultivating pearls and his will left provision for the construction of an unusual monument, to be called The House of Pearls. A concrete structure studded with real pearls, The House of Pearls was intended to ensure his enduring memory. For a very brief time it was the most beautiful building in the town. But the idea to use real pearls was a rank stupidity, and it was vandalised before it could be officially opened. Who could be trusted to leave the pearls intact? People couldn't believe their luck, as they winkled out a pearl or three; in a short time The House of Pearls was a scabby, pockmarked bunker that resembled, from a distance, someone with an horrendous case of acne. Some said the stolen pearls would bring bad luck to the thieves, though in such a blighted town it's hard to know how their luck could have been worse.

The official opening was a fiasco, so many of the pearls had already been stolen, and as a memorial to a dead man it only hinted at the deep deficiencies in his character. Ernie found it had retained a certain beauty, despite being stripped of all its pearls. The grey pockmarked concrete, the dirty interior, never swept.

Most people avoided it. Ernie thought it had become a concrete oyster, clamped on its hill, an introverted place. A place for serene thinking. He sometimes took a broom down and cleaned it out. Needing a bucket and hose to shift the grosser eliminations, the drunks who pissed in there or dropped their pants and defecated.

Ernie borrowed a bucket, scrubbing brush and mop from Les, walked back down to the gorgeous ruin, and cleaned the whole place out. Then he sat on the steps, on the small hill behind the bay, with the partial view of his raucous homeland, his poor Salvation and Ruination.

Ernie loved The House of Pearls because it had taken a beating. The gritty life of the town had disfigured the monument, yet it had survived and somehow absorbed the shock. Neglected, ruined, stubborn, a place of difficult virtues. Ernie saw so much of himself in it he felt embarrassed, that he might identify so closely with a concrete bunker on a hill.

IF HELL EXISTS ...

John Gobblelard was a keen butcher, a trade he had learnt from his father. Les Gobblelard found this business made him squeamish, something John always teased him for. Les was happier grilling steaks than slicing them off a fresh-killed carcass whose throat he had just slit. As John was no cook, they felt they were a perfect team.

'People look up to a butcher, son. They're all afraid of death, and to see a man administer it to some long-suffering beast makes them sure a bit of God has rubbed off on that butcher.'

John had never forgotten his father's words. He took pride in the fact that his knives were sharp and his movements swift.

When Gunter died he left his knives and leather aprons and wooden benches, the entire rudiments of his trade, to John. Whenever John closed his hand around the handles of those knives he thought of Gunter, and would kiss the head of the sheep he meant to kill and begin weeping, never sure if he was weeping for his father, himself, or for every living creature whose only certainty was termination. The days he wept while slaughtering he was careful to ensure the speediest departure for the beast. Oddly enough the steaks seemed most tender if killed on John's weepy days.

John Gobblelard enjoyed wrestling with the animals he slaughtered in the courtyard of The Bluebottle, Prawn and Oyster before he cut their throats. He felt a thrill like no other when he locked his arms around a beast. The sweet confirmation that he was much stronger than the animal once he'd brought it to the ground, knowing he was about to turn the thing into a carcass. Had he not become a publican he would have been a butcher. As it was he took great pleasure in what he felt was his perfect hobby and obligation. He always whispered in the creature's ear, 'You're dead meat now,' and kissed it on the head, before he slipped his slaughter knife out of its leather sheath and slit the neck. Amazed that the joy he found in this simple act seemed to be the closest he ever came to absolute pleasure. Making him feel godly, or as close to God as he ever got. If God was the great Maker, John became at that moment the great Unmaker. Convinced the Church had lost its way when it stopped making ritual sacrifices of live beasts. If it had still been the custom he might have become a priest. In a rare unguarded moment he'd once confessed this to Jean, and they'd both been embarrassed by how powerfully she'd embraced him. She had been surprised to think that he might, in his way, be a spiritual man.

He loved the sight of hot blood spilling from the neck, and the sweet smell coming with it. Loved it best in winter, when the steam rose from the gash, locking his thighs around the beast to thwart its struggle. The more it struggled the more powerful he felt; he liked a beast that put up a good fight, dismayed if the animal was too compliant. If it kicked or bit it only added to his pleasure, seasoning his joy with some revenge, loving even more the miracle of steam that billowed from the neck. He never had trouble eating meat he had slaughtered. When he ate the meat others had slaughtered he always swore the meat was tough.

'You didn't take enough pleasure in the killing. That's why your meat is tough. Either that or you forgot to look into the belly of the beast. You killed the thing too lightly.'

He found such action criminal.

After the slaughter he'd drag the beast across the courtyard, then string it up to bleed, slitting the belly and abdomen once it was hanging. Always felt thirsty then, stepping into the pub for beer, sending Les outside to hose the blood away — the job Les hated most in the working week. As Les was hosing, John felt once again surprised that there could be such rightness in the world, the pleasure he found in slaughtering redeemed so many failings. And glad as well the time had come for another visit to Jean Flinch.

Jean Flinch had sex with John Gobblelard once a week in return for a regular supply of fresh-killed meat. He always brought some tender steak, a bit of eye fillet and some chops. She didn't need to love him to be happy with the pact. Jean thought she had the better of the bargain, as she satisfied her hunger for two different kinds of meat, and would have slept with him if he'd arrived empty-handed. Some men tried wooing her with flowers but a tray of meat was much more practical. She'd heard of people eating flowers but was of no such inclination.

She thought him best on the days when he had slaughtered, possessed of greater vigour. If it coincided with her days of bleeding, their arousal seemed the more complete. Whispering in his ear, 'You're dead meat now!' Feeling him shudder as the involuntary spasms set in; he'd lose control and smother her in profanity that coupled with his greatest muscularity, and Jean would lose control as well, feeling this was some stranger she now gripped. It made her arousal utterly complete, more powerful too. She'd tell him 'I'm your butcher now' — that always got Jim spurty. She only thought of him as Jim when she was coming.

The strangeness of their encounters always made them thrilling. She didn't want a man with brains when she was fucking, she wanted brawn and vigour, not conversation.

John Gobblelard was not a jealous man, and Jean thought it was another aspect of his virtue. He couldn't see beyond the satisfaction guaranteed by their arrangement. What she did between those times was of no concern to him. It never occurred to him to feel possessive. Sent to her as a blessing by a horny god, perhaps, her compensation for the tribulations she'd known in love and sex. Saying a small prayer quickly, amazed she'd never been troubled by infection and diseases.

'If hell exists it must be full of ones like me. And if it doesn't I might as well have my fill before I'm done.'

A SPAT-OUT FROG

John Gobblelard let Ernie eat a few meals at the pub, but despite a muted affection for the boy, he made it clear it was time the lad learnt to stand on his own feet. In any case Ernie had mixed feelings about The Bluebottle, Prawn and Oyster. He didn't like getting drunk, yet it seemed a prerequisite of his presence there.

Ernie had become the entertainment, John lifting him by the jaw onto the bar, where he was plied with drinks; and every time he pleaded to be set down, trying to dissuade John from making him drink again, great guffaws burst around the room. When he finally crawled or fell off the bar he felt giddy, weaving around the room, bumping into people who laughed and pushed him away, sending him reeling into another drunken group who laughed and pushed, until finally he either collapsed onto the floor or found himself propelled through the door, tripping over the steps that led down to the street, lying on the ground, unable or unwilling to stand up. It was not unusual for him to sleep there, woken by someone spitting or pissing on him. An anger coiling in his gut, making him feel oddly sober. When the drink wore off he'd be appalled to think he'd harboured the desire to set fire to the pub, or to some man who'd pissed on him. Straggling back home, washing his clothes and person in a trough of water in the garden. Standing naked and shivery as he looked around at the old ruined house, the little shed. Glad that if nothing else he was at such times free of villainous company. Yet he found the loneliness hard to bear, and at night he'd find himself drawn back to the pub, preferring the humiliations and the jaundiced routines he performed on the bar to the utter dejection he felt those nights he stayed at home. When he grew weepy he'd walk quickly to the door, then run past the house, speeding to The Bluebottle, Prawn and Oyster.

His round would begin again, glad to play some small role in the communal life, he never had to pay for drinks, always someone to hit him on the back, run their fingers through his hair, clap their hands as he drained his glass. Though he never felt they had become his friends.

Always waking with a headache, feeling nauseous. It had become his constant since his parents died. He'd not been reared on alcohol, it curdled his appetite, and he was glad of this, spared the worry of what he'd find to eat that day, at least for several hours. And then he'd feel the anxiety mounting, as he wondered what to do with himself, what stratagem he might devise or what stroke of good fortune might await to help him find enough to eat and make it through another day.

He was hungry, but couldn't bring himself to show his face once more at the hotel kitchen. John had grown less indulgent, finally offering the boy a slice of bread spread with dripping.

It made Ernie's mouth taste oily, appeased his hunger briefly, while making him feel nauseous within the hour. Deciding to head down to the market square, perhaps he'd find some vegetables that were too ripe to sell but would make soup.

The market in Salvation was the usual proliferation you find in any town. The most expensive foodstuffs were always those in short supply — the rare birds, animals and sea creatures believed to be already extinct. There were stalls selling second-hand clothes, some of which, it was rumoured, gained all their stock through shady deals with the morgue attendants. There were street entertainers, beggars and other enterprising folk who hoped to transform some curious attribute into a money-making virtue. One man had turned himself into The Human Pickle, immersing himself for hours in brine and vinegar. His skin had erupted in a terrible rash, and had grown so wrinkled he looked more like The Human Prune than any pickle. When he finally stepped out of his vat to count the small coins in his box, and towelled himself dry, it was not unusual for large pieces of skin to peel off. Yet he persisted in his odd vocation. Another man called himself The Pincushion Man, and after sticking various needles in parts of his person invited the curious into a small tent where, he claimed, he would proceed to puncture himself in the most intimate and tender places. There always seemed to be one or two of the more discerning types who followed him inside. When asked why he did it, he invariably replied, 'It's a prick of a business but it's living.' Ernie avoided The Pincushion Man as he'd once watched spellbound during the preliminary display, then blurted out, 'Are you going to stick a needle down your willy?' The Pincushion Man assured him that should they ever have the pleasure of meeting again he'd stick one down Ernie's. Ernie didn't care to find out if he was a man of his word, and hadn't meant to say as he walked off, 'Two needles through the lips would shut me up, would that not be more effective?'

The short distance between his brain and tongue got him into all sorts of strife, as he uttered things he instantly regretted. Yet it was this very proclivity that set him on what he later recognised as his true path. He was standing in the marketplace, belly rattling, wondering if it would be too unseemly to put his hat onto the ground and start to beg. A young woman was passing by with her newborn child. It had been born two months premature, and yet survived. She'd just left the hospital to take her baby home when Ernie saw her. He meant to compliment the woman and her baby, but when he saw the ruddy little creature he heard himself blurt out, 'It looks like you just spat a frog out of your body!' and on the instant the woman slapped him on the face. They were both appalled by their exchange, and as they floundered with their apologies the woman pressed a banknote into his hand. Ernie had been about to give the money back when a burly stranger brushed the woman aside and said, 'I'm next!'

The man had seen the slap and money changing hands; in the midst of such sights as The Human Pickle and The Pincushion Man, the notion of a man you'd slap and pay for the pleasure seemed quite in tune with the intriguing local culture. He'd just arrived in the town and wanted to sample as many of its delights as possible.

Without another word he slapped Ernie twice, exclaimed, 'Now that's a public service!' and handed Ernie two notes, laughing as he said, 'One for each cheek!' He then strode off, humming, to peruse the other marvels of the market.

In the confusion triggered by this brisk exchange Ernie had forgotten the woman with a babe who looked like a spat-out frog, yet when he looked for her she too had gone. Two young boys were staring at him; the taller of them said, 'We want to have a go,' and without really knowing why, Ernie kneeled down to bring his jawbone to a height that could accommodate these young enthusiasts.

'We've only got small coins.'

'Small coins will do.'

The vigour of the blows seemed to exceed the stature of his clients, and yet the hunger in Ernie's guts made him grateful for their modest contribution as they dropped their small coins in his palm. Getting to his feet he felt giddy and off balance, trying to acquaint himself with some aspect of his equilibrium. He'd had four customers in four minutes for a service he didn't even know he was providing.

Moving his jaw he was relieved to find it was in full working order. He already had enough to buy his lunch, yet trade had been so good he decided to labour on.

After an hour he knew the time had come to take a break. With prudence he had enough money to feed himself for a week. When he tried to walk he noticed an alarming stagger in his gait, and could hear the sound of laughter following his ungainly progress. And yet he was not unhappy with this un-expected turning of events. He chewed a sausage while glancing at The Human Pickle bobbing in his vat. The sting and throb-bing of his face felt like some small glimmer of hope, or confirmation, though of what he could not say. How many people might he service in one day? What were the long- and short-term risks of such an occupation? As he mused and muttered between each mouthful he felt a curiosity and con-tentment. Deciding he would go back to work at once, and as he stood in place he marvelled at the fact that he'd already called the accidents of the morning 'work', and felt a strange thrill, as if he'd just achieved some act of private recognition, or definition. Hoping his afternoon might prove as fruitful as his morn.

His first customer after lunch needed no persuasion, having spent three months fattening a piglet, only to have it stolen within minutes of arriving at the market. The man jumped at this opportunity to vent his anger; he haggled about the price and then exclaimed, 'In all my days I never thought I'd know the joy of letting fly at a slapping man!'

His first blow knocked Ernie to the ground. Getting up slowly, he was disinclined to hurry. Feeling himself winded by some odd force of recognition.

When he got to his feet he knew he had already changed. He might have been a weedy boy when he fell down, but when he stood he had become The Slapping Man. The surge of this new identity was so full of motive and conviction he felt elated, and with each blow his elation grew. Happy to let the thwarted pig farmer indulge to his heart's content. It was not the pain of the blows that fuelled his pleasure, but the sheer force of an identity of his own: as if up to that moment his sense of self had been provisional, and finally the boy had come of age.

He felt the pig farmer had been midwife to some strange rebirth. Wanting to thank the man he'd been insulting, 'My God, you stink of pigshit,' and thought the man might slap him once again. 'No need to rub it in,' the man replied, before they briefly shook hands. 'Come back any time,' said Ernie, 'and you can have three slaps for free.' The man looked so content that Ernie felt a sudden wash of joy flood through him. He'd just done something utterly useful, of his own volition, and felt at peace. It was an unfamiliar sensation.

Walking home from the market Ernie was full of a brisk animation. Realising, to his surprise, that he felt glad. As if a hole in his innards had been plugged, and he was no more the leaky lad he'd been. Convinced he had finally come into his own, he had grown up in the space of a single day.

That night he printed up a little sign, *The Slapping Man*. His hands were shaking as he painted, it gave the letters a pleasing tremulousness, making them squiggly and slightly comic. Ernie liked the effect.

While the paint was drying he noticed that his hands were still trembling, and it was not long before his entire body began to shake. It was not wholly unpleasant, though it made him think of his drowning parents. He closed his eyes, and wished he hadn't, as he saw once more the image of the sodden Burner. Convinced his father had fixed him with a vital stare in the moments before he finally disappeared beneath the frigid waters of the bay. As if his father hoped that by holding onto this vision of the son who watched upon the shore he might find some stable point to clutch at and so defy the watery forces of gravity that pulled him down.

Ernie had been dismayed by his impotence, and the disdain that had appeared on his father's face when it became clear that his son was unable to save him. The Burner unblinking as his open mouth began to fill with water. His nose going under, and then his head. The fur hat he wore floating on the surface of the water for a moment before it too disappeared from view.

Ernie opened his eyes then, he was still trembling, and bent to touch the lettering of his sign. The paint was wet, he smudged the letters. Cleaning up his smudges with a rag, trying not to cry, knowing that at any moment he would erupt into a little howling ball pushing water from its eyes.

SPRUIKING

The next day he was back at the market, sure that some more authentic aspect of his life had just begun.

At first people were confused, unsure what to make of this new apparition. He didn't like to engage in idle chatter on the job, yet found he had to do a bit of spruiking.

'Don't be sad, no need to frown, The Slapping Man has come to town!'

Inventing a philosophy and creed for his new craft on the spot, regaling passers-by with a new lucidity as he explained the dangers of pent-up emotions, the fatal risks of unexpressed rages, and the greater life expectancy of those who let their anger fly. He was their willing target. For no extra charge he was happy to oblige those who needed to be insulted to refine their motivation. He called one woman The Ugliest Bitch In Town, and wondered if he hadn't overstepped the mark when she let fly and dislocated her little finger in the process. The woman demanded her money back and would not countenance attempting another blow with her other hand. Did he need to invent a code of ethics? At the very least he'd need to make some provision for the welfare of his clients. He'd start providing gloves for those who needed them.

The more he thought about it, the more he was convinced he'd stumbled on a noble vocation. He'd always wanted to do something useful, something for the common good. Despite the dull throbbing in his jaw and head after the morning's work, the sense that he had finally stumbled onto his true path was more than adequate compensation for these small discomforts. When he stood in the marketplace, his strong jaw jutting, he felt he became some other man, or perhaps the essence of the man he was. No longer poor Ernie, he was somehow exalted, no ordinary human, but some new and awesome creature, The Slapping Man. Whenever he felt a twinge of doubt he only had to feel his jaw to know he did not delude himself, but was clearly born for it.

That night Ernie took himself to The Bluebottle, Prawn and Oyster, feeling an awkward pride in the fact that he had money of his own, and felt a tremulous confidence as he nodded to John, who was serving at the bar. John seemed almost demure as he placed the drink in front of Ernie, and took his coins. He cast a cautious glance around him, surprised to find that he was not pushed and buffeted by other thirsty souls eager to get more swill into their bellies. It seemed there was a small, peaceful zone around him, which none dared enter, nor disturb. He knew that people were looking at him strangely, averting their eyes when he turned his head to survey the room. No one approached him, or attempted to haul him up onto the bar and fill him with booze. Ernie had another drink, and then a third, lost in a pleasing quietude while around him the usual noisy brawlings and disputations erupted. He had a lovely skinful and felt at peace. He'd earned the right to a little rest.

His second day at work had been eventful, there'd been a steady trickle of business. Many more had gathered to look at him, read his sign, shaking their heads, only to return an hour later as if they'd perhaps misread the sign, unsure of its implications.

'Is he really a Slapping Man?'

'So it says.'

'What, pay him and he'll slap you?'

'I rather fancy it's the obverse.'

'Slap him and he'll pay you?'

Ernie's voice piping up then,

'Feel your life's a horrid trap?
Just step up and take a slap!
Use some caution, or you'll groan —
my mandible's a stunning bone!'

Unleashing then an extraordinary patter. 'It is a well-known, nay proven fact that those who are unable to vent their anger slowly choke on it, as it causes the bones and arteries to harden, until the entire body has become a hard lump and the blood is unable to travel and then they die, and all because of their inability to embrace one of life's greatest pleasures, to whit the total spasm and release at the moment of expressing all their pent-up rage and anger. If any would care to step up now, at no charge to themselves, I'd be delighted to give them the opportunity to experience the rare thrill of which I speak. You could kick a door or wall, but what's the use? The door might break, the bones of your feet crack and split, and then you'd be angrier than you were, and left horribly exposed to the risks of which I've spoken. Whereas I am a Slapping Man. Who'd doubt it? The riddle of my birth finally solved by the good people of my own town.'

Turning his jaw in profile then, jutting it out to enhance its impact. Slowly doing a half-circle with his whole body, that all might take a closer look at that extraordinary specimen, his jaw. He was a persuasive little bugger, and any doubts were easily dispelled when you took the time to look at him. The skin on his jaw was as tight as a tuned snare drum, but where the snare sits over air, the skin on Ernie's jaw was stretched by the mass of bone. He had strong teeth as well. As some might twiddle thumbs he'd chatter those teeth when bored or nervous, if business was slow you'd hear that clicking sound, it was not pleasant, and some people were inclined to step up and slap him just to stop his teeth from chattering.

There were some who doubted The Slapping Man's utility. One could kick a dog for free, or hit one's spouse, or failing that just take a shot at some nearby child. Why pay for such passing pleasures?

Then John Gobblelard gave Ernie his blessing. Ernie felt indebted to John, who'd been so kind in the wake of his parents' death. Having stumbled on his vocation, and recognised it as his calling, Ernie beseeched John to come and chance his arm on The Slapping Man's jaw, as a mark of his appreciation. Ernie issued the same invitation to Les, though Les merely giggled and said, 'A Slapping Man? And where might he slap me?' Les seemed a little disappointed when Ernie explained that Les would have to do the slapping, and then only on the jaw.

John finally relented in the face of Ernie's invitations and pleas. He slowly walked down the slope from the pub to the market, stretched his arms and farted while yawning, surveying what he felt was his domain.

When Ernie saw John arrive, with a small army of curious drinkers who had followed him out of the pub like a brood of chicks following the hen, Ernie felt a thrill of pride, to think John had come to pay his respects. Ernie standing straighter, with out-thrust jaw, like a soldier bristling as the general passes by.

'What's this I see? The Slapping Man?'

John laughed then, and all within earshot laughed with him. Ernie was trying so hard to impress John, his brow had grown wrinkled. John rubbed his jaw, then reached a hand out to sample Ernie's.

'You say this jaw of yours is the hardest in Salvation? Harder than mine own? Do you think that if you slapped me in the face, then I slapped you, I'd be the one left lying on the ground?'

'My boast is simpler,' said Ernie. 'I only say my jaw is built from such stuff that you'd best beware not to strike me too hard for fear you break your bones, unless you'd like to wear a glove. I'd recommend it.'

'A glove? You'd recommend it? You insult me, boy!'

There's no doubt that whether by accident or design Ernie had a certain shrewdness. John lost all desire to quibble and immediately struck Ernie a solid slap. Not with his full force, just enough to make it clear who was master. Ernie did not flinch, and it was clear from the stunned expression on John's face that he was shocked to find Ernie's boast quite true. He slapped again with the other hand, standing close, and Ernie made a mental note that in future he might need to wear a mask or handkerchief over his nose rather than be so exposed to unpleasant odour. A third resounding slap John landed, and then the big man started laughing. This splendid game! John was immersed in a startling reverie of pleasure, letting fly a flurry of quick slaps, playing Ernie's cheeks like a conga drum, dabbling with different rhythms, having such fun that his laughter struck a note of childish pleasure.

True, by now Ernie's face looked somewhat red where John had laid his hands, though Ernie did not seem in discomfort. There was a determined set to that jaw, and a glint in his eye, as if he knew this was his moment of truth, a test he must not fail if he was to pursue his chosen metier with success.

'I think my hands are warm now, little man. You say your jaw's the equal of mine. Would you care to strike me before I split that jaw of yours in two?'

Ernie bowed, there were hoots and whistles among the growing crowd. Then he stood erect once more, and said, 'The Slapping Man is ever at your service!'

He'd barely finished speaking when John let out a terrible cry and launched a blow that knocked Ernie to the ground. To Ernie's relief it didn't hurt at all, though his skin was stinging. As he stood and dusted himself off he could see John staring at his hand in disbelief, and wondered if they were really tears that had gathered in the corners of the publican's eyes? Then John was laughing, rubbing his hands together, and beaming with contentment.

'By God, son, that's a mighty bone.'

He picked up Ernie then and kissed his jaw. To Ernie's relief he only kissed him once, though even that proximity to John's foul breath was more than ample. Catching a low note of rotting gums mingled with high notes of stale beer and whisky. Then John set him back on his feet.

'The Slapping Man!' said John, and walked off laughing. A sprightly gambol in his amble that was quite at odds with his usual gait.

There was a great red print on the side of Ernie's face, as if John had left his imprimatur on The Slapping Man's jaw. Ernie felt a thrill of pleasing certainty.

Clearing his throat he announced, 'For three hours only, The Slapping Man will make a special offer. One free slap to all who are willing to test themselves upon his jaw.'

There was a moment's hesitation and then, to Ernie's delight, a queue began to form.

The arrival of The Slapping Man in Salvation caused both curiosity and trepidation. They were used to people touting strange wares, but they'd never heard of such a thing at this.

Was it an appeal to their best natures, or their worst? They quickly realised it was the kind of thing that happens rarely in a life, to be seized at once. They had to admit it was a spectacular vocation, which none would care to emulate. Though who could emulate that jaw? One might have contemplated changing places, just to know for one moment how it might feel to be The Slapping Man. Yet there seemed a greater promise in his invitation: the chance to take revenge on the many slights and slaps suffered in a life. The simplicity of Ernie's prescription proved irresistible. The odd thing was it seemed to work.

Ernie was intrigued when people begged him to stop. Denying the charge that he was leading them into some kind of immorality. Though when had that ever been a problem?

'What would you have me do? We are born with different talents. I'm a professional, and have my ethics. Who am I to quibble with God's gift?'

His logic infuriated those who begged and pleaded, and he took most satisfaction in being slapped by them as they became determined to teach him a lesson. They were the ones who got a lesson — once they had slapped him they could not claim they were meek and passive, and had to take their place among the common herd.

THE MAN WHO NEVER LAUGHS

The marketplace was full of strange characters. One man claimed that he had never laughed and was immune to any antic that might provoke this disposition. For a trifling sum anyone was free to tempt his laughter. If they succeeded they'd receive a large amount of money. Each week the sum grew larger, as he added to the jackpot a little of his weekly takings.

Petros Agelasti had not laughed for so long his insides had begun to petrify. He had also lost the ability to cry, as a result of his intense professionalism. People tried tickling him with duck feathers, singing bawdy songs, lighting their farts, but he was a gifted man and had never been seen to smile, let alone emit that intake of short breath which sometimes precedes laughter. Even a giggle, let alone a guffaw, would suffice to carry off the prize.

And yet each week went by, and there was no sign that anyone would ever penetrate his humour. It was true that he'd once been told a tale of a family who perished by starvation, having eaten the leather of their shoes, then boiled the laces to make soup, before the inevitable death by emaciation. For an instant his lower lip had trembled. It seemed The Man Who Never Laughs was about to smile, and at that instant the world appeared suspended. Though if there'd been a subtle tremor at the corners of the mouth it was of such short duration that a moment later people were convinced it had been an illusion, triggered only by their desire to see the big man smile.

People attempted the most lamentable pranks, until The Man Who Never Laughs was forced to erect a sign which indicated that some ruses would incur a greater fee than usual: among these the showing of bare buttocks, particularly if the cheeks were spread. He felt he'd become an unwilling expert in some aspects of human anatomy. Why were so many people convinced they could make their fortune by revealing their posterior dimensions? He was intrigued by the variety of the human form, and like snowflakes no two backsides were the same. He was glad to take their money, it boosted his takings. Sometimes whole football teams turned up, paid a group fee, and on a prearranged signal bared their cheeks. It never failed to provoke the mirth of those who watched, with the single exception of The Man Who Never Laughs.

The fact that he would not laugh made people angry and frustrated. Ernie noted with pleasure that his trade prospered as he worked in close proximity to The Man Who Never Laughs. The more people tried to make him laugh the more frustrated they became, and they usually paid for several slaps before regaining their composure.

One morning, arriving to set up, Ernie winked at the man and said, 'I know you. You're laughing all the way to the bank!' It was early in the morning, no customers around, and The

Man Who Never Laughs had smiled. It was a moral victory. Ernie was glad The Man Who Never Laughs had only smiled; he was too good for business. Ernie knew that if the man laughed even once, his reputation would be shattered. People would have no interest in seeing if The Man Who Had Laughed Once would laugh again.

Ernie was sure the man's secret was simple: knowing that to laugh would bring immediate ruination, he had only to contemplate this doom to be immune to anything as trifling as good humour. Ernie thought The Man Who Never Laughs a paragon of discipline, a true professional, and did his best to emulate the features of such unflinching dedication.

JEAN LETS FLY

Ernie was accepted as The Slapping Man, which took him by surprise. He felt an unexpected equanimity and pride, he had somehow found his place among the rabble of the noisy market spruikers. He did not feel as ugly. Not when he was standing with jaw thrust out, touting for trade, or briskly practising his craft.

It looked like he was doing some kind of slapping dance each time he was hit. It made him appear somewhat mechanical, like a little slapping machine. Which, in a way, he was.

On the rare occasions that he was knocked to the ground, or slipped and stumbled, a cheer went up. He'd regather his composure, make a small bow, then say 'Next!' Shaking hands with his new customer, enquiring after their wellbeing, taking their money as he took their measure.

There were days he noticed Jean Flinch eyeing him. Ernie wanted Jean to slap him, he was sure it would help her come to terms with the sadness she still carried from Beau's death. Yet Jean refused his offers.

Jean had been one of the first to implore Ernie to cease trading as The Slapping Man — it seemed to offend her notion of human dignity. It didn't bother her that she had none herself, she just couldn't stand to see the small man being set upon. Doing his giddy little dance as he was struck and spun around. Yet Ernie laboured on, even asking her if she would like a free slap or three. She thought he was being cheeky, and almost slapped him for his rudeness. The more she observed him, the more she was struck by his equanimity. Though she never said so, she wondered whether some strange saint had wandered into town and this was his martyrdom.

Jean had appeared every day for a week, watching for a while, then disappearing, returning with a loaf of bread under her arm, or a broken umbrella she'd bought at a bargain price. Shuffling on her feet, wanting and not wanting to join the queue. After days of hesitation she finally took her place in the line, only to quail at the last minute. Returning the next day, finally screwing up the courage to test her arm on Ernie's jaw.

Ernie was delighted she'd finally yielded to his overtures. Bowing low, he could not help smiling, delighted that Jean had finally given her blessing to The Slapping Man. The corners of her eyes tightening as she asked him, 'Are you sure?' Not quite reassured when he replied, 'I am The Slapping Man! A man who's made for slapping, that's what I am! Do not doubt my stunning trade, Slapping Men are born, not made!'

She only slapped him once and for a moment she felt transported beyond her griefs and woes. Glad she'd taken his advice and worn a glove, even so her hand felt sore. It had been as thrilling, in its way, as the first time she kissed Beau, some illicit thing, a liberty that felt quite transgressive. It was only later that she felt herself settling into a profound remorse, worrying that she'd been party to some profound violation of the man's humanity. Ernie's insistence that he was born to the work had countered her reluctance, though now her misgivings had resurfaced and mingled with a more contrary feeling — she'd enjoyed the moment of the slap so much she wanted to return to the market at once and slap The Slapping Man again. For the briefest moment she'd felt avenged for the many slights she'd suffered at the hands of the town. The death of Beau, her immersion in the baptismal waters of Jean Flinch, had dissolved, just for a moment, and that one moment seemed to hold such ease and completion she wondered how she'd cope if she never felt such ease again.

The next day when he was finishing work, Ernie was surprised to see Jean arrive at his stand with a bowl of warm water, into which she poured some fragrant oils. For a moment he thought she meant to wash his feet, and was embarrassed. His feet stank, he knew; he didn't want to remove his shoes and reveal their mighty reek. He was so relieved to learn she had no business with his feet that he acquiesced at once to what might otherwise have struck him as a strange request. Might she wash his jaw and rub it with oil? It was not the kind of request he'd had to field before. Closing his eyes as Jean went about her quiet work, the warmth of the moist towel so soothing after the hard work of the day. Then she rubbed his jaw with oil that smelt of basil and rosemary, working her supple fingers into the hinges. She made him sit on the small stand he used while working, and between the day's fatigue and the pleasure of Jean's work, Ernie fell asleep.

When he woke, Jean was gone, the market nearly empty. A few stray dogs sniffing and pissing, or foraging for food among the scraps. An old violinist scraping out tunes, though there were few passers-by. Ernie felt confused, rubbing his jaw, then smelling his fingers. The lingering aromas of the oils made him smile, and he slept that night with neither dreams nor night-mares, and woke feeling a strange levity. He was astonished by Jean's gesture, wanted to thank her, though had no idea what he might say or do. And so did nothing, though the memory of Jean's apparition stayed with him through the day. That night he worked much later than usual, though trade was quiet, curious to see if Jean would come again. When she did not arrive, Ernie chastised himself for thinking she might appear, yet he could not help feeling sad as he slowly made the journey home.

BESOTTED

It's true some people became convinced that Ernie's jaw contained magical abilities. It only took one person to recover unexpectedly from a cold after visiting The Slapping Man for word to get about. It made life rather hazardous for the man himself, suddenly finding that in the midst of an epidemic of influenza every sick bastard in town was standing in line, coughing and spluttering, when they should have been home in bed. Those not well enough to walk either crawling or else supported by family members. Ernie seemed blessed with an invincible constitution despite his weedy body, rarely succumbing to infection, though he often took the precaution of covering his nose and mouth with a large green handkerchief. It only accentuated the mighty jut of his jaw, making him look like a creature of stunning potency. In their reduced physical condition his slappers were never able to hit with much vigour, yet the satisfaction they gained from the act only bolstered Ernie's conviction that he had a stern duty to the town, one he dared not shirk.

'Feeling poorly, sick or weak?
Just come down and crack my cheek!
Joints are aching, bones feel sore?
Take a chance on The Slapping Man's jaw!'

The drinkers in The Bluebottle, Prawn and Oyster now tried to best each other with tales of miraculous cures from fevers, aching teeth that no longer throbbed, or arthritic joints that no longer caused them grief, all attributed to the benign office of The Slapping Man. One man who'd suffered badly from haemorrhoids and had never been known to drink while sitting down surprised his boozing colleagues by slipping onto a stool to join them at the bar.

'You're sitting, Harry?'

'It were The Slapping Man. I gave myself a cure of three slaps daily for three weeks, one each at morning, noon and sundown, and my arse is now as sweet and tender as any flower. The pity is I had to wait so long for the splendid man to come among us. All those years of painful shitting — well, thank God they're now behind me.'

There were quiet murmurs along the bar. No one expected, nor really wanted, the man to whip his trousers down and reveal the dainty features of his dimpled arse, but there it was, and not a pile in sight. Their astonishment grew when the man then shouted a round of drinks, yet it only underscored the virtuosity of that marvellous creature, The Slapping Man.

It was as if the clumsy boy Ernie had never existed, or else had been utterly subsumed by his potent Other. Small details from Ernie's childhood were seen with new eyes, as people sought some confirmation or an inkling of the prodigy's prowess and early promise.

'You remember that giant fish Ball Harmsworth caught on Whisky Rocks? Ball hadn't even set his bait, had merely thrown the line to clear a tangle.'

'And what has that to do with The Slapping Man?'

'Ah. The boy had crossed his path that morn, and Ball had given the lad a swipe across the chin to be getting on with. The way you rub a hunchback's hump for luck. That fish fairly jumped onto his line.'

Wise heads nodded up and down the bar. The Man Who Never Laughs had knocked off work for the day and had caught this latest gobbet of town lore. Clearing his throat, spitting on the floor, then calling for a beer before he launched his own contribution.

'Well, I'll tell you something that is absolutely true. I knew the boy's mother. She told me that a horse kicked him on the jaw one day and the laddie didn't flinch. In fact the horse hobbled off, and it was a damn shame, because it was bred from champions. Irene swore me to secrecy, but as they say, you can't defame the dead.'

To Ernie's delight business was booming. True, he often felt a little giddy by day's end, but the hitherto unknown joys of steady money and self-esteem were most adequate compensations. A swagger in his step that seemed another beacon of his prosperity. Though to his consternation he discovered there were now imitators who tried to usurp his role in the marketplace, Mr and Mrs Bruise the most lamentable of these imposters. Ernie had mixed feelings as he watched them setting up in the market, standing beneath a gigantic purple banner with yellow print. Observing their winces as each new blow was struck. Ernie was relieved when after a short hour's trading they realised their folly and retreated in disgrace. Mr Bruise had a nasty swollen eye that would be black before nightfall, and both he and Mrs Bruise had copped some terrific blows to the arms and legs and shoulders. They were clearly unfit for such stern labours.

As each new hopeful retreated from the field it only underscored the extent to which Ernie was clearly a man of special talents. Yet he had somehow become unapproachable; even as he was exalted in the eyes of his fellows, he felt cut off when he wished for nothing more than human contact. A touch, a hug — anything but slapping.

There were attempts to avoid Ernie's modest fee, and have a free swipe. As he was walking home one evening three men grabbed him and began to punch him in the head and torso. One man punched him on the jaw three times, and each time Ernie heard what he thought could only be the sound of knuckles splitting. He was almost right, except that with the third blow the man had broken his wrist, which now seemed oddly floppy.

When word got out about the incident Ernie was relieved to discover that the demand for a free shot after hours declined dramatically.

Some days he noticed that his ears would not stop ringing. He told himself the high-pitched sounds would fade in time. It was no great discomfort, there were many people worse off than him. The market was full of people limping, hobbling along, people with only the use of half their bodies. Others were covered in scars and lesions from diseases whose names he didn't want to learn.

He had always been a funny-looking man, but now he looked quite odd. His ears swollen from the many times people missed his jaw, and thumped his ears instead, so that he looked like a runty boxer. Moved like one too, a little punch-drunk. Some people who saw him for the first time thought he must have been a sailor, and he'd answer, 'I've been at sea my whole life and never left dry land.'

Still, Ernie was besotted with his new identity. Strutting around his shed at night, talking to himself. 'I am The Slapping Man. I AM The Slapping Man!' He knew the work was draining, but would not countenance stopping. He had a duty to continue. Was it possible that he'd been born in Salvation because Salvation had a terrible need for someone like him?

PART THREE:

A DANGEROUS TREND

THE GOD OF COITUS INTERRUPTUS

For all his ghastly bravado, John Gobblelard had his tender side. He just did his best to hide it, knowing the cunning eye the locals had for any weakness, which quickly became a source of gossip and hilarity. John's father had impressed upon him a simple rule: 'Strike first! Your best punch is the one that's unexpected! At worst you'll scare the living daylights out of some bastard who's preparing to insult you, at best you'll earn a great deal of respect.'

John's father, Gunter Gobblelard, developed such a reputation for unprovoked attacks that people either avoided him completely or spent the duration of any conversation with him preparing to duck blows or else dispense them.

Frequently Gunter would go to shake someone's hand, only to find they thought he meant to strike them and decided to strike first! This only fuelled Gunter's belief that people were untrustworthy bastards, and made him all the more determined to get in early. People absentmindedly raising a hand to brush hair from their eyes, or nervously pick their noses, would be punched and kicked, and in their dazed confusion would hear Gunter's voice, 'You thought you'd beast me, you bastard, who's beasted who?'

He was not a big man, though he was stocky and strong. A good butcher, he passed his skills onto his eldest boy, while lamenting the fact that young Les would never turn out right. Spending his time in the kitchen with his mother when he should have been outside with the men.

Gunter had a squeaky voice, perhaps for this reason he was a man of few words. His testicles had been slow to drop, and his voice remained locked in the register of a seven-year-old boy. Gunter had become so used to being ridiculed as a lad that he'd grown testy despite the laggard progress of his testes, and even then had been quick to hit and kick.

He loved butchering, once he discovered the respect he earned from the business. No one laughed at him when they stood beside him as he slit the neck then calmly dissected the carcass.

Gunter's squeaky voice had been the reason why he'd decided to break a family tradition and become the first Gobblelard not to work in the pub. He'd only to ask, 'What's yours?' and some ugly punter would laugh in his face, before stepping back to avoid the inevitable swipe. The bar thwarting Gunter's desire to nobble his mocker. He'd been known to poison drinks through his own thirst for revenge; it was clear the man had no calling as a publican. He was too exposed to ridicule in such a public domain.

Gunter Gobblelard never made peace with his voice. Feeling betrayed by his body, trying to compensate by being quick-witted and fast-fisted, though his witticisms often provoked laughter because of their squeakiness rather than their wit. Gunter tried to speak with a low voice, spending hours attempting to locate some previously unknown corner of his anatomy where the long-lost low tones of his larynx lay in hiding. Never achieving anything more than a comical impersonation of the bass noises he aspired to. In a dismal moment he overheard two men doing impersonations of his speaking voice. Gunter, refraining from his usual practice of administering kicks and punches, went home and cut his throat. John found the body, and decided then that as a mark of filial respect and devotion he would perfect his father's craft, before calling Les outside to break the news, and getting him to hose down the yard.

When the two men who'd insulted his father later failed to return from a fishing expedition, John nodded sagely, while mumbling, 'Stupid bastards must have decided to go swimming!'

John, who'd started drinking early, took control of the pub at the age of twelve. One reason, perhaps, why John had such empathy with the youngest drinkers at the bar. Gunter's father, John Artemis Gobblelard, had lived till he was ninety, and Gunter's two-month reign over the pub was seen, in hindsight, as a kind of interregnum. It was a relief to all when John made his quick ascension to the throne as publican of The Bluebottle, Prawn and Oyster.

John was feeling as tender as one of his steaks. He'd spent the morning briskly slaughtering for the week ahead, and had found himself weeping once again, thinking of his squeaky father as he clutched the knife. Telling himself it was the effect of the winds that had been blowing since dawn, making him feel wrong-headed. Or was he feeling more in tune with himself than he usually permitted? The familiar griefs and uncertainties. Surprised that he wanted to talk to his mother, curious to know more about his father. Wondering why, when Gunter died, his mother made him swear never to ask for information, or talk about his father in her presence. John felt a certain rage that she'd deny his father what he felt was Gunter's due — the guarantee of an afterlife, the departed living on in the memories of those who were dear to them.

John had not realised that his parents had lived such separate lives. He was too busy in the pub to pay much heed to their affairs. The final rupture had come when Virginia decided to stop eating meat. Gunter still presented her with the choicest cuts each week, and each rebuttal kept his sense of injury fresh.

To make matters worse, Virginia Gobblelard had decided to go back to her maiden name of Birdeater. Her great-great-grandparents had stumbled on a nest and eaten seven birds, in the first days of Salvation, after the *Good Hope* had gone down. Known as Birdeaters since that time. They didn't mind the change — it seemed more promising than Slag.

When she was young Virginia had sworn, 'One thing I'll never be is a Gobblelard!' Within five years she'd fallen in love with Gunter. He had a roguish charm and a guaranteed income. Or was it just the rum? He was a hard-working man, and Virginia had been a meat-eater in those days.

John asked his mother if she had loved Gunter and was stunned by her answer.

'He was a man, no worse, no better.' His mother paused then added, 'If I had my time again I'd never have children. Count yourself lucky — you and your weedy brother. If you want to give thanks for your life, you should say your prayers to the god of coitus interruptus.'

John was appalled to think that he owed his life to such a random chance as his father's inability to withdraw before he spurted. It affronted his sense of importance. Seeing himself as some resplendent gloryman, product of King Sperm, his birth predestined, not an act of spontaneous emission.

Wondering if he'd ever celebrate a birthday again, hating his mother for her directness and unnecessary honesty. Granting him his birthright of futility.

John did his best to avoid the subject from then on, though he could not stifle his desire to know more about his father. Deciding he'd leave his mother alone and talk to his father's friends. Discovering that his father had no friends, or none who wanted to talk about the man, post mortem. At best the men he approached would mumble, 'Gunter was a good butcher. What more can I say?'

John had no idea, and only wished his informants might grow more eloquent, though the more he plied them with free drinks the more taciturn they became. Still Gunter grew in his son's estimation. Dedicating each fresh carcass to the memory of His Father, Good Butcher Gunter. In John's mind Gunter's voice began to drop, and John wondered if the town had ever known such an exemplary man.

The more John thought about his father, the more he felt a certainty brewing in him: if nothing else, he'd ensure the town would not forget John Gobblelard when he died.

A DANGEROUS TREND

Ernie was becoming increasingly alarmed by what he felt was a dangerous trend. Following the initial enthusiasm for The Slapping Man, many people now needed more than one slap to satisfy themselves. As if he was a drug to which they'd become accustomed and needed a greater dose. Yet the need for more slaps meant his business was turning over briskly.

He had a core of regular customers, many of them arriving each day to have their go at The Slapping Man. Had he spawned a brood of addicts? Some people were spending as much money as they earnt on The Slapping Man, their families pleading with Ernie to deny them his services. Ernie did his best to act with integrity, only allowing them three slaps. This made the thwarted slappers more angry than they'd been when they arrived to slap him, and thus negated his entire rationale.

One man arrived with a large bag of coins, placed them at Ernie's feet, then grunted, 'I'm not leaving till that bag is empty.' When Ernie tried to dissuade him from this plan the man clenched his fists and threatened to beat him. 'I won't punch you on the jaw, I know your gizzards and kidneys are as tender as any mortal's!'

Ernie let the man have thirty slaps, and then announced that was the maximum allowed on any day. Others waiting in the queue became increasingly agitated, both from the time the man was taking and from the sight of someone able to afford a reckless indulgence they'd not dreamt possible. Thirty slaps! The man had strong hands, with skin worn hard from years of labouring with pick and shovel. Ernie thought the man's eyes had begun to water by the end, and felt a glint of pride that his jaw was more than a match for a man with such work-hardened palms. The man alternated blows between his left and right hands, and his left-hand slaps were not as hard. By the end of the thirty slaps Ernie knew the man was not using his full force. Sure the man had begun to wince each time a slap landed. Ernie grew cheeky then, asking if perhaps he'd care for another ten.

'No, no, I think you're right, thirty is plenty for one day.'

Later that day Ernie was distressed to learn that the man had stolen the money from his wife's savings. The wife arrived at Ernie's booth, wanting her money back. She also begged him to refuse her husband any slaps in future. He felt his kidneys spasm as he contemplated the likely beating he'd sustain to all the wrong parts of his body. In the end they made a deal. Ernie would refund half the money, on condition that the transaction was made out of hours, and if she breathed a word of it to anyone he'd let her husband have a hundred slaps or more if he so desired. Ernie could imagine the riotous scenes and schemes that would break out if word spread about his weakness for benevolence.

THE SLAPPING MAN

Ernie had not reckoned on the moral dilemmas posed by his profession. There seemed no end of tricky permutations. He was just The Slapping Man, he was no philosopher of ethics. When the man returned the following day Ernie let him have three slaps, then sent him on his way. The man looked tense and stroppy. As he walked off he kicked a stray dog in the ribs, and the cracking sound that issued from the canine abdomen made Ernie feel he was responsible for the cruelty. When he finished work that day he found the dog lying in a corner of the market, whimpering each time it breathed. Ernie bought the dog a bloody steak. The dog eyed him curiously, as if it had no precedent for such an act of generosity, and began to chew. When it swallowed it emitted a curious long whimper, the distress in the animal's whining too eloquent for Ernie's comfort. Ernie squatted on his haunches beside the beast, stroking its head as the dog chewed and whimpered. The dog had been unable to swallow more than two mouthfuls before deciding that the pain thus incurred was greater than the pleasure of eating fresh meat. Not knowing what else to do Ernie walked off then, telling himself that in time the canine ribs would mend. Wondering if this was just a lie confected for his comfort.

LORD OF THE BAY

John Gobblelard fancied himself a kind of lord of the bay, yet he never ventured onto boats. He preferred to spend his spare time at the fish-scraping yards, where the fish caught by his boats were gutted and scaled.

The fish-scraping yards stank, though seagulls loved them, circling then descending to eat the guts that were thrown onto the ground. Blowflies and maggots were also partial to that stinking feast. John avoided the yards in the hottest weather, though found the sex there thrilling when the catch was in. The fish wriggling in their boxes, coated in goo and slime. The agitation as they thrashed around excited him. His shark-tooth necklace gleaming in the light as he scraped away with some lively female against a wall. Always someone glad to duck the work and have a scrape with him instead. He'd always wanted to have sex in the bleeding shed behind the pub, though never found a volunteer, and had to lend himself a hand instead as the carcasses were draining. Glad he had more success at the fish-scraping yards, it appeased what he felt was a fundamental appetite for sex in the open air, with the smells and sounds of dying creatures to help propel his vigour. Still hoped he'd find one day a bleeding woman who'd do him in the killing shed.

John Gobblelard felt he was in competition not only with all the living residents of Ruination, but all the dead as well. He wanted to achieve a level of success unprecedented in the town, that he might truly know he was the First Citizen of Ruination for all time. It would need to be some extraordinary exploit, so that those yet to be born would still be unable to surpass his reputation.

John loved hearing the terrible stories that circulated about The Gobblelard Clan, and was glad to do his best to help the family legend along. Embellishing new details when he felt that they were needed. He was troubled by one thing only: Artemis Gobblelard had been such an exemplary forebear and founder of their dynasty it was hard to surpass the man. John wanted to eclipse the reputation of the great Captain Cook, but had no idea how to do so. At times he wondered whether he needed to make a string of human sausage and devour it in public, it made him salivate with curiosity, yet he knew this was nothing more than a pale imitation of his ancestor. And Artemis had not been alone in his epicurial exploits. John wanted to achieve the exploit, if not the life, that made it clear to all that he was The Gobblelard Majestic for all time. As if he might digest the family name and make it utterly his own. Wanting to make it impossible for anyone to hear the Gobblelard name without thinking immediately of him. What could he do to become an exemplar, the most extraordinary man who'd ever graced the shores of Ruination?

VRONSKY'S SLOPBUCKET

Ernie started worrying that he was doing some kind of psychic harm to the populace, appealing to their worst natures and pocketing the proceeds.

It was due to this distress that he decided to visit Doctor Vronsky, Salvation's only Counsellor of Grief.

Vronsky had a small windfall each year when the footballers suffered their annual humiliations and lost by new record margins. Coming to him for counsel at the end of each season. He always seemed so cheerful as he explained that football was really about the nature of defeat and how the townsfolk coped with it.

'Look,' he'd explain, 'there's only one team who wins. All the others lose. All the players, supporters and loved ones of all the other teams are plunged into remorse. The nature of the game is to lose. Winning is an aberration.'

His logic brought a comfort to the listener, and he quickly developed quite a reputation. At first he didn't like to charge for his services, yet invariably would be repaid. A dozen bottles of home-brewed beer arriving on his doorstep, a box of mudcakes, or some oysters. People thought of him fondly. That in itself was unusual. As more people began to seek him out he felt compelled to start charging them, there was no time left for other work. He preferred it to cleaning fish for John Gobblelard, and the pay was better.

Everybody knew he had no medical training. The handwritten slat outside the door was a grateful joke from an early patient. Back in the days when he helped his friends, before he began to think of them as 'patients'. The sign painted up, stuck on the wall at the front of the house. The name had stuck to him forever more, and so he became a 'Doctor'. And slowly began to see himself that way.

Vronsky didn't know who his parents were, and had been found crawling through the streets clutching a small bag with the name *Vronsky* written on it. It was the brand name of the satchel, and he thought it funny that he'd been named after it. Calling himself 'Satchel' when he felt in good humour. It was as good a name as any, and no less arbitrary than if he'd been named after some dead actor or a fish.

He still had his little satchel, and when he became Doctor Vronsky he had the bag updated to accommodate his new title. *Doctor Satchel Vronsky*. He felt he'd finally perfected his identity. Yet he still got a surprise when people asked him, 'Are you Jewish?'

Vronsky had a special chair he used when people came for their first session, a chair designed to fall apart when sat upon. Vronsky was convinced he learnt a lot about his new client from their reaction once they hit the floor. Would they explode with fury or sit, resigned and weepy, suddenly emptied of their life force? Ernie was the only one who started laughing when his arse hit the floor, and Vronsky knew straight off he liked the little man. He listened, intrigued, as Ernie explained the full extent of his new vocation, and the ethical and moral dilemmas it now provoked. Vronsky was convinced that Ernie embodied a selflessness quite at odds with the prevailing winds of the town's temperament.

It seemed an extraordinary martyrdom, and Vronsky wondered how such a small man could take such a large burden onto his shoulders, or his jaw. Ernie's dilemmas were so unprecedented, Vronsky had no idea what to suggest.

At the end of their session he went to shake Ernie's hand and said, 'Good luck with your moral dilemmas!' Ernie was as surprised as Vronsky when The Slapping Man slapped The Counsellor of Grief, and then said, 'For your arrogance!'

An awkward moment then, ruptured by Vronsky's laughter, which coincided with Ernie's bursting into tears. The two men hugging each other without deliberation. It might have been that hug which forged whatever bond of intimacy they established. The hug disturbed by Vronsky's laughter once again as Ernie said, 'I hope that I'm not turning poofy!' and instantly regretted it. Was an affectionate punch in the stomach as close as the men of Ruination could ever come to admitting that in the male bond there was scope for love and kindness? Something he and Vronsky now discussed, and it was not the sort of thing Ernie had ever heard over the back bar at The Bluebottle, Prawn and Oyster.

Vronsky had never laughed during any of his sessions, usually he found the self-obsessed outpourings began to bore him or make him angry; if he felt like laughing he always suppressed the impulse. He didn't charge Ernie for his time, and the two men started meeting regularly, on an informal basis, Vronsky sometimes dropping round to visit Ernie in the little shed out in the garden.

Vronsky was surprised to find he had befriended The Slapping Man. He preferred to keep a professional distance between himself and his clients, even when they had formerly been friends. The intimacy tainted by an excessive familiarity, making him more isolated and adding to his grief. Not that he ever showed it, apart from when he whinged to Ernie.

Vronsky ate and drank whatever he wanted. As if this was his compensation for the rigours he endured while working. Ernie admired Vronsky's gusto, the glee with which he sat down to steak and eggs, a bottle of red wine, and smoked with contentment as he drank strong black coffee after his evening meal. Like many men and women in Ruination, Vronsky welcomed insomnia.

Ernie could understand Vronsky's need to whinge and moan. Needing to find some relief from the constant tide of horror and discontent that washed around him. His waters muddied by the effluent of the town's guilts and tragedies and consternations. Sitting together in the shed, or beside The House of Pearls, as Vronsky aired the many ailments of the townsfolk. Ernie was unsure what obligation he was under, if any, feeling some onus of confidentiality now passed to him. Wanting to talk to someone about the horrid things that Vronsky loaded on him, while convinced he must tell no one.

He would always be The Slapping Man. The stories Vronsky blurted out were like fresh blows, though they were different to the ones he fielded with his jaw. These blows of Vronsky's seemed to cop him in the tender places of his innards, penetrating to the core. Feeling resentful, wishing Vronsky might choose a different target, yet he also felt flattered. He'd become Vronsky's slopbucket, into which was poured the filth and muck of the town's worst features. The man who pulled his gizzards out of his belly after opening his stomach with a razor, while saying, 'Well, nurse, what will you do now?' The woman who'd killed two strangers and used the bodies to stop her boat from leaking.

Faced with such tales Ernie could never bring himself to add to Vronsky's load, and almost found it amusing that the one man he could not ask for counsel in his grieving was his good friend The Counsellor of Grief. Ernie had never made peace with the guilt he felt over the death of his parents. Trying to console himself with Vronsky's free advice, 'Cheer Up!'

After his whinge Vronsky always felt lighter, Ernie could see his step was springier as he walked off. Ernie always felt worse, often drinking for several hours after Vronsky had staggered home, and sometimes drank till he threw up, as if it was some necessary purge. Needing to find a way to hurl the horror stories from him, and if they merely dribbled at his feet, that was already far enough.

JEAN WITH GODWINGS

Jean was having the most intense orgasms with total strangers. Unsure what implications there might be, if any, for her personal theology. She enjoyed it, mostly, and when she didn't she thought of the pain she got in her knees when scrubbing the marble convent floors, and knew she preferred her current situation.

She had not expected to surprise the rector in mufti by The Virgin Wall. The man had not recognised her until after he'd muffed her. Muffling his protests and dismay, his cover blown long before he had.

'You used to act like your shit was too good to lick. You don't look like that now.'

The man was flabbergasted, had no idea how to reply.

'I used to go to you for a service. Now you've come to me for one. Things don't change, do they?'

For a moment she saw herself with a white dog collar, a dazed and naked priest. She made the man kneel then while wondering exactly what she wanted him to do. Did she want to put a collar and leash on him? Did she want to say the sacred prayers? Watch him emptying himself over a bowl? She wanted none of these things. Might they have access to any aspect of the sacred at that moment?

'Do you have your collar with you?'

'It's in my bag.'

He was looking nervous, and a vein in his temple was pulsing too rapidly.

'Give it to me.'

The man's trousers were still around his knees. His pale haunches wobbling as he bent and rummaged. The man gave her the collar.

'You.'

She hadn't meant to command such authority.

'You put it on me.'

It occurred to her that the man might try to strangle her. But he made no such attempt. She felt her gaze had strengthened. An elevation in her chest that caused her breasts to tilt a little. She felt a movement in her plexus, as if the stiffened cartilage was now loose and she could breathe more deeply. She felt that she was smiling, could see the wind tossing the palm heads and rippling the water.

'Will you pray with me?'

The rector nodded. He felt bewildered, compliant. Unable to leave, alarmed by the implications of his staying. And yet he knelt beside her.

She closed her eyes and could not think of anything to say. And so they knelt, the confused pair, and felt the wind on their faces. As if this might have been their common act of prayer. The man pulling his pants up then over flaccid haunches.

As he picked up his bag to leave Jean held his hand, and was glad to feel his fingers briefly squeezing hers. It seemed more intimate than their rutting by the wall.

Surprised to hear him say, 'Those who have not sinned will only know the minor of what we feel.' Pausing before mumbling, 'You can keep the collar.'

Jean wondering what she meant then as she said, 'Sometimes when I have sex it feels just like another form of prayer.'

Taking the collar off, handing it back to the rector.

'I don't think I'm a collar sort of person. It reminds me too much of a penis ring.'

She felt the most surging wonderment when she had sex, and felt sure some days that this intense contact with the divine was the thing that drove her in her sexual encounters. Her lower lips become a pair of godwings, speeding her to pleasure.

CHEER UP!

Vronsky knew he was on a winner with grief counselling. Amazed that in such a place no one had thought to do it, given the internal climate of the town. It was as good as making bread, he told himself, or better. It satisfied an essential appetite, and he didn't need to bake or knead. Needing nothing more than his own scone. Nor did it bother him if at times his thinking was half-baked: he did the best he could for a man not blessed with an IQ to match his ego.

Agonising at times as he wondered if he really did his best, or had he just grown complacent? Still, he knew grief counselling was a good lurk. There was no end of grief in Ruination. He had been threatened by angry wives, husbands, sons-in-law and lovers. He'd been physically assaulted, accused of quackery and deception.

'What's his advice? Cheer Up. That's it? How much do you pay him?'

Vronsky tried to keep his sense of humour, not always easy when sporting two black eyes.

All those woes poured into his ears like a liquid poison, seeping into his brain. It was a tricky business, being a grief counsellor. The constant woes made him despondent, yet he'd become accustomed to the cash and comfort. To the identity he had as Doctor Vronsky, Counsellor of Grief. Doubted he'd ever summon up the courage to walk away from it. At times he envied those who came to him for counsel, wishing he might give himself some good advice.

The grievances of Vronsky's patients had slowly become his own. As if he was a lake who had been slowly filled by the tributaries of sadness flowing into him each day. All the while he smiled, and nodded, holding his feelings in. And yet he'd had his successes.

The daughters of Harness Wilson were cheered immensely once they'd seen him. He'd only needed eight words, had seen them both at once and charged them both his standard fee. They were out the door in under half a minute. He thought he had a genius for the work.

HARNESS WILSON AND HIS DAUGHTERS

Harness Wilson was called by that name because he had been born without knee-caps and couldn't walk. His body collapsing when he stood. To rectify this fault in his design he built himself a chair on wheels and, when his twin daughters were old enough, put them into harness, hauling him along. Resisting all efforts to persuade him that it would be more seemly to use a dog or horse or other beast. 'Why,' he would answer, 'when I have two healthy daughters?'

The mother had left when the girls were three years old. Nobody blamed her, as he was known to have foul habits, though they thought it was unfair to leave the young ones in the care of Harness Wilson.

Harness was never shy of arguing what was fair.

'Life is not fair. If life was fair I'd have been born with kneecaps. The girls have kneecaps, they can walk. Putting them in harness seems fair to me. What would you have me do, drag myself across the ground like a human worm? Would that strike you as fair?'

It was a difficult argument to refute. Harness had always wanted to have a drink at The Perseverance, but the hill was too much for his daughters. A lifetime's aspiration that would never be fulfilled. He was a big man, and because he never walked, had never known the joy of running, and was not prone to any form of exercise, he became bigger with each passing year. His daughters were hauling a bowl of human jelly, and the jelly bowl bawled at them, venting his anger at his life's misfortune. Who could blame him? Who could tolerate it?

The girls were known as Sweat and Blood, and no one was surprised when, aged eleven, they ran away. It was a pitiable sight, to see Harness Wilson propel himself in his trolley-chair, using a wooden pole as if he was the ferryman of some poor land-bound gondola. The surprise was that the girls came back six months later. They felt too guilty, though once returned they instantly regretted it, as Harness seduced them into putting on the harness once again, then with the help of his large stick beat them soundly and chained the girls together. He never let them out of sight or out of harness. Keeping them like a pair of badly treated dogs, or worse. Though no one intervened. Perhaps this was because the girls were only seen when they pulled Harness out of doors, and no one realised the dreadful state of things behind closed doors.

It came as no great shock when, on the thirteenth birthday of Sweat and Blood, Harness Wilson was found at the bottom of a cliff the locals called The Last Embrace. A favourite spot for suicides. Sweat and Blood insisted that their father had wanted to visit that haunted place, needing fresh air, ignoring their complaints that the hill was too steep, and the trolley might be difficult to control where the hill sloped down towards the cliff.

If their report was true, poor Harness and his trolley had gathered speed, attaining a frightening momentum, and it was only what the girls called an act of God that enabled them to hang onto the cliff as Harness and his trolley disappeared at speed over the edge. It was as well they had the foresight to bring a small knife to cut the traces, or the three of them would have perished. Poor Harness, smashed to blubber on the rocks. Discovering the vital truth of The Last Embrace as his gizzards wrapped themselves like tentacles around the sharp serrations of barnacles and molluscs.

Sweat and Blood were now Bruised and Bloodied. A guiltiness informed their footsteps. Perhaps the shock of losing their dear father had only now begun to register, and it was grief, not guilt. It was then that a well-meaning acquaintance suggested they visit Doctor Vronsky.

As they began their story he held up his hand to silence them, being fully cognisant of the details.

'The dead have long memories, but no fingers.'

For some reason it seemed the very thing those girls needed to hear. They'd become very pious after the accident, going to church every day for both matins and evens, walking hand in hand. After seeing Doctor Vronsky their attendance waned. They suddenly grew taller, and their bodies blossomed. By year's end they were grown women, as if their bodies had only needed to be freed of the father's shackles to find their true stature. Vronsky thought them a testament to his natural ability.

FOOTIE

Jean was an attractive woman, though she was not confident in her beauty. She was overeager to please, and this was her greatest vice, or was it a weakness? How else could she have ended up in the arms of so many members of the football teams? Telling herself she could now play all the positions. Though she never let men kiss her. Propelled by something greater than her sexual appetite. A terrible determination to succeed, or to exceed. Wanting to please. Developing her sexual talents as she discovered this was the way to win the heart of any man. Only realising the folly of her thinking when it became too late to change the image of herself that she'd created.

In time people stopped calling her Jean Flinch and simply called her Footie. Passed from hand to hand, fondled, mauled and fingered. She thought she'd enjoyed it at first, would smile and shake her finger, as if the one who called her Footie was merely being naughty. She seemed unable to comprehend the malice that lay behind the name. The disdain.

Footie would not have said she was the sexual genius of Ruination, though she was. Footie had full use of muscles many women didn't know existed in the female body. She'd developed a mastery of her organ that was truly prodigious, being able to clench and grip, lying utterly still while pumping a man's cock internally. Most men had never known the like before, had not dared presume it was in the realm of the humanly possible, and thus let Footie take liberties with their persons that they would not otherwise condone.

She was unrestrained when it came to foreplay, using fabrics, fruits, liquids, or any object that came to hand. If she found herself swathed around an upright man wearing a green silk tie she'd slip it off his neck and wrap the silk around the throstle, deep on the stem; it kept the men hard, and stopped them coming. Footie was artful in her way, though utterly untutored, learning as she went, instructed by her curiosity and carnal pleasures.

Sometimes she took them, sometimes she left them gasping, begging her to take them in hand, or mouth, or body, aching for relief. They'd do anything then, like performing animals, kneeling on the ground, standing on a table, they were foolish and Jean didn't want to fuck them. She wanted to humiliate them. Telling herself it was not her greatest virtue, yet if she chose her subjects carefully she could live with herself. Belittling those who had inflated opinions of themselves, or who Jean knew to be villainous. Watching with satisfaction as their cocks began to tremble, and the slippery bead of transparent slime oozed out of the tip. Then she'd announce, 'Actually I've got a bad disease, or several, and one of them's that I don't fancy you at all ...'

Loving the sure knowledge that she was the best root in town. Jean wanted to smell life's rump and butthole. She'd slip her finger up the rump of some eager men, it scared them, and gave her a sense of power. Knowing that she was brave and they were timid. She wanted to fondle the testicles of her life, and was not content to lie on her back while the world heaved and shuddered over her. Could sex really be a kind of prayer?

She knew her sense of the sacred had not died, she just felt thwarted, not knowing how she might express it. Wondering some days if God was not dead, but merely resting?

One of the strangest things was this: Footie had her revenge. She had the name emblazoned in red letters across the jumpers of the local teams. Wearing the colours of The Tempest at the start of the game, then changing into the black jersey of The Dead Men at half-time. When people called her Jean she corrected them, 'My Name Is Footie!' Earning a grudging respect through her obstinate embracing of the name. She laughed a little wildly when she said it, and there was something quite alarming in that laugh. People knew, when they heard it, that they'd lost whatever power they might have once enjoyed over her.

Out on the ground the ball the lads were playing with was a constant reminder of the girl, and their abuses, as if the ball itself was emblazoned with the name in bright red letters. Jean didn't need to attend the games to bring the lads undone, their guilts and consternations were ever present on the field. The players didn't want to touch the ball, there were passages of play where the ball would just lie on the ground, the players pretending to be engaged in some tactical manoeuvre, the ball could stay like that for minutes at a time; needless to say the crowds evaporated — who'd stand in the mist and rain for such a spectacle? For the first time in the history of Ruination an entire season passed and not a single point was kicked. At season's end all of the teams were declared to have won the wooden spoon.

There was a curious curse in place. People started talking about the death of football. Vronsky was doing a roaring trade. Refining his theories, inventing new ones, unaware of the truth as he never went to watch a game. He hated football, but he loved his theory. He never tired of telling anyone who'd listen that the game was derived from the practice of kicking a severed head around a field. The ultimate celebration of defeat.

'The players kick the ball-as-severed-head in the ultimate triumph of the living over the dead. Though as the ultimate destiny of all who play is to die, in time they'll share the defeat of the one whose head is being kicked. Cheer Up!'

Oddly enough his advice did not make his clientele grow cheery.

During the off-season a lot of the players took a new interest in swimming, 'To keep in shape,' they said. The Octopus took a few. In fact, The Octopus was so diligent that the following season the number of teams was halved, as clubs were forced to merge due to reduced numbers. To make things worse it had become impossible to entice new recruits from the young lads who were now old enough to play. Some people said the town was Doomed, and for a few weeks it became the new name.

Threats were made on Footie's life, but she was immune to fear. Possessed of a strength she'd never known was hers. She'd begun to find this strength when she started laughing at herself. Ernie thought she had become quite marvellous. He also knew he was her beneficiary, as so many of the players and supporters stood in his queue that people had to wait for hours, and he'd been forced to put his prices up. It had been Vronsky's idea, and a good one.

Jean seemed unable to cultivate a necessary cynicism, she was too trusting of people. It wasn't just the sex, though she quite enjoyed it. She didn't know that grief could send the sexual motor into overdrive. Always expecting something that was never returned, some gentler aspect of the species that she glimpsed and gave her heart to on the spot. Always feeling sore and chafed when she discovered that tenderness had been withheld.

Many of the women felt a compassion for Jean and withheld their sexual favours. There was an alarming decline in the birthrate. The cruder men lamented that they could no longer score on or off the field. Trying to sublimate their sexual urges by drinking; becoming frustrated, maudlin and angry, depressed and violent. Accusing each other of being the cause of their downfall, before they lurched out of The Bluebottle, Prawn and Oyster to have yet another go at The Slapping Man. Jean's thighs were closed for business and The Virgin Wall had fallen silent.

PART FOUR:

A BOWL OF PERIWINKLES

ERNIE WAVES WHILE VRONSKY WAIVERS

Ernie hated saying goodbye. The act of waving reminded him of his parents drowning. Whenever he waved he felt like crying. Shaking hands was fine, it was only when he saw people at a distance that he had a problem. Friends and customers were often affronted when they waved to Ernie only to see him turn his back and stride off. Thinking the little man was rude, when he only wanted to spare himself the grief that seemed to surface so readily in him. It was not so bad for business, as it made those who waved determined to go back to the market and take another swipe at The Slapping Man.

Ernie's inability to wave goodbye was something he discussed with Vronsky, and the esteemed Counsellor of Grief insisted Ernie spend whole sessions waving goodbye to imaginary friends, or to his parents. Ernie spent the entire time weeping, his arm growing numb and heavy. Vronsky thought he was clever to have devised this simple stratagem, until he realised that all he'd achieved was Ernie's forced immersion in a grief that was all-consuming. At the end of their third waving session Ernie asked, 'Am I making progress?' as he wiped the tears from his eyes and cheeks and jaw, and Vronsky answered, 'Yes. You've helped me realise what a fool I am.'

They embraced warmly then, and Vronsky joined Ernie in his weeping, glad of the release, while wondering if he was taking advantage of the little man. Provoking Ernie's tears because he was the only person Vronsky could weep with. It made him feel guilty, yet he found the weeping such a benevolent release he didn't mind the guilt so much. Forcing Ernie to recount once more the details of the double death by drowning, that Vronsky might grieve for his own parents, the ma and da he'd never known. Vronsky always meant to confide his guilt to Ernie though never felt quite strong enough to do so. As Ernie told his tale once more Vronsky imagined that his own father's head was disappearing beneath the cold waters of the bay, and that he and Ernie were both waving to their dead parents. Vronsky assumed his parents were dead: having no information to the contrary it seemed a reasonable expectation.

Satchel Vronsky was so used to the fact that he had no idea who his parents were, it had become a stable part of his identity. Never expecting to solve the riddle of his parentage, he told himself this might have been a stroke of good fortune. There was no guarantee that his forebears were in any way exemplary, and he may have thus been spared the trauma of learning that his mother and father were exemplars only in their capacity for villainy. Or was he the product of a benign and fruitful union? Relieved that his family history was a clear slate. Freed of a burden. Or so he tried to tell himself, on a daily basis, while the question gnawed at him like a patient mouse in a winter pantry.

ERNIE WAVES WHILE VRONSKY WAIVERS

At the end of their third waving session both men were so overcome with grief it was obvious there was no point in continuing with this approach. To make things worse, as Ernie left he winked at Vronsky, smiled, then said, 'Cheer Up!'

VRONSKY'S LOGICAL DIRECTION

Vronsky sometimes tried to make his clients more depressed. Hoping his gambit might force them to cheer up, unable to sustain the weight of their depression. Listening to them whingeing about their ugliness, their lack of hope, their excessive weight, their lack of humour, their lethargy, their inability to lead effective lives. Nodding his head, agreeing with everything they said.

'You're a hopeless case. Have you considered suicide?'

To his surprise, so many of them had. The most hopeless cases were the ones who'd tried several times yet never managed to bring the fatal business off.

Vronsky wondered whether people made up stories to tell him, as if the more graphic their account the greater their relief, regardless of whether it was true or false. Not always sure he could tell the lies from the true stories, though the true stories were usually the most disturbing. One man had called his daughter Money in the hope that she'd attract his fortune. He was bankrupt within a year of the christening. He thought of working her as a child prostitute when she grew older, though didn't want to give his uncles and brothers the clap. Telling Vronsky he had some scruples.

Vronsky wondered whether he needed to devise a system that would allow him to rank the various horrors he heard according to their degree of villainy. Which was worse, to kill someone without reason, or with reason? Were some reasons better than others, or was there no possible justification? How might he construct a scale? Did he need to concoct a set of guidelines, giving each deed a score out of five for a range of criteria, then add the total?

When working with clients it was not unusual for him to remain utterly still for the entire session. The more still he was, the more animated the confessions of his clients, something he thought useful. Occasionally he would break his silence and commence a rapid dissertation. This unexpected animation left his clients stunned, particularly as he'd immediately resume his silent immobility. He wouldn't even grunt or nod, and his clients would wonder if they'd really heard the man talking or had begun to hallucinate through their need for some kind of response. Had he fallen asleep with his eyes open, or slipped into a coma?

Vronsky liked the idea of a coma. Telling himself that the less he did, the less chance there was of committing some villainy, whether by design or accident. Envying the stillness of rocks, and the wooden posts of the wharf anchored deep in the mud and sand of the bay. Hoping he might yet attain something of that eternal torpor.

Vronsky had a distaste for physical exercise. He preferred the great indoors.

He found The House Of Pearls a pleasing place for meditation, though the breezes which passed through the structure made his ideas fleeting, and hard to remember. No sooner thought than it seemed they'd blow out of his mind. A room with no open windows was, he felt, a prerequisite to the retention of cerebration.

Vronsky found it easiest to think in small rooms. Asking himself if the smaller the room, the greater the thoughts? If so, then the most trivial ideas would be those conceived out of doors. Did he need to design a special room that would inculcate his most intense thinking? He decided to be logical about the entire enterprise. He slowly reduced the volume of a spare room in the middle of the house, six inches at a time, and monitored the changes of intensity in his thinking. To his delight his premise proved accurate, until finally he bought a coffin and stood it on its end, that he might still think standing up. As he expected, his thoughts achieved their maximum intensity at this point, as close to 'pure' thought as the human brain could achieve. Though he hadn't reckoned with the obvious: for every 'pure' thought there was another quite impure. He'd never known his sexual fantasies to assume such intense and overwhelming proportions, and in such a confined space it was difficult to masturbate. He had once entered what he called 'the smallest room in the house' utterly naked, and ended up chafing himself against the lid. He'd toppled the box from the vertical to the horizontal, and considered himself lucky that he'd only sustained minor injuries to himself and his intimate person, including several large splinters.

'Three millimetres to the left and I might have severed a vein and bled to death!'

Unsure whether he was delighted or appalled by this prospect, he wondered whether it would be best to conduct all future research fully clothed.

Once inside his box his thoughts often led in one direction: suicide. So many of the people he admired had killed themselves he wondered if he was under any obligation to follow suit, if he wanted to die with his self-respect intact?

Vronsky sometimes complained about his work so much Ernie would ask him why he bothered, would it not be easier to go back to scraping fish? To which Vronsky would reply, 'Ah, but they need me, Ernie,' and the two men would nod in unison, feeling a growing bond between them, the bond inspired by the curious burdens of their professions.

A CONNOISSEUR OF SLAPS

Ernie had become a connoisseur of slaps.
Convinced at times that he could read his slapper's soul from the fine calibrations of their blows.

Each time he was slapped he looked like a man who'd just been struck by some vital truth, or a glint of self-awareness, the force of which had left him momentarily speechless. It was hard not to laugh. Ernie made no attempt to compose his features. He was, somehow, naked.

While there was something comic about the little man, that was not the only attraction. In a town full of liars it was something to see a man who was struck by truth not once in a lifetime but, on a busy day, every few minutes for hours on end.

It was not unusual for people to spend hours sitting in the market, watching Ernie go about his business. Cracking jokes, spruiking up a bit of trade when necessary, delivering insults to those who demanded to be insulted. Mostly though he just stepped up and took it on the chin.

To Ernie's dismay some of his fellow toilers in the market no longer spoke to him, and averted their eyes when he looked their way. The Human Pickle and The Pincushion Man fell silent when he approached, only to resume talking the moment he was out of earshot. The low tones of a dark laugh reaching his ears, he'd turn back then, and they'd fall silent, the laughter choking in the air. Ernie had not reckoned that he might become too successful and that the more The Slapping Man prospered the worse his rivals would fare. The Pincushion Man was keeping a jealous eye on Ernie, noting that the young upstart could make more in a day than he made in his best weeks. The last time The Pincushion Man had spoken to Ernie he'd said, 'You're killing us, man! I've lost three stone since you started working; will you not be happy until I've shrivelled into bone? I'm The Pincushion Man, not The Walking Skeleton — if there's no meat upon my bones, what am I meant to push the needles into?'

Ernie had no idea how to react, and offered The Pincushion Man three free slaps a day. Dismayed when The Pincushion Man strode off, muttering, 'You're no good for this town. You're just too good at what you do.'

To make matters worse, The Pincushion Man was threatening to change his name to The Human Pincushion, and The Human Pickle wasn't happy.

Ernie wished he'd never boasted that the great difference between The Slapping Man and The Pincushion Man was that The Pincushion Man never let you push the needles in. Word filtered back and The Pincushion Man decided to tackle The Slapping Man head on, letting his customers push the needles under his skin, though they tended to get too excited, and wanted to push them in too far, at great risk to his essential organs.

Ernie wondered if he should cease trading as The Slapping Man rather than do such injury to his fellows.

He found it increasingly difficult to look at the people who were slapping him. Invariably he knew more about them than they realised, usually from Vronsky's ramblings. If he blurted out some family secret, such as, 'Are you still cheating on your wife?', the slapper invariably went into a rage that required many more slaps to defuse.

Ernie started keeping his eyes closed when working, to still his tongue by denying it ammunition. His ears sharp enough to know whether a coin had clinked into his box, or some other worthless object had been inserted.

'No, that's a button. Perhaps your pocket's broken? Try the other one.'

He preferred working blind. Being spared the knowledge of the identity of his slappers made it easier to sleep at night. Instead of lying awake wondering why Mrs Beaker, who'd never been to see him, suddenly felt the need to administer seven slaps. Convinced that such unnecessary knowledge could only harm his ability to provide the best possible service to the populace.

Yet there came a time when Ernie could tell the identity of his slapper even when his eyes were closed. Recognising the particular music of their coughs and shuffles, their certainties and hesitations, the force they used, the angle of the blows, the calibrations of the calluses on the palm. It only enhanced the mystique with which he was already regarded, farewelling customers by name, having kept his eyes shut for the duration of the visit. Realising that it was stupid to keep his eyes shut when his ears were still wide open.

JEAN WITH GAWKERS

Jean was eating like a woman who thought every mouthful might yet prove to be her last. The habit of setting a meal for both herself and Beau having fuelled her appetite, she no longer set two plates when she ate at home yet still ate enough for two. As if by stuffing herself she hoped to consume more of the world, taking in as much of life and experience as she could before her inevitable demise. Gorging on sausages, a plate of periwinkles at the pub, followed by two servings of mashed potato and bacon, a large steak, three pints of stout with dinner, just to help kick-start the night, and a double serving of apple pie, jelly, or whatever else Les had on the menu.

Even with her belly full to bursting she felt her appetite was not sated. She seemed to be regressing, constantly toying with her lips, sucking and eating. The more she toyed the more she salivated, the salivation made her want to eat again, and she was putting on so much weight she worried her bones would break under the strain of this new-found bulk.

A certain delirium seemed to have possessed young Jean. A curious dereliction. She no longer tried to make herself look pretty, her hair a tangle of knots, painting her mouth with a wild streak of red that made her lips look gashed and livid. Staring at men she'd known with a coolness and detachment that made them feel like specimens in a wax museum, or the aborted foetuses of different animals laid out for some scientific study. She wondered what were the constants in these men, beyond their desire to bed her, or get their momentary thrill before they parted company? And why did they later avoid her, or laugh at her, treating her with a disdain that was in such contrast to the intensity with which they clutched at her before they came? It puzzled her, and she never found an answer to her confusion.

Sometimes Jean's self-disgust seemed so familiar she wondered if it was the glue that bound her sense of self together. Feeling she was being 'nailed' every time she felt the cock being driven in.

She wanted to be abused, and disabuse herself of any notion of some spurious better self. Preferring her dereliction and iniquity, finding a strange peace at such times, sure she had at last come to terms with the most difficult essence of herself.

She'd propelled herself into so many encounters, and was now marked by them. She was Footie. There was no denying it. It had been good to feel wanted. Now she was the town slut, would be forever more, even if she never slept with a man again. And yet she had enjoyed some crazy liberty, and truth to tell she had enjoyed the sex. Not sure whether it would be better to become celibate, or continue on her sexual rounds.

She expected to feel anger, instead she just felt empty.

A phrase going round and round: 'Those who've never sinned will only know the minor of what we feel.'

Jean was lying on her bed, staring at her body as if it belonged to someone else. The dimpled contours of her flesh she found displeasing. She had put on so much weight she found it difficult to walk. Could not remember when she'd last tried running. When had her body billowed? Hating the way people stared in the street, their eyes caught by the great movement of her body as she waddled. She found it hard to resist the desire to abuse the gawkers, grew testy, and was dismayed when the gawkers ran away as she approached them. Trying a new tactic then, smiling and nodding, engaging them in banal conversation as she approached, or asking if they'd lend a hand, she'd dropped her purse and could not bend to pick it up. If they were foolhardy or kind enough to approach, she'd wait till they were within arm's reach then grab them and start to squeeze.

'You think I'm a big fat woman? You think I'm fit for gawping at? You didn't think I'd be strong enough to crush the life out of your bones, did you?'

Her laughter never brought comfort to the ears of those she squeezed. The more they tried to wriggle, the more she flexed her arms. The strength she felt at those moments made her briefly forget the dismay she felt at other times. When they began to quail and protest that she was killing them she only laughed harder. The more she squeezed the stronger she felt, and kept squeezing until she heard the whimpers and gasps as she forced the last air from the body that had stopped wriggling and become strangely inert. Then she'd drop them at her feet. She didn't always manage to resist the temptation to kick them. If, as they wobbled to their feet, they were foolish enough to kick her back, she felt an unruly righteousness spread through her. Pulling her sleeves up, she'd start throwing punches that carried the full weight of her bulk. She tried to restrain herself when confronted by people who were less than half her body weight. She enjoyed these stoushes, enjoyed them most of all if she was hit at least once. She felt she had an unfair advantage, as the great wads of fat that covered her frame gave excellent protection; at worst she sustained bruises which she admired in the comfort of her room. Feeling thwarted by the lack of any decent opposition, making do with the poor challengers that came to hand.

In time people made a point of crossing the street if they saw her approaching, or if they passed by they kept their eyes lowered. Jean's anger began to change course. Where she'd been offended when people ogled, now she became furious if they refused to meet her eye.

'Look at me, you bastards! Am I so disgusting?'

Grabbing the very ones who tried to respect her by not gawping; if they were lucky they'd escape with a good shaking. If they were unlucky she'd sit on them until they apologised. She was a weighty woman.

It was not uncommon for people to burst into tears if they saw Jean in the near distance, fearing the consequences of this inadvertent meeting. On the rare occasions she stepped inside a hotel, or went out shopping, a silence would fall as she walked through the door. Jean loved the air of expectation that greeted her entries. If she nodded to the assembled company and quietly muttered, 'Good day to you all,' and then left, there was an edge of disappointment and relief that followed her out. She'd step back inside then, saying, 'Which of you bastards is in need of beasting today?' and laugh.

It never failed to delight her as she watched the numerous gestures of discomfort that then broke out around the room. Men who hadn't picked their noses in twenty years would start to fidget with their nostrils. Others would shift from side to side, discovering a previously unknown interest in the cracks of the floorboards, or an out-of-date calendar featuring horses who were all dead.

JEAN WITH GAWKERS

People began running away from her when she appeared in public. Jean stumbling round the streets saying, 'Talk to me, please talk to me,' as people moved as far away from her as they could, afraid that at any moment she'd grow violent, they'd fall into her grasp and be beaten, bruised or bloodied.

THE UTILITY OF THE USELESS

Vronsky was convinced that the most important things were those commonly regarded as useless.

'These are the things we choose to make important. We grow potatoes because we are hungry. But there is no need to sew a ring of red flowers on the hessian sack we use to carry the potatoes. It is precisely then that we make our small meanings. Devoting our efforts to something of no practical use. Sewing threads to represent a ring of flowers, that is beauty. Defying the futility of our days and nights.'

Vronsky was intrigued and puzzled by the fact that the useless had its uses. He was standing in his office, fiddling with the satchel after which he had been named. He took the satchel off his shoulder and stared at the gold letters. *Doctor Satchel*

Vronsky. What could be more useless than gold letters on a satchel? Being named after them?

What if he had no name? Or had a different name? Would he be a different man? What if he'd been named after a fish? 'My name is Spine Fish, but you can call me Spine.' Would he be more erect in his bearing, or utterly spineless? What if he'd been called Blubber? Would he be prone to constant fits of weeping, or immune to the jellied feelings he sometimes felt in his belly? What name would he choose for himself?

Without realising it he'd begun to chew the leather strap of his satchel, a habit he'd formed in childhood. The strap bore the indentations of his teeth along its entire length. If he looked closely he could see the history of the development of his teeth preserved in the worn leather. The small bite of his milk teeth, the bolder indentations as his canines and incisors achieved adulthood. In places he'd chewed too hard and almost bitten through the strap. Where he'd sucked the leather it had become dry and brittle.

Sucking the strap always induced the same reverie. He saw himself wandering around the quay and markets, a lost laddie with no mummy and no daddy.

He had no recollection of their demise. Perhaps they'd left him in the shade of a tree while they went swimming, and The Octopus had claimed them. He often wondered how they died. Tried to avoid it, told himself he rarely thought about it, yet there were days he couldn't get it off his mind. Telling himself there were some consolations. He could invent and reinvent his family history according to his whim, or need. His mother one of the most beautiful women to set foot in Salvation. The charming hilarity of her laugh so forceful and beguiling that whenever she laughed in public whole crowds were hushed by that sparkling sound, and went about the day feeling refreshed and lighter. Perhaps her name had been Hilarity. His father a coward and a thief, continually perpetrating minor frauds and other acts of dereliction to support Vronsky's mother, with her habit of walking into shops and buying only the most expensive items. The ripest cheese, the double creams, dresses of silk and voile, hats plumed with the feathers of birds who'd been the last surviving examples of their species.

Arriving on the morning boat, taking a brief walk around the bay before eating a modest lunch, taking shelter in the trees of a secluded cove. Deciding to bathe, leaving their plump and chirpy boy under a bush, well protected from the risk of enscorchment by the blazing sun. His mother keeping her undergarments on. His father more bold, swimming confident and naked, the pair of them enjoying the ease their bodies felt, the dust of the journey washed away, inspiring a love for this strange place they hoped to call their home. Stroking out into the wide mouth of the bay, enjoying the colder currents that now wrapped around them like the tentacles of some great beast, not realising how strong those currents were, nor how icy, and only too late did they appreciate why the locals called those currents The Octopus, a phrase they never lived to hear, though they experienced its power, its cold grip pulling them down into the depths.

His reverie broken by the sound of someone knocking loudly on the front door. Vronsky blinked. He'd bitten right through the strap of his satchel, and was glad at the anger he felt as he cursed himself for being careless. It distracted him from this grief.

If he could baptise himself he'd call himself Charm. Knowing the truth was simpler — he did not know his name. Didn't even know if he was a local or a stranger. And would he ever know?

He decided to rest from his theoretical labours and finally attend to the whingeing bugger who was still knocking loudly on his door.

THE CRAPPING MAN?

The spreading addiction to his services caused Ernie great distress. He decided to take a week off, feigning a grievous injury to his neck, in the hope that it might allow those who'd become dependent on his services the time to regain their equilibrium. It had the opposite effect. The market was full of thwarted souls who'd come to see The Slapping Man, disbelieving when told that he was not available. Standing in the queue, convinced the story of his absence was a rumour spread by those who could not be bothered queueing. That Ernie was merely having lunch, or afternoon tea. The Man Who Never Laughs found the whole thing hilarious, and feared he'd lose concentration and blow his jackpot. This thought was all he needed to defuse his repressed hilarity, though he began to grow alarmed by the rowdy scenes that broke out among the stubborn queuers. Some tried slapping each other, but lacking Ernie's jaw the one who'd been slapped was liable to throw a punch in return. There were scuffles and fist fights. Some were convinced this was a cruel and selfish prank of Ernie's, designed to make them more aware of just how vital a role he now played in the town's physical and mental economy. It made them all the more determined to teach the little man a lesson when he finally showed his face again. People threw handfuls of mud at the little sign that said, *The Slapping Man regrets he will be unavailable till next week.*

There were jostlings and insults freely exchanged, which did something to mitigate the frustrations of Ernie's clients, while only underscoring the unique talents of The Slapping Man. He did not poke you in the eye or threaten your intimates when you hit him, unlike one's fellow would-be slappers as they waited in a queue that grew longer and more disorderly with each passing day. The Pincushion Man was worried, the enthusiasm for pushing needles into parts of his body he preferred to leave unpunctured was threatening to leave him mortally wounded, as people tried to take revenge on his person for the absence of The Slapping Man. Even The Man Who Never Laughs was growing alarmed, as people stopped trying to make him laugh and hurled dreadful insults, handfuls of mud and half-eaten sandwiches at him in their frustration. At least he had no fear of laughing.

At the end of the fourth day The Man Who Never Laughs convened an impromptu meeting of the market workers. In a rare moment of unanimity they agreed that if Ernie refused to return to work they were all at risk of being beaten. They were having trouble restraining their desire to retaliate, and would have already done so were they not so overwhelmingly out-numbered. Someone had tried to drown The Human Pickle, and were it not for the acuity of The Pincushion Man, and his dexterity with long needles, calamity would have been certain. They all had similar tales to tell.

To Ernie's astonishment The Man Who Never Laughs came to visit that night, poured them both a glass of stout, and proceeded to beg, wheedle, admonish and threaten Ernie. All to no avail.

Ernie was not bothered by the insults and admonitions of The Man Who Never Laughs, but could not cope when The Man began to sob uncontrollably, blubbering, 'Don't you see? We'll all be dead by Sunday if you don't show your face! People are making plans to abduct you, march you down to the square, tie you to a pole and teach you a lesson! Can't you see how grave the situation is? Some bastard tried to stick a needle through the eye of Pincushion!'

At which point Ernie had to concede The Man Who Never Laughs was right. They finished the second bottle of stout in silence. As The Man stood to leave Ernie mumbled, 'We're born with strange gifts, and that's the truth. If I'd been born with a prodigious gizzard and could shit at will, I might have been The Crapping Man and this whole dismal business would not have happened.'

The Man Who Never Laughs froze in midstride, his progress to the door suddenly interrupted. He seemed to be wrestling with some foreign impulse, freezing every muscle in the hope that he might restrain the tremor in his diaphragm Ernie's parting shot had inspired. A full minute passed before he deemed it safe to continue his forward progress, though he was moving in slow motion, so carefully did he ease himself out of Ernie's shed.

Ernie wished The Man goodnight, and closed the door. As The Man walked down the path beside the house Ernie heard him say, 'The Crapping Man!' and strained his ears, sure that he detected some foreign sound. The gurglings of a laugh quickly aborted? Or had The Man Who Never Laughs collapsed through nervous fatigue and was now sobbing under the bushes in the garden? Perhaps he was just regurgitating his stout? Ernie was about to step outside, but changed his mind, deciding to leave The Man in peace. Ernie heard a loud belch then, followed by a series of farts that grew quieter as The Man Who Never Laughs made it safely to the street.

The next morning Ernie was back in the market, determined to work overtime if necessary to clear the backlog. The fact that he'd made such a speedy recovery from his terrible neck injury became just one more example of his extraordinary powers. In the middle of what seemed the longest afternoon of his slapping life, he noticed The Man Who Never Laughs was staring at him oddly. He winked at Ernie, stood up and for a moment pretended to shit in that position before sitting down. Then he bit his lip so hard Ernie expected to see blood begin to trickle down his chin.

The Crapping Man! It made Ernie laugh, though his laughter was cut short by an impatient customer.

'You won't be laughing when I've finished with you!'

Ernie's customer was wrong, as Ernie laughed and giggled right through the several blows he fielded, and the more he laughed the harder his customer tried to wipe the smile off his face. At the end of this exchange Ernie turned his head, hoping to catch the eye of The Man Who Never Laughs, but The Man was nowhere to be seen.

THE GOBBLELARD MAJESTIC

Ernie wished he'd never seen John Gobblelard weeping. Some things, he felt, were best left unknown. That John Gobblelard had been smoking on the toilet at the time only amplified Ernie's sense of having violated the ungainly publican. Ernie had only meant to step outside and get some air. The air was not as fresh as he'd expected.

'If you tell a soul I'll slit your throat while you are sleeping!' It was a curious promise John made as he sidled up to Ernie at the bar after his visit to the john.

'My mother died this afternoon and it's got me feeling poorly. A good woman, she thought I'd wasted all my talents. Though she said the same thing of my father, may he rest in peace. Never displayed a gleam of delight at my abilities as a slaughterman. She was a vegetarian. She choked while chewing pumpkin seeds, can you believe it? Now, what are you drinking?'

John was bewildered by the manner of his mother's death.

'A pumpkin seed! Can you believe it? A pumpkin seed! A gunshot wound or a knife-slit throat I understand, but I'd never thought a pumpkin seed might be a dangerous thing. Are we never safe?'

He'd sworn off eating any vegetable, he'd live on meat and beer. He'd been tempted to make an exception for the peas he loved in his soup, before coming to his senses.

'A pea, a pumpkin seed, there's not much difference. It only takes the one pea that's not cooked, and there you are, a dead man in your shoes. Even an apple, now there's a mouthful of treachery. My mother used to make me eat them seeds and all, she swore it was good for a body, but I wonder now was she not trying to kill me?

'I'll not die from a piece of fruit or some vegetable, what a ridiculous end for any man or woman! My mother deserved a better death than that. Killed by a pumpkin. Not even a whole pumpkin. A seed, man, a bloody seed! She's been belittled by that pumpkin! You've got to think about the manner of your death, you can't leave yourself exposed to the villainies of chance. If she'd been washed off a boat and taken by The Octopus, at least it would have been a traditional way to go. It's no disgrace, the bay's a mighty thing and The Octopus a force of deadly reckoning. But a pumpkin seed? It's a mockery. What am I to do, plant a pumpkin vine on her grave to bless her memory?'

Something in his logic seemed to stall the tidal wave of grief that had been spilling over Ernie as he sat on a stool, sipping beer. There was a strange gleam in John's eyes as he leant forward, speaking quietly, as if he'd just perceived the truth.

'They'd be sweet pumpkins, though, that's certain.'

'The sweetest pumpkins called Death Themselves.'

Ernie felt his ears ringing with the volume of the publican's laughter. John reached over the bar, hauled Ernie to him and hugged so hard Ernie thought he had just discovered the preposterous nature of his own demise. His perplexity undiminished as John Gobblelard started shaking him while calling out, 'I love you, Ernie, yes, yes, the sweetest pumpkins!'

The next day John was by his mother's graveside, planting pumpkin seeds. Handling them with the care that others might handle an unexploded bomb. Finally his curiosity got the better of him; he placed one between his teeth and crunched it slowly. Grinding the seed into a thorough paste before he dared swallow the treacherous morsel. As he swallowed he felt he had triumphed where his mother had failed. Feeling he was a better human being than she was, no matter that he loved her, no matter that she never told him what a subtle man he was as he deftly slit the throats of bleating creatures. She was no match for a pumpkin seed.

By the end of that summer Les had won a new respect for the delight inspired by what became a permanent fixture on the menu: Mum's Pumpkin Soup.

John, meanwhile, began experimenting with the slaughter of a startling range of beasts — his mother's demise had filled him with the realisation that he too was mortal, and he wanted to have the pleasure of slaughtering as many different kinds of animal as he could before he died. Lizards, snakes, previously unknown kinds of sea creatures and rare birds were all considered fit for his sharp knife. Arranging the different tastes and textures in his mind as a painter might garner shades of colours. It was his personal artistry, he felt it demonstrated his feeling for the sublime. He never lost the thrill that came from seeing some previously unsighted set of gills or gizzards. Keeping the skins or shells of each new creature, displaying them in different parts of The Bluebottle, Prawn and Oyster. It was a pity they lost their vital sheen, yet they inspired in him such a sense of wonder at the array of living forms, he told himself and all who'd listen that The Bluebottle, Prawn and Oyster was the equal of any church or museum as a vehicle for rhapsody. Something that would survive him.

PLUMP LABIA

Jean was sitting in the market, listening to
Ernie's ramblings, wondering if this truly
was some saintly martyr who'd begun to minister to the town.

'There are always those who slap, and those who are
slapped. Slapping is a fundamental reality. Slapped when we are
born, slapped by the fact of our mortality, and the panic this
causes in us all. The fear that our lives are founded on nothing
of substance, that we are as ephemeral as the waves that rock the
boats along The Birth Canal and dissipate upon the shore. We
are slapped by life, why then refuse the vital pleasure of slapping
back? Who's next?'

His presence seemed to calm her, and her violent in-
clinations were subdued as she sat at his feet listening and
nodding between blows. Though she had no desire to join the
line and slap him again.

Ernie felt a strange agitation. Jean was staring intently at him. He held her gaze, held it too long, then looked away. When he looked back she was still staring at him. He met her gaze again, before lowering his head. At the end of his working day something of this exchange stayed with him, and he could not get that gaze, and some strange sense of contact, out of his mind. It made him feel uncertain and jumpy, and he wished now that he had not looked away, had held her gaze until — what? Some vital intimacy that seemed suspended between their mutual gazes had been made manifest? Not knowing what import it might have, yet feeling some unfamiliar surge, or urge, a tremulous thing, not wholly pleasant, yet the agitation it brought provoked a pleasing vitality. There'd been desire in Jean's glance, at least Ernie thought so. He was not certain, it lay outside his experience, yet that uncertainty was thrilling. Not knowing how to proceed, wanting to go to her, or find her in the street, not daring to, and castigating himself for being so cowardly. So nervous he could not eat, feeling a nausea that was not the nausea that came from eating bad seafood, nor the nausea that came from drinking too much booze. What was it, this confusion in his gizzards?

Jean was angry with herself. Something was moving beyond her control. Feeling an attraction for Ernie. Was this another of her manias, or some finer pulse?

A tenderness in the man — was there no cruelty in him? Jean felt an odd trepidation. For all her boldness she grew shy when close to Ernie. She could not voice her admiration. A selflessness in him she envied.

Ernie was walking home one night when he saw Jean approaching. Jean smiled at Ernie, it brought him to a standstill. It seemed unprecedented. People slapped him, hugged him, wept on his shoulder. But they did not smile. Standing there, watching Jean smiling at him, Ernie felt suffused with a strange warmth.

PLUMP LABIA

The lips, the lips, she could not take her eyes off his lips. Why had she not noticed them before? Her labial aversion meaning that her eyes fled from close inspection of the mouths of those she met. Preferring to stare at the eyes, until people felt they were being subjected to some terrible scrutiny. Or else she stared over their shoulders, or at their feet. She was struck by the plumpness of Ernie's lips. He had a sensual mouth. His jaw so prominent it dominated one's vision, yet now she'd taken time to inspect his lips she felt an overpowering desire to reach a finger out and touch his labia. Ernie stood mute and bewildered; if she'd slapped him he would have felt at ease, but he did not know how to react, and so he stood, jaw hanging slackly off his skull, which only emphasised the plumpness of his lips in Jean's eyes. Tracing her fingers around the rim of his mouth, then across each lip, gently prodding each one in the middle, it tickled, Ernie didn't mean to flinch. Jean withdrew her finger for a moment, Ernie noticed the way her eyes tightened in the corners, then she cautiously began to stroke his lips again. Ernie felt that he was being slowly undressed, he was quivering slightly, as if his body was being stirred by some small breeze, though the agitation came from inside him, down in his belly. He closed his eyes. When he opened them again Jean had gone.

Yet something of Jean's presence, and her strange actions, stayed with him. His lips tingling. Licking his lips, then biting them softly. Jean's tenderness had aroused some unfamiliar sensation. Perhaps it was the gentle touch she had? Something of her curiosity provoking a curiosity of his own.

Her touch so unlike the slaps that had become his daily meat and bone. When he got home Ernie undressed in the garden, and ran a finger over his lips, his eyes and nose and jaw. Jean had somehow opened him, exposing a nerve of feeling that he did not want to close again. A vulnerability. He began to weep, standing naked in the overgrown garden, and could not fathom the reason for his tears.

A BOWL OF PERIWINKLES

Ernie wished he'd never called himself The Slapping Man, or been baptised with that name by a stinking pig farmer. Every time someone said, 'How's The Slapping Man today?' he felt angry. Why did they never say, 'Hello, Ernie'?

When people stared at him they only saw The Slapping Man, as if he had become his jaw and nothing more. Appalled to think his life had shrunk to a single ability, wishing he could reinvent himself, though he'd not invented his jaw, his jaw had invented him. He'd fallen in love with a vision of himself as The Slapping Man, devoting all his energies to that potent creature, only to find that like a parasite it had devoured his essence.

He was sitting in The House Of Pearls, staring at the bay. Deciding he'd put his toes into the waters. Taking off his clothes and wading in, expecting that at any moment the sure tentacles of The Octopus would drag him under. He was cold, but there were no currents pulling at him. Standing in water up to his chin, then ducking himself under, wondering if he could end his life this way, and rejoin his parents in the bay. Feeling oddly calm, despite the cold. It was only when he ran out of breath that he observed his knees pushing him up and out of the water, his lungs grasping the air. Discovering then that it was hard to drown yourself. He walked out of the water and stood dripping on the sand. Wondering if he'd wanted to kill The Slapping Man, or was The Slapping Man trying to mortify him?

When Ernie got home he packed a little bag, there was still time to catch the evening boat. Walking slowly through the backstreets, feeling brisk and yet nostalgic, wondering if he'd ever see the town again. He wanted to say goodbye to Vronsky, but Satchel was not at home. The thought that he might not see Jean again also conspired with his nostalgia.

He was surprised to find John Gobblelard lounging against the pier. John did not seem surprised at all, and Ernie had the distinct impression that the publican was waiting for him.

'Good evening, Ernie. You're looking well.'

'I'd say the same of you if it were true.'

'Did you know the boat's been cancelled? Here, give me your bag.'

John didn't wait for Ernie's answer, but took the bag and dropped it out of sight behind him. He ran his fat and greasy fingers through Ernie's hair, before taking hold of the hair by the scalp and twisting Ernie's face up, from which point of view Ernie had an excellent sight of the publican's hairy nostrils and gloating face.

'I don't think you'll be going anywhere, my little man. I own you as surely as I own The Virgin Wall. You're too good for business!'

John let go of Ernie's hair then, though if Ernie felt relieved his relief was short-lived, as John now placed a hand around

Ernie's jaw and lifted him clear of the ground in a single, elegant manoeuvre. Ernie was as docile as a kitten caught by the scruff as he dangled helplessly from John's arm. John was gazing at Ernie's jaw with the intent admiration that a jeweller might bring to some precious stone he'd not seen before.

'By God but your jaw's a rare thing, lad. A real work of nature's art. Even if your talents are unnatural. You might be the best thing to happen to this town since the founding of The Bluebottle, Prawn and Oyster — excluding the fact of my own birth, of course. I'm watching you, Ernie. My scouts keep me well posted. I know what you eat, I know when you shit, I even know when you fart at night in that damp little bed you call your own.

'You were born to die here, Ernie, you were born because we need you. Believe me when I say that you will never leave this town. Can you imagine the heartbreak should we ever lose our favourite son? Can you imagine the consternation, the remorse and ruination should The Slapping Man desert us? Do you want to be responsible for the mass suicide of the entire population? You don't want that on your conscience. I'm thinking of you, Ernie, I know you want to die a happy man.'

Ernie was relieved when John finally set him back upon his feet.

'This town's been good to you. If it turned on you you'd be torn apart — it would be such a tragic waste.'

To Ernie's dismay the publican now clapped a hand over his cock and balls, and was squeezing rather hard. Ernie was speechless, and rooted to the spot. For a brief moment he thought John Gobblelard meant to kiss him, the publican's face so close to his, the aroma of sour beer and rotting teeth quite overpowering.

'I've got to protect you from yourself, lad; it's not as if I don't already have enough to do. Some nights I cannot sleep, such is my consternation when I contemplate your welfare. You look hungry. Come back to the pub and have a feed. Les has got a nice fat cray for you, he wants to thank you for all the good you've done. Says you're the most public-spirited man alive, with the exception of myself. So you see, lad, we've got a lot in common.'

John was laughing now, and his rotting breath enveloped Ernie in a foul fog. The harder John laughed the harder he squeezed Ernie's testicles and member. Ernie had turned quite pale.

'What's the matter, boy? You're looking ghastly. I know that altruism's a hard weight to carry in such a godforsaken town. You need a feed. Here, let me carry your bag.'

Ernie was glad that John now liberated his privates. And so the two men headed up the slope to The Bluebottle, Prawn and Oyster, John looking like a giant beside the runty little man trotting beside him.

Ernie was trying not to weep from fear, frustration and humiliation. Could not prevent a few tears from leaking out. John wrapping a massive arm around him as they walked, the force of it landing on Ernie's back causing him to stumble.

'Ah lad, you've had a hard life. Your mammy and daddy dead out in the bay. Too bad they decided to go swimming. Don't you set foot in those treacherous waters again, The Octopus will wrap a tentacle around your ankles before you've even got your willy wet. Your mother was a good fish scraper, your father was a fool, and so are you if you ever think of trying to leave this town again. You can have a good life here among the ones who need and love you, or you can end up feeding fishes on the bottom of the bay, with your throat cut for good measure. It's the simple choices that are the easiest to make.'

They were now standing outside the pub.

'Welcome home, boy. Salvation loves you, let that never be in doubt. If some bastard gives you grievance, I'll have his throat cut before you've finished saying thank you.'

John pushed Ernie inside the pub. There were no free tables and so John simply grabbed a man by the ear and threw him out into the night. Then he placed Ernie's bag underneath the table, pulled a chair out and pushed Ernie's head so that he landed sitting.

'I'm bringing you best porter, and Les is going to boil that cray. Would you like some periwinkles to tease your gizzards?'

John took one look at Ernie and started laughing. The wet stains of suppressed tears that had leaked onto the cheeks, the look of bafflement and impotence. John kissed Ernie on the forehead then, the way he kissed a lamb that he was just about to slaughter, and whispered in Ernie's ear, 'I love you boy, I fucking love you!'

John turned his back then, humming and laughing to himself as he strode through the crowded bar, knocking people to the floor as he went if they were foolhardy or unfortunate enough to block his way. Letting out one loud fart for good measure, as if to announce his forward progress, the way a boat might make use of its foghorn.

Ernie knew in his bones that John was right. He had a duty to the town. He could not shirk it. When, a short time later, Les appeared with a glass of stout and a bowl of periwinkles, Ernie set on them with glee.

Some hours passed and he was still drinking. The bowl of periwinkles now nothing but shells. There was no sign of the cray. No sign of Les either, though John was keeping up a steady stream of stout. Ernie burped and tasted bitter gas. Sucking the last salt juices from the shells, and chewing on a little leaf of parsley.

Les knew how to cook a periwinkle. Ernie thought he knew how the tender creatures felt, convinced he'd just become John's periwinkle.

PART FIVE:

A LOAD of BULL

IN THE SKIN OF A RHINOCEROS

There was a commotion down by the wharf. John was overseeing the docking of a barge which contained an old rhinoceros in a metal cage. A crowd had gathered to watch. Ernie could hear shouts as a work gang began hauling the rhino up to the market on a massive trolley. John was going to slaughter the ruined animal, a circus castaway. Before he did he was putting it on display in the market.

Ernie took the chance to stroke the creature's flank. He was working so hard his face had grown quite leathery. His skin was getting close to that rhino's toughness, he thought it an accomplishment. Laughing for a moment as he saw himself inside the skin of a rhinoceros.

It was the only pleasing thing about his visit to the rhino. The creature was housed in a tiny cage. Barely room to turn itself around. No space to walk, or run. No chance to gain the speed that it would need to charge those metal bars. Ernie didn't know what sound a rhinoceros made, yet he was sure the whimpering cry he heard was not its full expressive range.

He wanted to hear the grey beast trumpet, moan or bellow, yet the rhinoceros seemed to be in a state of terminal depression, as if it had been born in Ruination, and not arrived that afternoon.

Ernie was appalled to learn, later that week, that John Gobblelard was serving rhinoceros steaks at The Bluebottle, Prawn and Oyster. Word was they were horribly tough, though who knew when the chance might come again, if ever? Ernie wondered whether he could ever eat red meat again without grieving for that poor rhino.

That night Ernie looked out the window and thought he saw a ghost or gooly monster. He felt naked in his bed.

John was staring in through the window. To make it worse John was smiling, which showed off his rotten teeth to good effect. John was tapping on the glass. He had the charismatic determination of the drunken. There was nothing to do but let the big man in.

'Ernie, my boy, I cannot sleep. Every time I close my eyes I see that rhino. It had such big grey eyes. True, the whites were horrid yellow, though so are mine. Perhaps that's why that rhino's got me, we've got the same eyes. I feel as bad as if I'd killed my own brother. By God it was tough meat. I needed a saw to hack through its neck, and that's tiring work. I'd always wanted to butcher a rhino, never thought I'd have the chance. I'm having its head mounted, but the eyes follow me round the room. No wonder I can't sleep. I'm going to put it in the back bar. The Rhino Bar. Or The Horn Room? That'll spark The Virgin Wall! I was going to have its penis mounted, my God what an organ! Though it might scare the men away, if they start comparing notes with that beast.

'Would you mind if I kept the head here for a day or two? I'll be back before the flies.'

John had pushed his strange cargo along in a rusty wheelbarrow. Ernie insisted John leave the head in the ruined house, and was relieved when only a few hours later John was back, wheeling the creaky barrow down the path beside the house. He could hear John mumbling under his breath, 'Sex has died in Ruination…we need to learn how to rut again …'

To Ernie's surprise John was right, and the transformation of The Moonfish Bar into The Horn Room restored The Virgin Wall to its former glory. John's voice booming out, 'FREE WHISKY SHOTS TO THE FIRST SIX COUPLES TO GET IT UP AGAINST THE WALL. WHAT'S THAT I HEAR? THE VIRGIN WALL IS SQUEALING.

In no short time it was.

FISH HEAD SOUP

Jean hadn't had sex in a month and was feeling proud of herself. She was also feeling terribly aroused, knew she was ovulating, and was tempted to tie herself to a chair in case she started drinking then headed out the door, inevitably lingering near The Virgin Wall with one clear intention.

She didn't need to look at her vulva to know it was swollen, yet once the idea presented itself she couldn't resist her curiosity. It was just as she expected, as she inspected herself with the aid of a small hand-mirror. Admiring the supple form of her distension, and the budding erection of her clitoris. Looks like a red meatflower, she told herself. She felt like a small glass of ale, her throat was dry and water only made her thirstier. Ignoring that voice in her which counselled abstention, wanting to wet her whistle then wrap herself around some sturdy gristle.

Feeling confused and slutty and excited she forgot about tying herself to a chair, walked out the front door and slammed it behind her. Pausing at the gate, wondering if she looked far too keen, her primary intention all cock and balls. Deciding she'd avoid the pub and walk down to the pier isntead, perhaps she'd sit inside The House Of Pearls and try to calm herself.

When she finally arrived at the pier she squatted uncomfortably on her haunches, before straddling a pole that ran the length of the wooden walkway. She felt she was sitting on a meaty cushion, and the sight of the long wooden pole stretching out from her thighs focused her attention too clearly on things she didn't want to dwell on. About to desert her post she halted when she heard a familiar voice behind her.

'Jean, Jean, don't be mean, come into the garden where we can't be seen!'

John Gobblelard, wooing her with his subtle ways. Holding a tray of meat under her nose as another man might proffer flowers. Placing the tray at her feet, leaning his cheek against hers, wrapping his arms around her midriff. His forearms firmly wedged beneath her breasts. In an odd way she felt glad, as John's presence and behaviour made her lose all interest in sex. Or was it the way that he'd begun to grope her? Grabbing his hands to stop him as he pinched her nipples. She didn't bother turning to face him as she said, 'I'm sorry John, but I've decided to become a vegetarian.'

She half expected to hear John running after her, and was relieved when she made it to The House Of Pearls with no interruption. She paused when she saw Ernie mounting the steps to the House, carrying a mop and bucket.

Both nodding, smiling awkwardly, not knowing what to say. Jean wanted to give the man a cuddle, or be cuddled by him. Instead she found herself helping him scrub and wash the walls free of grit and grime and shit and piss and slime of such dubious origin it was better not to speculate, just hold the breath and scrub and wash.

When they'd finished Ernie thanked her with such sincerity that Jean felt confounded before cursing her stupidity and swearing at Ernie.

'You little prick, how did you trick me into this? I've got enough to do at home without hosing out the crap and spew of every drunk in Ruination!'

Ernie apologised at once, which only made Jean feel worse. When he invited Jean to eat with him at home she accepted with alacrity. Trying to make conversation she asked him, 'What's to eat?'

'Fish head soup.'

Jean almost turned heel on the spot. When they arrived at the ruined house she caught a whiff of what she could only describe as a delectable aroma. Had her ovulation made her sense of smell more acute as well? The closer they got to Ernie's shed the more aroused her sense of smell became. Stepping inside she inhaled so deeply that Ernie asked, 'Can you drink steam, Jean, or are you merely ravenous?'

'No, no.' Stopping herself then as she felt her stomach contract and her mouth fill with saliva. 'Well, perhaps a little. Tell me, what do you put in this soup of yours?'

'It was my mother's favourite. It's mainly fish heads. A little basil, some chilli, the juice of two lemons. Oh, and a pair of lobster tails, a dozen large prawns, two cups of white wine, a handful of whitebait, green peppercorns, a bay leaf, grated lime rind, a little oil and a dash of vinegar.'

Ernie paused, before asking Jean, 'Are you all right?'

Jean recovered her wits and brought her salivation under control, mumbled, 'Oh, fine' and wished her saliva hadn't dribbled onto her shirt as she did so.

'Then won't you close the door? There's a draught.' Ernie

noticed Jean was trembling. 'Are you cold, Jean? I've got a jumper, or a shawl if you would rather.'

As she closed the door Jean began to sob with such profusion that she felt her knees give way, and she was sobbing on all fours, guts heaving like some dog trying to regurgitate a poisoned bait. She calmed herself sufficiently for Ernie to ask again, 'Are you all right?', though he felt a fool, it was so clear she wasn't. Jean looked him in the eye, and opened her mouth to speak before sobbing once again. Ernie put his arms around her then, surprised by her strength as she hugged him tightly while trying to speak.

The best sense Ernie could make from the sounds was this: 'And you don't even want to fuck me!' Ernie held her tightly then, feeling they'd both been had by their villainous town. After some minutes of these exertions he was distracted by the overvigorous clinking of his soup pot upon the stove, and gently disengaged himself from Jean's embrace. Taking the lid off the fish head soup, dropping it into the sink, mumbling, 'Needs to reduce a little bit', before pouring Jean a glass of cold white wine.

Handing it to her he noticed she was staring at him, and there was such directness in her gaze he stopped abruptly and felt the wine slop on his hand and saw it spill onto Jean's arm. Feeling so stupid he couldn't even apologise for his clumsiness. Jean still staring with her wet eyes, taking the glass from him, licking the wine off her arm then sipping from the glass. Drying her eyes with the damp front of her shirt.

'I'm sorry, Ernie.'

She laughed briefly, and Ernie laughed a little with her. Jean drained her glass then gave him a look he could only describe as horrid. He felt the blood draining from his face as she suddenly threw her glass against the wall, then shouted, 'That's all you want, isn't it, you want to feed me up and fuck me! Tell me that's not true! Go on, tell me!'

Yet Ernie didn't have the chance, as Jean suddenly left, not even bothering to slam the door behind her. Ernie was dumbfounded. Going to the door, calling her name, looking down the path beside the house. Jean was gone. Walking back inside he closed the door and smelt his soup. It was ready now. Oddly enough he no longer felt like eating.

He was relieved when some minutes later he heard a shy knock at the door.

Jean felt utterly foolish. Mortified by her unruly exit, relieved she'd found the strength to show her face once more at Ernie's door, apologising for her conduct. Jean smiled awkwardly then joined him by the stove.

'Where are the fish heads?'

'They're in the stock, Jean, they're in the stock. You don't think I'd give you fish heads for your tea? What, sucking their eyes out for the meat?'

Ignoring the broken glass shards on the floor he poured Jean another glass of wine. Jean was glad of the comfort as she felt Ernie's bony arm around her shoulders while he stirred the soup with a long wooden spoon. The small man nattering on as if she'd never left the room.

'My mother said it was the one good thing about scraping fish for the Gobblelards.'

'What was?'

'Getting the fish heads for free. Though she said that the women had a deal. If one of them cared to have a scrape with John while the others were scraping fish, they'd steal some lobster, or some crabs, and the woman who'd been scraping John could have her pick of the stolen crop.'

Ernie wondered what he'd said wrong as he observed Jean's lower lip trembling slightly. She seemed to make some kind of effort, before tipping the rest of her wine down her throat. Ernie was hoping she wasn't about to break her second glass.

'Do you know, Ernie, I was feeling so horny before I left

home I'd thought to strap myself to a chair just so I wouldn't go to the pub and have a fuck against The Virgin Wall!'

Ernie was tasting his fishy soup and was only half listening to Jean.

'Is that the truth now?'

'When I'm ovulating my vulva swells up like some meat-eating flower and all I want to do is fuck.'

Ernie was grinding more peppercorns into the brew, tasting the liquor of his soup and smacking his lips, while trying to keep the conversation flowing. Though he hadn't really heard a thing she'd said.

'Go on! Is that a fact? Would you like to taste this soup?'

'It's not just a fact, it's the delight and bane of my life. Have you never seen a fanny in full flower? It's quite a sight.'

Ernie was busy getting bowls and spoons and bread set on the table, he'd lost the drift of the conversation, but felt it safe to burble back, 'Oh, make yourself at home.'

To his astonishment he looked up from the table to find Jean perched against the bench, knickers down, skirt up around her waist. Leaning her hips forward to accommodate his point of view.

'Have you ever seen anything like it?'

Ernie was flabbergasted, and blushed so deeply he could feel the blood swimming in his cock.

'By God, it looks like a firm, plump mussel. Only redder.'

He turned away then, so confused by this unexpected revelation he had no idea what he'd just been doing. Relieved when he heard Jean laughing, then saying, 'It's all right, I'm decent now.'

'I would not have said you were indecent.'

'But I am. I know I am.'

She joined him at the table and they began to gulp their soup. Ernie watched Jean suck the juice out of a prawn head then pull apart a lobster tail.

As he filled their glasses once again he wished Jean had not spoken. Yet she hadn't said much. She'd simply sighed before mumbling, 'I wish I could be like you, Ernie.'

'How so?'

'Sexless, so utterly sexless, with no need at all to feel the warmth of a body pressed against your own.'

Jean too was wishing she'd not spoken. Now that she had, she'd no idea what to say next, or how to comfort the little man whose tears threatened to spill out of his eyes into his soup. And so they finished the meal in silence, finished the wine, and then she left. Holding Ernie briefly at the doorstep, she said once more, 'I'm sorry', then stumbled out into the night.

Walking down the pathway by the house she wasn't sure if she could hear a cat mewing for food or Ernie sobbing in the shed. Standing by the dark and ruined house, rubbing her arms for warmth, puzzling as she asked herself which way virtue lay — should she return and comfort Ernie, or was it best to leave the man alone? Perhaps she'd done enough damage for one night. Rubbing her arms, feeling the goosebumps rising on her flesh, the hairs standing on end to trap the warmth remaining in her body. Afraid to knock on Ernie's door, convinced she'd find new ways to humiliate a man who'd done nothing more than proffer solace and treat her simply.

Swallowing, tasting the chilli on the back of her palate. Walking silently to his doorstep. Glad he'd stopped crying. Went to knock, then froze. It was a pity her horny fit had passed. If she had still felt horny perhaps Ernie would let her make amends. But she didn't feel horny. She just felt cruel and stupid. Tiptoeing away, not wanting him to find her standing by his door. It was only then she realised she'd just eaten fish for the first time since Beau had died. She needed a drink. Perhaps The Bluebottle, Prawn and Oyster was not such a bad idea after all. She'd spare poor Ernie the villainy of her company, she'd only find new ways to bring the man undone.

That night Ernie cried himself to sleep. He hadn't realised he'd become so utterly sexless, and the realisation only fuelled his sense of isolation. Had Jean forgotten she'd once possessed him by The Virgin Wall? Ernie wanted someone to cuddle, wanting some winter warmth amid the dark. His nose felt numb and frigid in the cold air of the shed.

The greater the distance between herself and Ernie, the more Jean wished she'd had the courage to knock, and sit with him.

Instead she picked up speed as the lights of the pub came into view. She'd have a drink or three, and if The Virgin Wall was calling she'd follow the drinks with a well-primed cock or two. Feeling confused, midway between her disgust and her desire. Yet even as she dithered she swore that she could feel her cunt growing hairier and her lips swelling.

Later that night, having finally found her man and lost him once again, Jean felt sated and disgusted. Wishing she had more self-control, or that she was not such a sexual creature. Walking home, feeling chafed and oozy as the remnant sperm drained down her legs. Lying in her bed, wondering why she'd felt such ease in Ernie's presence that she'd displayed her ripest plum to him. Wishing she'd been more solicitous of his welfare. It helped her disgust reach some kind of peak, as if it might take solid form and keep her company right through the night. Yet she slept fitfully, and in the morning woke feeling exhausted. Rising to pee she avoided looking at herself in the mirror. Later that day, to her surprise, she kept turning on her shadow, pulling faces, and enjoyed the fact that with each grimace some essential ugliness seemed to be confirmed. Thus might her truest features be displayed to the world.

Jean felt numb. What had driven her in her sexual odyssey? Had she been attempting to annihilate some part of herself? Mortifying the physical self in the hope she'd penetrate some deeper spiritual core?

Yet she felt dirty and confused. Heading down to the wharf, removing her clothes, throwing herself into the water and swimming furiously. She was surprised how far she was able to swim, some anger propelling her much further than usual. When she stopped to look back she wished she hadn't — the brief rest as she trod water all it took for the frigid waters of the bay to make her muscles freeze. She tried to swim and felt her body tightening. She was sinking. Surprised to discover how easy it was to drown. She knew that if she panicked she'd disappear beneath the water within seconds. Trying to keep calm, breathing as deeply as she could, floating on her back with just her air to keep her buoyant. To her relief she felt her muscles starting to overcome their seizure, she could move her arms and legs enough to keep her head above water, and propel herself slowly like a jellyfish. After thirty seconds she could move her arms and legs enough to swim with strength again, though her confidence was dented. When she made it to the wharf she wept as she pulled her clothes back on. Remembering how Beau had lit a fire the first time they had made love, and how she'd rubbed the warmth into her skin, then dried her hair, looking at his nose and lips as he worked intently, repairing nets.

Walking home, sobbing as she went. Feeling that if nothing else she could finally accept just how much she felt cheated by Beau's death. Wondering to what extent her sexual feeding frenzy had been an attempt to prove to herself that she no longer needed him. Or was it a way to punish herself for feeling so disgusted when she saw his body at the morgue?

From the moment she denied him access to her body, John could not get Jean out of mind. As if the muscles of her cunt still gripped him tightly and he could not break their grip. So used to having his way he could not cope with being thwarted.

He needed Jean, not from any excess of tenderness or passion, but to assert his sense of potency, rather than feel himself become some toy that Jean had cast away.

To Ernie's dismay he discovered that Jean had goaded John, saying, 'Ernie's my man now, to tell the truth I always found your cock a little small, where Ernie is much bigger than I suspected ...'

John had fumed for half a day before appearing in the market, unconcerned by any queue, marching to the front, pushing Ernie's customer out of the way, then letting fly with a series of back and forehand swipes. Ernie ducked when he finally heard the knuckles split, and was unprepared for the kicks John then unleashed to his head and body. Ernie heard a scream, and thought for a moment John had cracked his foot on The Slapping Man's jaw. But it was Jean, in a rage provoked by John's pounding of the little man. As the publican prepared to launch another kick Jean punched him in the crutch, and as he staggered she grabbed his hair and butted him in the face. She let his hair go then and was glad to see him crumple. Then Jean picked Ernie up and ran from the market, as if he was her prize.

John was stunned by this development. Trembling as he wondered how he'd sunk to such a state, feeling Jean had somehow managed to castrate him.

VRONSKY'S QUEST

Vronsky's hunger to know himself better began to gnaw at him, and he frequently lost track of his clients' morbid ruminations as he mused upon the possibilities of living a new life with a new identity.

One bastard had surprised Vronsky inside his wooden meditation box, moaning to himself. Scaring the wits out of Vronsky when he suddenly rapped loudly on the coffin. Vronsky had been so stunned he'd simply said, 'Come in', and to his mortification the coffin door had opened.

'What are you doing standing in a coffin?'

'Trying to conquer my fear of death.'

Glad he'd thought of that, relieved his fly was not undone. There'd been no further discussion on the matter of the box, and Vronsky's moaning. Though the good doctor knew, from the way his client's eyes had opened wider, that the man now held Vronsky in ever greater esteem. Nor had Vronsky demurred when the man muttered, 'By God, Vronsky, you might be the only genius who ever lived in Ruination.'

He had no intention of disclosing his conviction that the most intense thinking might only be done in the smallest rooms. He didn't want any other bastard stealing his ideas, and discovering that they too were capable of intense thought in tiny spaces.

He was standing in the smallest room in the house one morning when he was struck by a most odd notion. He'd kept files on them all. Before Ernie had become his earhole it had been the only way Vronsky could put some distance between himself and the livid entrails of the town. It had remained his habit. To satisfy his curiosity he had even begun delving into the town's macabre past. He'd amassed a hideous mound of information, was often tempted to burn it, yet never found that fiery volition. It had never occurred to him that there might be a more obvious path of action, until now.

He'd kept his notes in chronological order. Yet there were so many common links that defied chronology. Standing in his box he suddenly saw a way of ordering his life as Doctor Vronsky, Counsellor of Grief, and was convinced that at this moment he'd finally attained the truest intensity of his thinking. And so he began to compose another version of his notes, arrayed in alphabetical order according to theme, like a perverse catalogue of human failing. Organising what he realised had been his life's work. Astounded to think that at last he'd found an outlet for his grief.

He wondered what he might call such a monumental volume. Telling himself it would take an entire encyclopaedia of betrayal to do justice to the inmates of the town. He felt such a flood of rightness as he pondered that one phrase, he knew he'd found his title. *The Encyclopaedia of Betrayal.* Stepping out of his coffin then, stunned to find that he felt positively jaunty. It was an unfamiliar sensation.

It would be a most unusual document. Vronsky hoped it would bring him some relief from the ghastly stories he had heard during his years of grief counselling. He was convinced it was the only way he might find some peace before his death.

Vronsky was at once concerned and delighted to think that he had overstepped some limit. It was clearly a gross breach of confidentiality and professional ethics. That only heightened the pleasure he took in his new task. He felt increasingly un-burdened of all the horrid stories he'd soaked up

Ernie had never known the good doctor to appear so sprightly, yet had no idea what had triggered such a change in his friend's mien. Some aspect of his puzzlement had finally come out right. Vronsky wondered if he was committing some villainy, yet always felt reassured when he muttered, 'It's the truth, Satchel, it's just the truth', and was amazed that such a simple dictum could appease his grosser doubts; it seemed enough, no longer caring if in the process he'd be blessed or damned.

A LOAD OF BULL

Given his dismay at the manner of his mother's decease, John Gobblelard would have been quite happy with the manner of his own demise. There was a big celebration at The Bluebottle, Prawn and Oyster, though Ernie felt it fell a little short of a wake. With the exception of brother Les, there seemed a common satisfaction at John's death.

The big man had grown cocky, some felt he had contravened the essential spirit of the town: the town of the second best did not take too kindly to anyone who claimed they had excelled in their chosen profession.

John had started boasting that the beast did not exist he could not wrestle down and slaughter, and he had started tackling animals of increasing size and vigour. A small crowd would gather as he tested his arms against large sheep, cows and horses, without the use of ropes to tether them and provide some small security. He thought it would be cowardly to do so. People began bringing their most obstreperous and intractable animals, and didn't need to dare him to grapple with them, he saw it as a test of honour and self-worth to take them on. Bets were laid. John Gobblelard had progressed from sullen rams to grumpy geldings until one day a man had brought a bull for him to try, tired of hearing the Gobblelard boast that he was the equal of any creature that was mobile on four legs.

The size of the bull had set John back; he didn't like to admit that for the first time he felt a bit of fear move in him when he saw the fine prongs of its horns. He'd never had to deal with such great horns before. The bull much bigger than him, and surly too. The knocking of its hooves against the pub wall where it was tethered made it clear the bull was not happy with its current situation, and had no intention of accepting with docility whatever fate now lay in hand. John Gobblelard finished his drink slowly as he heard the knocking of the hooves; he felt unsettled by the eyes regarding him as he put his glass down on the counter. The sight of so much money changing hands did not put him in a sweeter frame of mind, particularly as the bull was a clear favourite. Deciding it was best to back himself, he offered odds of three to one that he would have the beast slit and bleeding in under two minutes. Nodding to Les, who was looking worried, instructing him to meet all bets with cash straight from the till. There was a rush as John Gobblelard announced, 'Last bets', and then headed out, ready for the bull.

The man who owned the bull, Greedy Harris, had wagered a huge stake on the affair; to be precise, the full amount of an unpaid bill for ales and champagnes following the wedding of his only daughter. The thirst of the wedding guests had outstripped his worst imaginings, and he would not be able to pay the bill without selling his house and all its furniture. He had procured the bull at auction cheaply, due to its reputation for a vile temper. No one had been able to work the animal, and Greedy Harris had bought it specially for John Gobblelard. He thought the bull might be an astute investment. The creature had a name that augured well, the Hooves of Heaven. The publican announced that it would not be just the hooves but the whole damn beast that would quickly be dispatched to paradise, ably assisted by his trusty slaughter knife.

John was eyeing the bull, still safely tethered, albeit cranky; he decided to give it a hard kick in the flank, and then announced, 'This will be a royal battle between the Blade from Hell and the Hooves of Heaven, and I've no doubt that Hell will triumph once again!'

Greedy Harris wasn't bothered by that kick, he thought it foolhardy because it only fired the bull's anger. Where it had previously been intractable, even a little roguish, now something in the beast had clarified. Greedy Harris thought it was some aspect of that bull's fury.

The crowd inside the pub had spilled out into the court-yard, many others preferring to lean out of windows, wanting the pub walls for security. Les was looking fidgety, busy counting on his fingers as he calculated how much they stood to win, and how much they might lose. Wondering if it might not be more prudent for his brother to concede that for once he'd met his match, before he came to grievous harm. Whispering in his brother's ear. His whisper had the same effect as the kick had on the bull, John pushed Les away so hard Les scraped the skin off his nose and chin as he hit the court-yard paving.

The scuffle seemed to arouse the bull, for it bellowed then, and for reasons best known to itself started getting an erection. John Gobblelard seemed to take that as an insult to his person, for he bellowed back, and strange to say there seemed to be an awkward movement in his trousers. He bellowed once again, and was surprised to see the bull lift its tail and evacuate its bowels. The action caused a momentary loss of purpose in John Gobblelard, and then he bellowed a third time and yelled, 'Untie that bull, you cowards, and let me have him!'

Greedy Harris was afraid of this moment, and had procured a long wooden harpoon that allowed him to slip the rope without having to set foot outside the pub. He'd bought the bull on the condition that it be delivered directly to The Bluebottle, Prawn and Oyster, with strict instructions it be tethered in the courtyard by a window. Glad of his foresight and acumen. The bull did not notice his ministrations as the rope was worked free of the head. It seemed the bull had also forgotten its anger, becoming distracted by thoughts of God knows what. Flicking its tail, a bit of drool flowing down the chin. Presenting it haunches to John Gobblelard.

It offered an irresistible invitation to the publican. He was of a mind to show this mob just what a man now stood before them, and did not want the thing to look too easy. He could have snuck up then and slit the beast's throat with ease, instead he took a run and gave that bull a kick so hard it broke three small bones in his foot. He'd hoped to make the bull hit its head against the wall, but the bull was far too big for that. It staggered forward half a step, then trotted around quite daintily to get a look at the source of this annoyance.

It seemed John and the bull were joined in a common purpose, deciding whether it was best to charge or hold their ground. To the publican's dismay the bull trotted off, and there was a momentary panic. No one had considered the possibility that the bull might simply run out of the yard and make the town its own. There was no gate. Here was a contingency for which they had no plan.

Thankfully the bull trotted to the rear of the courtyard. Had it escaped, not only would they have the problem of rounding up the bull, but all bets would be off. As it was, John Gobblelard now stood between the beast and its liberty.

Given the dimensions of his opponent, John decided to make a small change to his usual technique, and slipped the Hellblade from its sheath. He had intended to wrestle first, imagining he could get the bull in a headlock and tip it to the ground. He was no longer sure of this. He wasn't certain that it was strictly following the rules of the wager, but had in mind some degree of self-preservation, feeling the essence of the bet would still be sound.

John Gobblelard and the bull made their rush at the same time. John was glad he had that knife as he felt the wind knocked out of him. Managing to get one arm around the bull's head, he hadn't meant to be so clumsy as he stuck the knife in, but he'd been off-balance and ripped the throat on impact. It was not enough to kill the bull at once, and it was a pity John then fell to the ground. The bull's temper not in the least improved by this sudden goring, it decided to repay the compliment in full, and gored John several times. The publican seemed too shocked to shriek or whimper, nor was he alone. It seemed the bull had knocked the breath out of them all, there were no cries or shouts, and no gesticulations.

The bull was in poor shape; it buckled at the knees, regained its strength, and staggered to the back of the courtyard. It was a cool day, and steam rose off the blood that was coming from its neck. The Hooves of Heaven collapsed, and no one dared go near it.

Les ran to his brother's side, but when he saw the belly open to the sky, and the gruesome colours of his brother's gizzards, he knew there was no point in having John hauled inside.

Within a span of twenty minutes both man and beast were dead. A funny harmony achieved in the sounds they uttered as they died. Les had to hose the yard and he felt odd as he watched his brother's blood mingling with the bull's before it ran into the gutter. Deciding then that if nothing else they'd carve the bull and eat it at John's wake.

No fortunes had been made, no money lost: by common consent the contest was a draw.

UNFLINCHING

After a few more drinks at The Bluebottle, Prawn and Oyster, Jean asked Ernie if he'd mind walking her home. Under the circumstances he felt he could not refuse. When they arrived at Jean's he also felt obliged to accept her invitation to take tea, the least he could do, to comfort one so recently bereaved. Assuming as he did that Jean felt some glimmer of bereavement. Holding her hand, keeping her company as they drank the brew. Both of them troubled by the day's events, feeling buffeted by the gory demise of John Gobblelard. Shaking their heads at his stupidity, and the way he'd fallen victim to a fatal vanity.

Ernie was unprepared when she popped the question, staring at him with a gaze that held fierce purpose.

'Are you a brave man, Ernie? Have you never felt there are

things you have to face to find some peace before you die? Some aspect of your fear perhaps?'

Ernie was lost for words, so many things came to mind all he could do was nod while holding his jaw, so that the jaw remained in place as the cranium tilted up and down.

Jean gave him a look then that he could only describe as queer. It made him feel uncertain, and he wondered if it had been a mistake to walk her home and drink her tea. Feeling he was entering waters of a depth to which he was not accustomed.

'Will you kiss me, Ernie? Will you kiss me on the lips? It's something I've not done since Beau died. Don't ask me why, but tonight I feel I have to. Perhaps John's death has filled me with a vital sense of my mortality. You're a good man, Ernie. Forgive my being blunt, but I'm dearly hoping you'll oblige me now and kiss me. No more than that.'

Ernie wanted to run away, yet knew he couldn't. He'd never thought that kissing might fall within the brief he'd set himself as Salvation's Slapping Man. Though he could see some strange connection given Jean's history. She was gripping his hand so hard she was white-knuckled.

'That's my hand you're throttling, Jean.'

She relaxed her grip. 'Is it not a simple thing I'm asking? You only have to kiss me, Ernie. Am I so disgusting?'

Jean was trembling, appalled by her boldness and her need, having lain herself so bare, so open to rejection.

'Might we have a drink while we consider a path of action?' Ernie countered.

'There's only cooking sherry.'

'In that case I'm partial to it.'

Ernie did not know why the deed seemed so hard to countenance. Feeling the request was a violation, though he wanted to comply. It seemed the smallest thing that he could do, to help another find some glint of resolution in a life that had been more than full of bitterness and consternation. If she'd asked to slap him he'd not have hesitated. How then could he refuse a kiss?

'I don't know if I can do this thing at all.'

He felt a barrier form between them.

'Forget it, Ernie. It was not fair of me to ask. John Gobblelard was a quirky bastard, though he had his virtues. I think some inkling of a grief might have unhinged me.'

She paused, as if deciding whether to keep talking, then continued. 'My sympathies for John were rather strained after his mother died. Coming round, wanting to get in. Saying, "I've got your meat, Jean." I'd always tell him that I'd just had a roast. I let him in one night, he thrust so hard he made me bleed, and would not stop. I swear my bleeding just aroused him. Another bastard's dead, so what?'

Jean's outburst catching both of them unprepared. She filled their sherry glasses, they drank, she refilled them and they drained them once again. Ernie was feeling drowsy, knew it was time to go, yet felt disinclined to move. His back was hurting. Wanting to enjoy the supine comfort of the floor and straighten out his vertebrae. He shucked his shoes off then and slid onto the floor.

'Are you all right, Ernie?'

'I'm weary and feel the need to straighten up my bones.'

'Let me get a cushion. And, please, forget I ever mentioned kissing.'

The floor felt good, he could feel a pressure in his spine easing. Wondering if he'd dare relax and close his eyes. It would not do to fall asleep. He didn't notice when his eyes drooped shut, nor did he notice when Jean turned out the brightest lights, only opening his lids when she snuck a pillow underneath his head. Something in her expression was so sad it filled him with an overwhelming sense of failure. Telling himself he was not responsible for the sadness of the world, yet he felt guilty and selfish. He would not make this small concession, set aside his own flawed wants and meet Jean's need to find her little bit of comfort. As she began to massage his toughened jaw he felt a hardness in him soften, and pulled Jean down to meet him on the floor, his bony chest her pillow. A little bit of human contact, at the very least he could do that.

He felt her body weeping before he heard the tears. The agitation that gripped her torso as the weeping fit began. Wishing Jean would not apologise as she blubbered, feeling cheapened by his prim refusal. Every sob another kind of slap he'd not experienced. Telling her, 'If you apologise for weeping you might as well apologise for being born.' Wishing he had a greater gift for eloquence.

Her head was bouncing on his rib cage and then it settled on his chest as the tears died down. Rubbing her head at the place where the spinal cord became the skull. Feeling some small measure of his own self-worth returning.

'Are you nothing but a bag of bones, man? Have you no flesh upon your body?'

He had thought, when she started weeping, that she would set him off as well and they'd be coupled in common grieving. He'd not expected to feel calmer as her agitation grew. Feeling the calmness in his body slowly moving through her. The vibration of her sighs travelling through his body, as she lay, head on his chest, breathing and sighing. Rubbing the back of her head, and pushing with his thumb as if trying to release some pressure.

'That feels so good, like you couldn't know.'

His arm had stiffened, getting crampy. He stretched it out and thought to lie it on her back. Easy and friendly. But as he shifted his arm Jean shifted too, as if a moment had now passed and their common bones needed to find some new relation. She rolled a little to the side, keeping her head upon his chest, and instead of placing his arm across her back he was embarrassed to find his hand now landing on her belly. His arm sidling down beside her breast. The heat of the mammary charmed his bicep; it flinched a little and nudged her bosom. He went to move his arm, but Jean restrained him, holding his hand against her belly, keeping his arm in place. The contact of his arm against her breast now more pronounced. He could feel her arm resting on his thigh. Mortified to feel his small reaction, some movement in his groin that nudged her fingers, which responded with such gentleness he grew distended. Telling himself he should never have stayed for sherry as she curled her fingers round his corona and brought her eyes to face him.

'I knew I could trust you, Ernie, to come good.'

Was it too late to run away? Asking himself the question as his fingers tightened on her bosom, sure the movement was involuntary, feeling he was drifting with the tide, gripped by The Octopus, perhaps, as he closed his eyes and gave over to sensation. Could hear and feel Jean moving over him, kissing his eyelids and his chin, not relinquishing her grip, as she slowly licked his lips. Doing her best to conquer thoughts of sea lice eating labia. Her revulsion not as strong as her determination to reclaim some lost thing in herself, some thing she couldn't name, sensing it was the only way to make herself complete, freed of a misery. The sign of her completion would be her re-emergence as a woman who loved kissing. Easing her hips against the man who had become compliant.

Ernie was unsure whether the thing was right or wrong, or whether there were times a curious martyrdom was called for. His doubts unvanquished, his resistance washed away. Feeling he was undone as Jean slowly pushed her tongue into his mouth and down his throat. Feeling a fool that he'd come inside his pants at the very moment Jean had started weeping. Convinced the tricky business of human fellowship was one he'd never master.

Holding Jean tightly through her convulsions as the weeping fit subsided into sobs. She sniffled the snot back up her nose and swallowed, and to his surprise she started laughing. Looking at him with a tenderness and clarity he could only meet by answering with his eyes. Both of them smiling as Jean put her hands behind his head and kissed him gently once again, lingering now as if at last she could enjoy this moment. Ernie glad this time she spared the tongue. The pair of them feeling shy and embarrassed, Ernie blushing as Jean looked at him and shook her head.

'Sometimes a bit of wicked is the only way to do some good. Slip out of your pants now, let me sponge and dry them.'

For the moment it was as close as they could get to conversation.

Walking home, Ernie could not help wondering if he'd been raped. It was not true, though he'd felt some violation. Yet he felt a little gleam of virtue, and didn't mind that he'd been subservient to some force he could not name, nor control. Telling himself, 'Grief has quite strange effects,' as he sat down on his bed. He didn't feel like sleeping, and so he sat, staring at nothing, wondering what had got into them. He could not help feeling that for all the oddness, Jean had just shown him an unexpected face of courage.

PART SIX:
BREED!

THE LAST OF THE GOBBLELARDS

John Gobblelard's will gave Les full control of The Bluebottle, Prawn and Oyster, as long as Les respected the dead man's final wish: that his body, when stuffed and mounted, be displayed in all its glorious nudity behind the counter of The Horn Room. His shark-tooth necklace dangling from his neck. It was a pity he'd been so disfigured by the bull. No amount of careful stitching could mask the dreadful wound. Jean found it quite off-putting, standing in John's shadow, reminded constantly of the dead man's exertions and her own refrain, 'I'm your butcher now!'

John's flayed image also had a disquieting effect on the drinkers. It made them feel the need for constant drinking, as if the belated publican's voice was still ringing in the bar, 'Drink Your Fill! We're Not Closing Till The Kegs Are Empty! You're

A Long Time Dead!' And so they took him at his word — in death he was living proof of his fatal predictions — and the till kept singing.

Les had been sure that with the brother gone his fortunes would collapse. The fact that the eternal image of John Gobblelard had increased the thirst of their customers filled Les with a profound admiration. The suspicion that this might have been John's intended legacy was another intimation of his brother's genius.

Had some aspect of this genius rubbed off on Les? Since John's death, business was booming. They'd had a good trade before, but now that John stood behind the bar in perpetuity, the graph of weekly consumption had achieved a verticality hitherto unknown, nor dreamed of. Ernie thought the true cause might have been the fact that so many people were glad to see the end of John, even if they had to view his loins at an excessively intimate distance to get a drink.

Following John's death the behaviour of Les became increasingly erratic. He was convinced the family was doomed — his mother and brother both were dead, and in a span of months.

He'd be the next dead Gobblelard, there were no others left. Trying to calculate how many days, minutes or seconds he might have left before death claimed him. He felt guilty because he missed the brother more than his mother. Or felt John's absence most, having depended for so long on his stern guidance to shelter him from the difficulties of daily life. When Les felt lost he'd only had to ask, 'What should I do now?' and John would give him a clip on the side of the head before issuing some fresh command, and thus Les never felt the need to be decisive.

Now he was utterly lost, become vague and anxious. Ordering far too many periwinkles and not enough oysters; the periwinkles remained uneaten and began to rot. He had to find someone to butcher the animals, and the customers complained the meat was tough. The butcher hadn't taken enough pleasure in the killing.

Les was terrified one night to find he was alone in The Horn Room with Jean, the other drinkers having already stumbled out into the night. Jean mumbling what Les thought were threats against his vulnerable person. As he tried to sidle away into the relative security of the kitchen he heard her calling after him. He froze, while wondering if it would be too unseemly to run and lock himself in the toilet.

'Les, come back, you coward. I'm not going to hit you, kiss you or fuck you. I hated you when Beau died. Now John's gone too. Who's next?'

Jean hugged him then and for a moment Les wondered if her words had been a ruse to stall him and now she'd either kiss or beat him. Holding each other in the shadows, looking at each other briefly, both glad to quickly look away again, having no idea what they might say or do. Yet it seemed some fundamental transaction had been made. To his surprise Les heard himself asking Jean if she'd help him in the pub, now that the brother was gone and he was struggling. Relieved when Jean accepted his offer, certain she'd prove adept at dealing with the most obstreperous customers.

Les felt the pressure of a terrible certainty: he would be the Last of the Gobblelards. He'd been sure that John would spawn a brood of Gobblelards, and had never thought that he, the youngster, would be faced with such a problem — to father a male child or be responsible for the extinction of a dynasty.

Les didn't care to admit it, but he liked the idea of being the Last of the Gobblelards. It was an awkward achievement, but an achievement nonetheless. Who'd have guessed that he'd be singled out by destiny? He and the legendary Artemis forming the bookends of a defunct dynasty. They'd go down in history together.

Les wondered whether he'd have to abstain from sex in order to achieve his wayward plan. He'd certainly need to keep his spawn well distant from the womb. Something in the plan's simplicity pleased him and renewed his sense of purpose. Its sheer selfishness suggested to Les that he might yet prove himself worthy of the Gobblelard name, even if he'd be the last to wear it. If he was the Last of the Gobblelards he'd eclipse his brother's reputation without having to do a thing. The dynasty would end as it began, in the hands of a cook.

Les couldn't help laughing then. Though a sudden noise from behind the bar cut him short. Was it a rat, or had the ghost of the brother just kicked the wall to indicate its disapproval of Les's line of thinking?

THE WORST OF TIMES?

Les was not the only one troubled by thoughts of dynasties and succession. Increasingly people were looking to Ernie as the only hope of Ruination. He had unwittingly become the town's star attraction. The number of fish caught in the bay had dwindled, and no one knew whether the fish had all been caught or had finally abandoned The Birth Canal in search of warmer waters. Crops were failing due to lack of rain, and when the rain finally came the land was so dry the water turned into floods. The topsoil washed away, leaving bedrock and mud. The rains had been a strange, muddy colour as the winds carried the little remaining topsoil up into the clouds. The rain filled the watertanks with a brown, sour-tasting liquid; even the beer tasted queer. The most devout drinkers now held their noses while drinking that muddy swill, with its dirty head that left streaks of grit on the inside of the glass and mouth.

Yet in these worst of times The Slapping Man still prospered, his trade growing brisker with every new disaster. People kept arriving from distant towns, having heard of the extraordinary man and his unique talents, wanting to know the pleasure of letting fly at The Slapping Man of Salvation at least once in a life that was too short. The visitors needed places to sleep, they needed to eat and drink. Inevitably deciding to extend their overnight stays by days, which sometimes became weeks as they in turn became addicted to Ernie's services.

The Slapping Man had become the basis for an entire industry.

Ernie had to employ three boys just to organise the queues in the marketplace. A new system using numbers had been put in place, and the boys were employed in relay, calling out the numbers around the market to keep things as orderly as possible. His assistants always suggested that the visitors have a go at The Pincushion Man, try and wrest the jackpot from The Man Who Never Laughs, or sample the other delights of the market rather than waste half their day standing in line.

The other marketeers were delighted to find that Ernie had become their drawcard, and they too prospered. No one had thought the blighted town might develop such a unique attraction. The decline in the numbers of fish meant that Les only needed one boat to farm the depleted waters, and the other two boats were busy day and night doing their best to navigate The Birth Canal as they ferried passengers back and forth.

Other boats from foreign towns brought their own loads of passengers. Boats still foundered and sank. Those who survived the most perilous journeys felt the greatest thrill when they finally arrived in the market, took their place in the queue and heard their number called.

Standing in front of Ernie, marvelling at the fact that the

little man had a jaw that exceeded the stature of his legend. Feeling they'd come close to death just for the pleasure of taking a swipe at The Slapping Man filled them with an astonishing vitality, and this intensity was attributed to some aspect of Ernie's potency.

When these strangers finally left town, the stories they told about The Extraordinary Slapping Man Of Salvation only boosted his already prodigious reputation.

There were stories of people who became so depressed when they returned home that they suicided rather than contemplate a life without recourse to The Slapping Man. Ernie never encouraged such rumours, nor had he ever been presented with concrete proof that they were true.

There were those who had decided to settle permanently in the town because they needed their regular swipe. After years of dwindling population the town had begun to grow at an unprecedented rate. Strangers were prepared to tolerate the worst humours of the town just to enjoy the essential pleasure The Slapping Man afforded.

Les had a constant supply of travellers holed up in the rooms of the hotel. It was a windfall he had never imagined possible, and he was not the only one who became convinced that the birth of Ernie in Salvation was a godsend. Anyone with a spare room had no trouble finding some desperate soul keen to pay an exorbitant price for a dry bed, with some dry bread and dirty tea for breakfast.

Ernie was so overwhelmed by the gushing fountain of his popularity it was all he could do to make it through each working day. So many people stopped to thank him, or stood back to let him make his way through the crowded market, or simply said, 'Ernie, you are Salvation's true salvation!'

He was astounded when he realised how many people now depended on him for their livelihood. There were those who gave hand massages to those yet to slap; others who bandaged fractured hands, or rubbed bruised palms and fingers with concoctions made from the secretions of cacti mixed with wild honey. Others wiped the sweaty brows of those who stood in the hot sun, or provided shelter from the rain using large umbrellas.

You could buy an entire 'Slapping Kit' if you wanted, with a small umbrella that provided shelter from the rain and wind and sun, a bottle of muddy water, some sandwiches, a brief history of The Slapping Man of Salvation, as well as bandages and ointments for use as necessary.

There was one major disadvantage to this curious prospering of The Slapping Man. It was much harder for the locals to gain access to that jaw. In retrospect the days before word leaked beyond the borders of the town seemed like a time of innocent luxury, when the queues were shorter and you could sate your desire for The Slapping Man without needing to spend an entire day doing so.

The most forward-looking members of the town, among them the enterprising Les, had begun to ruminate on what was inevitable: the time would come when there'd be no Ernie, no Slapping Man, the man was not immortal — and what would happen then?

SATCHEL'S SATCHEL

He had begun to think of his tome as Vronsky's Folly. It had consumed him, and he was beginning to realise the magnitude of the task he had envisaged. It was a fucker of a job. What to include? What to leave out? Needing to give the thing some finite dimension despite the infinite possibilities. Telling himself he'd know the thing was finished when he could not longer squeeze it into his satchel.

How might he garner the truth amidst the distortions of rumour, speculation, lies, braggardry and the like? Or were they the very truths he sought to lay at their communal feet?

Documenting a history of the town, knowing he was really looking for himself, some clue to his point of origin. Rummaging through any archive he could find, pretending he was only making notes for his immodest history, hoping he'd turn up some clue to his parentage, a bastard job, given that he didn't even know their names.

He found a new sense of purpose as he scurried around the cliffs, examining shipwrecks, rowing a small dinghy out to the reefs in the calmest weather. Pulling a handful of black mussels off the rock face at the tide line. Glad at least he had his dinner.

He was growing obsessive, sleeping at odd hours, only to rise in the middle of the night and get back to work on his opus. Going to bed again some hours later, sleeping soundly for three hours, waking at dawn. Alarmed at how long it was taking just to read all of his files. Wondering how on earth he might construct his summation. Deciding then he'd cancel all appointments — he'd take the whole week off. He hauled old files out of cabinets, unpacked old journals from boxes, and spread them onto every available surface, the great spills of paper covering the floor. Taking refuge in his coffin, glad of its quiet dark once he pulled the lid shut. No longer confronted by his sprawling sea of paper.

Satchel, swimming through reams of paper, drowning in their histories. Drinking so much coffee he became jittery and panicked, drinking red wine then to calm down. By four o'clock in the afternoon he was a wreck.

Vronsky felt a rage spawning in him. The whole of the town's history seemed an outrage perpetrated on the inmates. The filthy drains and gutters of their common horrors.

Grown stubbly after five days without shaving. Sleeping little, enjoying a growing delirium, some hysterical delight driving him forward.

He was tempted to burn the boxes of notes, the files, the journals. Instead he began to put things back in boxes. He was getting through the filing cabinet. Spurred on by the realisation that it was a finite thing, and he got closer to the end with each day that passed, each detail noted. There'd be an end to it.

Putting whole case studies into the draft. Glad his handwriting was legible, even if he was a doctor. To his delight the encyclopaedia now barely fit inside his satchel.

Heading off for a quiet stout at The Perseverance. The upstairs bar had the best view of Ruination. You could see the entire coastline, and see from the wall map the exact places all those ships had come to grief. It was Vronsky's favourite bunkhole, a quiet table by a window, the sun streaming through, or else the dark and menacing vistas of low grey cloud engulfing the headlands and inlets. The vistas feeding a fascination with disaster.

The walls were littered with paintings of shipwrecks, piteous sights of dread and calamity as those on board contemplated their certain ruin. Or would they yet tumble on Salvation? The walls and ceiling spattered with relics of all the boats that came unstuck on The Birth Canal, or other dangerous stretches of the coast. There were spars and rudders and other bits of boats that had been dashed on the rocks.

The prow of a small dinghy was breaching one of the walls, as if the boat had just broken through it. A nasty gash in the hull loomed over the heads of drinkers. The boat's occupants had all sunk. The drinkers knew the feeling, often ending capsized on the floor themselves by the end of a good night.

The publican was known as Perce, as was every publican who'd ever run The Perseverance. Vronsky and Perce were on friendly terms — Vronsky was not an angry drunk, and loved the late afternoons when the trade was quiet.

Perce liked Vronsky. Here was a man who actually took an interest in the family's historical collection. A man who happily sat and listened and sometimes scribbled as Perce spouted forth. Usually his punters expected him to shut up and listen to their blather while he pulled their beer.

Perce poured them both a cleansing stout. It wasn't long before they shifted over to whisky as Perce unleashed his own torrent of tales and rumours, licit and illicit exaggerations, and home truths.

The pub had smuggled its own history of Salvation within its walls. This included a habit worn then discarded by one of the stranded nuns when they'd finished their vigil and decided to copulate and cherish.

'She returned to the main camp in her underwear, ready to start on the task at hand; to whit, getting herself with child as soon as possible. She gave the others courage in their labours, and in time became a midwife, whispering encouragement to the womb-enquickened. Became known as the Mud Nun to some, the first of the fallen sisters to go hard at it.'

Perce had been a seaman before retiring to the family pub when his knees and joints had finally begun to give and seize. The pub had a collection of logbooks, detritus and trivia going all the way back to the first fleet of lifeboats that made it to dry land. And a bit of the *Good Hope* as well.

One dusty glass case held coins, some old money purses and a wallet, all part of the pub's collection of wreckabilia. When Perce opened the case and began his spiel, Vronsky was intrigued. The wallet held his eye, some familiar aspect puzzled him. Slowly realising that it bore a remarkable similarity to his satchel.

Vronsky drank, then swallowed. He did not know his name. He did not know his birthday, nor how old he was. All of the staple facts were denied him, all the little structures erected in the face of the great obliteration.

Vronsky held the wallet in his hands. The stitching and leather were not unlike that of his satchel. Worrying at the zip, slowly working it open. There was a single word embossed in gold on the lining. *Vronsky.*

'Ah,' said Perce, 'it were a wee small boat, that's true for starters.'

'Occupants unknown?'

'Not much is known on't.'

The white crests of a waterspout called The Gurgler caught the publican's eye from his window seat.

'A lot of boats gone down The Gurgler, and many lives lost down that rocky throat. This wee boat were one.'

Vronsky felt his own gorge rising.

'The name of the boat?'

'Well I'll be buggered.'

He poured them both a stout.

'No, I'm buggered. Might yet dig it out.'

A raucous sucking sound was heard in the distance as water squelched and squealed through seaweed while rushing up and down The Gurgler's throat. Was this his parents' burial water? Or was the wallet made by other hands? Who was this Vronsky?

He put the wallet down and sipped his stout.

'Is there nothing more you know?'

'Was it the *Air Purse*? It may yet come to me.'

'How did you get the wallet?'

'Before my time! I was a nipper. How's the stout?'

Vronsky drank, and mumbled sweet sounds through frothy lips. The two men sitting and listening to The Gurgler between swallows.

JEAN'S KISSING SPREE

Since kissing Ernie Jean felt she'd made an important discovery — that if she put her mind and body to it, she might yet heal the breach that had opened in her following the unsightly and untimely death of Beau.

Ernie had never heard of a kissing mania, but felt Jean's kissing spree had to be a mania. Her desire to conquer her fear of kissing had only begun the night she had kissed Ernie. Having coped with their first kisses Jean was keen to repeat the experience. One evening she dragged Ernie out to The Virgin Wall on the pretext of asking whether a cut above her knee had become infected. Once outside she didn't mention that cut again, instead she used her full weight to push Ernie up against the wall. He could smell the sweet and sour breath caused by tobacco smoke and sherry. Ernie felt appalled and inert. He felt it was somehow his fault, he should never have been accomplice to that first kiss. Had it deranged her?

He knew there was no point struggling. She had him pinned, he could feel the soft weight of her breasts and belly, using her pelvis to lock his hips against that infamous wall. He closed his eyes and tried not to whimper as she put her lips to his, her tongue slowly advancing until it occupied his oral cavity. He didn't mean to gag as she began to push her tongue down his throat, nor did he mean to bite her.

It brought the kissing to an end, and he was glad that Jean retrieved her tongue so quickly. He was shocked when she punched him in the chest after she had done so.

'I'm sorry, Jean.'

'So you should be. I'm a grieving woman! I could have you any time I wanted.'

To prove her point she leant against him, pinning him to The Virgin Wall once more. Her pubic bone a needle, and he her butterfly.

'I'm sorry, Ernie. I didn't mean to hurt you.'

Taking his silence as acceptance, she began to kiss him slowly, and Ernie hoped there might be some accidental virtue in his compliance. To his surprise Jean started sobbing. It was only then that he put his arms around her and they embraced with the strength of the grieving and forlorn. From a distance, as you heard the sounds and saw their bodies shaking, you'd swear the pair of them were making love.

Jean was immersed in her conquest. As if by mastering her fear of kissing she might conquer all her fears. Strange act of reclamation. Ernie was disturbed to see Jean, most nights, standing by The Virgin Wall kissing friends and strangers. Her lips becoming swollen and bruisy.

Ernie wondered whether Jean was sick, and if so, what might bring on curing. When he asked, 'Are you all right?', she always answered, 'Fine, boy, I'm fine.' Something hard and blinkered in her answer made him feel she was not fine at all. Yet he could not see the virtue in persuading her she was ill. She was only kissing.

He felt a certain admiration for Jean. A purity of sorts in her determination. A man had called her Kissing Jean as she pulled beers in The Horn Room, and puckered his lips. Jean kissed him and stuck her tongue down his throat, squeezing him as she did so. Then she lifted him off the ground, and threw him to the floor. Without hesitating she grabbed the discarded man's drinking partner and repeated the exercise. They were small men, no match for Jean. It looked as if she was going to make her way around the bar, kissing and discarding every man in the room.

'Who wants a big fat tonguey?' she said, and roared with laughter. She felt a thrill of power when she saw them all recoil.

She'd never thought that kissing might be such a vehicle for her strength or liberty. She felt sure she'd grown taller, her neck felt longer. Not just her neck, it seemed the whole of her had risen up. She'd always been a tall woman, yet only now did she realise she was the tallest person in town. She'd always been too slumped to notice. Surprised to find that when she rose to her full height she could look down on the entire population of Ruination. She'd always been embarrassed by her height, and could not believe it had taken so many years to yield its private virtue.

Men were scared of her. She found that quite delightful, giving her a confidence that some found terrifying. It made her laugh to think about it, and the laughter only underscored the terror she provoked.

Jean began kissing inanimate objects, and animals. On her knees, kissing every stone in the street outside the pub. Kissing every doorway she passed, every mailbox.

Some people thought she'd finally succumbed to an idiocy that had always been latent, though if they mocked her it was never to her face. A confused hilarity they shared over a beer in the pub at night, while wondering what possessed the girl, feeling a certain envy at the tranquillity which seemed now to enfold her.

Ernie was baffled. Was it a mania, or her way of blessing the town? It struck him as an unusual exaltation, though he could not say it was inferior to any other.

THE SLAPPING MAN'S REVENGE

Ernie felt haunted by his success. People always wanted to test their arm on The Slapping Man's jaw, or handle it like a scientific exhibit, whether he was working or not. Out walking, he'd find himself turning on total strangers, shouting, 'I am not The Slapping Man!' He'd begun to get cranky and cantankerous. When the chance presented itself he was not averse to bumping into people who had bent over to tie their shoelaces, tumbling them into the dirt. Reaching over to help them up, he'd mutter his profuse apologies while bumping his solid jaw into their tender faces. It did not make him feel noble, but it brought its satisfactions.

The ringing in his ears had become incessant, making it hard to sleep or enjoy the song of birds, and the din inside

THE SLAPPING MAN'S REVENGE

The Horn Room echoed in his head in a painful manner. It was something of a joke to see Ernie sucking his beer through a straw, fingers in his ears so that he could drink without feeling he was being deafened. He was spending less time at The Bluebottle, Prawn and Oyster, and more time sitting on his own inside The House Of Pearls, or just staying at home. Jean thought Ernie was avoiding the pub through fear she'd try to kiss him, and no matter how many times Ernie explained it was just the noises in his head, Jean never quite believed him.

The work had aged him far too quickly — he had grown old before his time and had not even noticed it was happening. Stunned one day to discover that the comforting thickness of his skin had started wrinkling. It still gave good protection, but it was not the skin of a young man in his prime. Perhaps it was not the slaps at all; the creasy definition of his face might have been prompted by the terrible tales Vronsky had ladled into him. A human slopbucket might be prone to growing haggard. He looked like he'd been out in the weather for too long and no end of mollycoddling would ever rejuvenate the man.

Telling himself he wanted some revenge for all the slaps delivered. Wanting to deliver his own mighty slap to the town. Imagined himself clasping a huge baton and whacking it over a line composed of one hundred pairs of naked buttocks.

He did not want to be a horrid man. Yet he wanted to wield that stick. Even once would do, as long as the blow he landed was a beauty.

Ernie was growing addled in his thinking. He didn't want to be an agent of unnecessary cruelty. He just wanted to slip out of the noose of being The Slapping Man. Yet he'd slipped that noose over his own head, and was paid for his work.

He felt entitled to some compensation. For what? His wrinkled face? The ringing in his ears? People told him his work must be character-building. It would be shameful if he did not share the small lessons of his craft with the world at large. One good slap, The Slapping Man's revenge.

He could feel the impulse lodge in him. He liked the sound of it: The Slapping Man's Revenge. Tantalised by the promise it seemed to hold. Though how might he achieve it?

THE GURGLER

Vronsky was dismayed. The lining of his satchel was frayed and torn. Should he replace it? Leave it intact? Worrying at the frayed edges, surprised how easily it crumbled at his touch. Even more surprised to discover that what he thought was padding had a line of scrawl on the top of it — a few pages inserted finely, and craftily, behind the waterproof lining. Holding the frayed paper to the light, trying to decipher the streaked and faded ink. *To My Son.* He blinked, then carefully tore the frayed cloth until he could remove the lining and the letter it concealed. Astounded by the obvious. His satchel had been, for all these years, a kind of safe, or envelope. He read on, then stopped, opened a bottle of red, poured a glass, said his prayer of thanks, drank some wine and began to read again.

When I first met Mira, your mother, she was hanging from a tree. She lived in the tree trunk. She'd been set upon and left hanging from a bough. But she was a big woman, and as the vagabonds left her to her demise she observed that the bough was slowly bending under her weight, until her feet just met the ground. She was still trussed and could not free herself, but had no immediate fear of strangulation. Breathing easier now, she waited. I was trundling along in a small wagon, which was full of my leathers and needles and satchels I had made. That's why they called me Satchel. I didn't realise she was hanging by her neck until I was much closer.

Her first words to me? 'You took your fucking time!' We both laughed then, before she burst into tears, clutching me to her and holding me for dear life. We never separated.

We met and made love and lived together in the hollow tree trunk. Then we sailed off, after wheeling our craft overland, building the hull and interior as we travelled. Converting the little covered wagon into a sailing boat, the axle made a small mast, the sails were made from the wagon's cloth covers. The wagon reborn, transformed into a creature of wind and water. A bough of the tree served as our boom. Finally dismantling the wheels and axle, the relief when the small craft floated and was tethered to the sands by quiet waters. We baptised it the **Wind Bag.**

We sailed off in that boat and lived for two years on a small island we discovered. In fact we were wrecked, but could salvage the ruined boat. We built a small shack at the back of the beach, lining the room with our sails. We repaired to the beach in search of shellfish and we finally conceived you, our darling babe. You were born in that shack, our love shanty.

Finally we abandoned our retreat, you were a nursling babe no more. I'd made a small store of wallets and satchels and small bags by then. I knew how to make good leather from a skin. I kept my knives sharp. We'd heard of villainies perpetrated — the false lights set to lure the unwary onto reefs.

Vronsky peering at the water-stained pages, trying to discern some meaning from the places where the ink was illegible.

> *Dropped sails and anchors, but the anchors did not hold. Upping sails we just failed to clear the reef ... dripping water from the limestone cave ...*
>
> *To feel this sad is no great achievement ... you were our boy, and we loved and blessed you.*

To think the answer to the riddle of his birth had been under his nose for all these years. And he'd not gleaned the slightest inkling. It made him laugh, though he got to feeling sobby when he thought some more. And his father's name? Satchel Vronsky — that was how he'd signed his brief epistle. He'd called himself aright all these years. It made him feel less orphaned. There'd been a strange coda to the handwritten note. The last page held just one line in the centre. *Suicide is not an option.*

Vronsky drank another glass of red. And then another. He still did not know how he had reached dry land. Nor the precise facts of his parents' demise. Making do with the little that he knew. It was too early to go to bed, yet he needed to lie down. He took another glass of wine to bed with him.

At around four in the morning he woke up laughing. Astonished and delighted, it had never happened before. He'd dreamt of a child by a river, a man, a woman. The woman giving the boy a toy the father had made. Little wooden rods and wheels, and a little manikin. When he blew on the tube the dancing manikin pissed in the wind, and they all laughed together.

Lying abed with the sounds of early birds, feeling baffled by his contentment. Even the bare crumbs of his family story could sustain him.

The satisfaction and delight Vronsky felt was tinged with a profound dismay — somehow he knew he'd hatched his history of the town, and now it was complete. He'd found what he was looking for. His personal footnote. He'd miss the footing his historical folly had given him, the sense of purpose. Feeling footloose and bereft. Deciding he'd go and visit his parents at The Gurgler.

He placed the encyclopaedia on his kitchen table, then put a couple of longnecks of stout in his satchel. Tied the manuscript with a purple ribbon, put it in a box and decided he'd have a glass of red. Halfway through the glass he suddenly grunted, scribbled a note to Ernie, tied the box with another ribbon, snuck the letter beneath it and smiled to himself. He finished his wine slowly then.

Slipping his satchel over his shoulder, putting his father's letter in his shirt pocket. Heading out the door and walking down to the bay in the grey, predawn light. Sniffing the sea air, a bitter aftertaste of red wine in his mouth. Stamping up the hill towards The Perseverance, then heading out along the cliff line. Enjoying the thrill as he stood closer to the edge of the cliffs than he usually dared.

The path was a narrow sheep trail, with hazardous stretches of scrabbly pebbles on sloping rock, difficult to cross if you didn't have four legs and cloven feet.

It was a place of appalling beauty, the human creature so unnecessary to it. A pair of deep gorges, with jagged columns of rock thrusting up from the seabed. The water banging and pounding against sheer rock cliffs. Impossible to climb; those wrecked would find no escape even if they made it to shore. Instead they'd be tossed and pounded onto rock, sucked back and lifted again and again, until their bones and bodies broke and flesh gave way. The Gurgler.

A small cove with a yellow sand beach and a deep cave at the foot of a cliff provided the only hope of landfall and refuge. It was an awesome place, the water rushing and gushing down deep channels between the looming spars of rock, or through archways formed by years of oceanic pounding. The ocean's constant action had forced tunnels through headlands, the water rushing and spurting out into some nearby inlet. If his parents had come aground here, they'd surely have been wrecked. Ground to a pulp and eaten by polyps. Yet if that were true, then how had he survived?

Working his way through the stout. Offering his small prayers to the memory of his parents. The sound of the rocks bumping and grinding at the water's edge and in the shallows. The ocean's great maw grinding its teeth.

He was less steady on his feet by the time he'd emptied both stout bottles. When he stood he didn't mean to stumble and wobble, his shoes skating on the pebbles; to his astonishment he slipped and fell onto a rocky ledge below, breaking both legs on impact. Hauling himself to the edge of the ledge, excruciating pain, wondering if he'd prefer a drastic thirty seconds to whatever now was to come.

Getting his head over the ledge, staring down at the awesome view. Surprised he was not terrified; he'd always thought he could not stomach heights, though this new vista was appealing. The pain in his legs seemed greater with each intake of breath, and he wondered if he'd pass out.

He shouted and heard no echo, just the dinning bash and thump of wave on rock. Shocked by the pain.

'Fuck!' he shouted. Broken highnotes of seabirds in the distance. Groaning to himself, 'I'm going down The Gurgler.'

And so it was. Les broke the news to Ernie.

'A shepherd found his body on the rocks. He'd missed The Gurgler by a bit. If he jumped. There's a scrubby pair of marks that make it seem he might've slipped.'

Les pushed another beer across to Ernie.

'There's a sheep trail that will take you down to him. Would you like to borrow a shovel?'

Ernie stared at Les, then blinked and nodded his consent.

EXIT VRONSKY

While Ernie had felt a certain confused sympathy for John Gobblelard when the publican died, the death of Vronsky plunged him into a state of genuine grief. At their last meeting they had been sitting in The House of Pearls, Vronsky talking as usual. There had been thunder in the hills behind the town, and Satchel had told Ernie a story about a woman he had seen that morning. Her father had come into her mouth during a thunderstorm, whenever she heard thunder she tasted semen in her mouth and became immobilised for hours. Ernie and Vronsky had started weeping together as the rain fell down. As Vronsky left he said, 'See you in the next life'. Ernie had thought it just another of Vronsky's awful jokes.

Vronsky had no family, and being the late doctor's closest friend, Ernie knew the task of putting Vronsky's affairs in order had just fallen to him. It was not a task he relished. To his surprise the rented house looked as if someone had just moved out, the cupboards bare, and only a few bits of furniture.

Vronsky had already put everything in order. His coffin was built, just waiting for the insertion of his corpse. Ernie had an uncanny feeling when he saw a box on the kitchen table, tied with purple ribbon, bearing a small note addressed to him.

> *Dear Ernie,*
> *Please find my modest contribution to our strange communal life. A perverse history, if you will. It's an alarming document, not the least for the fact that it's all true. I'd hoped to set the beast free, our poor history on its rampage. Might you not find some way to let it loose on your demise? If you are reading this, my time has come. Cheer Up!*
> *Yours,*
> *Satchel*

Cautiously undoing the ribbon and opening the box, his uncanny feeling turning into an intrigued sense of foreboding when he discovered what was inside. Ernie was alarmed when he saw the first page. *The Encyclopaedia of Betrayal.*

Ernie had no idea that Vronsky had compiled a history of the town.

Vronsky was not interested in the great figures of the past. *The Encyclopaedia of Betrayal* was a more fundamental and disturbing document. Using the intimate confessions he'd garnered in his office, he had compiled an exhaustive listing detailing every shortcoming and human failing of his clients, their families, friends, enemies. It was horribly inclusive. Perhaps the real betrayal was the extent to which he had betrayed the confidence his clients had placed in him. Where necessary he'd drawn from historical documents, and any other sources that would give his local history the most definitive dimensions.

Ernie read Vronsky's words with mounting trepidation, not sure whether it made his spirits sink or rise. Was it a wholesale breach of trust, or the most truthful account of local life he'd ever see?

He read the first few pages, flipped through the middle and end, and then sat down on the nearest chair. It broke beneath him and he landed on his arse. He could not believe he'd fallen for the trick one last time, yet such was his perplexity as he pondered the implications of Vronsky's secret history he neither laughed nor cried, didn't even bother to stand up, just sat amidst the pieces of the broken chair, lost in his bafflement. He had a new respect for Vronsky. In all their drunken rambles the good doctor had never revealed the existence of such a document.

The more Ernie read about his fellow citizens the more perplexed he felt. Feeling he had lived within such a narrow band of the humanly possible. He'd never had sex with a donkey, he'd never even thrown a punch in anger, and now he felt taunted by the fact that he had not lived his life to the full.

Ernie discovered that he needed to be drunk to persevere with his perusal of Vronsky's ledger. Even the footnotes began to fill Ernie with an unprecedented dread. In one there was a list of all the children who'd been molested by the local clergy. Vronsky had called the chapter: 'How a church became The Paedophile Machine'. Drinking himself into a pleasing numbness that made it possible to digest the horror stories. The force of the revelations would, he felt sure, provoke a riot.

He hadn't realised how many people had sought out Vronsky for advice, or just to have the pleasure of a willing ear. Remembering Vronsky's words, 'This is not a town of listeners, Ernie, that's why they come. They need an ear.'

It was a terrible document, no one was spared. Ernie had never thought the dead might know the living far too well. No one had kept their secrets from Vronsky.

EXIT VRONSKY

Ernie was feeling a growing agitation. He was terrified by the scope of Vronsky's project, it was such a wholesale betrayal. Yet Ernie could not resist the conviction that there was a rightness in it, even a necessity for such a thing in the town's life.

PHIL ANN THROW PISSED?

Les had decided to donate one half of one per cent of the weekly takings to some as-yet-unknown benevolent enterprise, in memory of the brother. He wanted to let Ernie in on the secret, and was intrigued when Ernie muttered, 'You've decided to become the town philanthropist?'

The sound of it pleased Les utterly. He assumed it referred to the fact that he made his money from getting people pissed, he didn't care who Phil and Ann were. He had, however, no idea what form this benevolent impulse should take and was rather hoping Ernie might help him. If brother John was still capable of diction he'd have seventeen ideas inside one minute. But as the brother was stuffed, Les was hoping the little man might fill the big man's shoes.

Ernie could feel his ears burning as he toyed with a terrible solution to Les's problem.

'That's an interesting, tricky puzzle, Les. It's hard to know what might befit a man like your brother. His unique qualities, you'll agree, deserve some unique gesture.'

Ernie tried to avoid looking sly as he then casually suggested, 'We could always write a history of the town.'

He thought it best to mention nothing of a Slapping Man's Revenge or *The Encyclopaedia of Betrayal*. It was a complex topic, and he didn't want to impose too much on Les's faculties. Les was beaming, mouth hanging open, his eyes shining. He had the fixed stare of a man who's made a decision from which he will not budge. Ernie was glad that Les quickly convinced himself the enterprise was his own idea.

'There is one difficulty, Ernie. Who might author such a thing?'

Ernie almost started giggling with nervous excitement as he said, 'I know the very man, though he's a shy retiring type, he'd want his name kept secret till the thing was done.'

They shook hands, and Les thumped another beer down on the counter. He walked off then, humming. Ernie was pleasantly drunk, drifting in a lethargy of beers.

Ernie had trouble sleeping that night, perhaps one of the oysters had been off? He woke feeling nauseous and to his dismay became a dirty human fountain, gushing at both ends. The attack came on so quickly he fouled his bed in a manner he'd never thought possible. Cleaning the mess of soiled sheets and shitty blankets he couldn't stop thinking of the phrase, 'an encyclopaedia of betrayal'. It had lodged deeply in his lobes, and the more he thought about Vronsky's death the more he felt some irrevocable bargain had been struck.

JEAN FLINCH IS NO MORE

Jean was stripping off, rubbing herself in black mud and adorning herself with sea weeds and sea flowers, before plunging into the waters. Returning to the shore in this, her new garb.

As she waded among the rocks an octopus tried to bite her foot and wrap a tentacle around her leg. She flinched, grabbed and grappled with it, and quickly turned it inside out. It looked like a bathing cap, on a whim she stuck it on her head. The tentacles still waving, as if the tresses of her hair had started dancing.

She felt spirited, and full of anima, ignoring or not feeling the occasional sharpness of rocks upon her soles. A long tress of seaweed barred her progress, she gathered it and draped the sea fronds around her neck. She began to rub sand on her body, scrubbing the dead skin off her, then plunged back into the cool water, and loved her body's surge as she stroked and stoked herself across the inlet. Flipping and lying on her back, loving the see-through clouds, the ripples splashing as the waters broke over her body. Dawdling through the kelp beds, walking slowly back to land.

Only noticing then that the tentacles no longer tweaked and slapped against her. The octopus was dead. She'd eat it now for dinner. Stripping it off her head, looking for a rockpool of clean water to leave it in while she made a fire.

Emerging fresh and sandscrubbed from the water, she felt reborn. Beau was dead, she loved him still, she no longer flinched at his memory.

'Thank God!' she said. 'Jean Flinch is dead, and I live on.'

Returning with renewed purpose to the task at hand, she lit off then, in search of firewood.

Out in the bay the fish were spawning, she could see the clouds of eggs on the surface, and the males swimming in strict lines as they fertilised the eggs in shoals.

Realising that in her way she been devoted all her life. Her fumbling sense of some animating power, which informed and infused the seas and winds and her. Wanting to put herself at the disposition of those natural forces, that fundamental animating power which lit the whole world's fuse.

BUTTOCK BOY

There was a foul smell coming from the fish-scraping yards, the foetid organs and decayed intestines of fish. Ernie could see a cloud of birds diving and feasting, the livid worms of fish gut in their beaks.

His jaw felt sore, and he had a headache which started at the base of the skull and seemed to reach up through his brain like a hand, squeezing the contents of his brainpan. It was not time for lunch, yet he already wanted to stop work. He'd thought he was somehow superhuman, with a capacity to withstand pain that outstripped any other. It had become an article of faith. Contemplating an early retirement from the rigours of his life as The Slapping Man, wondering what he might do instead. He could always join the men and women at the fish-scraping yards. Les might let him wash plates and scrub the floors come closing time. He'd be a most congenial menial, he was certain.

Ernie felt sure of one thing — he could no longer work as The Slapping Man. Whatever abilities he possessed in this regard had been finally extinguished. Going to bed each night with a head that throbbed and kept him awake, never quite believing when the sun rose that it was already time to start the working day.

He should never have mentioned his desire to retire to Les one night after closing time. Les had nodded and smiled, yet a certain creasing around the eyes made Ernie sure that the news was most unwelcome.

Word quickly spread about The Slapping Man's impending retirement. It triggered a panicwave of custom, and the length of time that elapsed before they got to slap him meant more people were breaking bones or getting profound bruises, as they hoped to land a slap that would satisfy their need of him for the rest of their lives.

Ernie worried that the extra punishment he now received might do irreparable harm. Was there not an increased risk of brain damage? Though he did not dare to stay away. As he thought about what might ensue if he failed to turn up, he also began to suspect that even if he wanted to retire they would not let him. He'd be dragged out of bed, put back in the market. What right did he have to deny them an essential service? A doctor must keep on practising, whether sick or well, and in all weather. But there were always other doctors. There was no other Slapping Man. Was there no way out?

As his desire to withdraw from public life became common knowledge, a great wave of depression slowly broke over the town. The inevitable passing of The Slapping Man would leave a shocking void. Were there no heirs? Had he not sired any bastards who might have inherited that jaw? Yet there had been no sightings of any child sporting such a mandible. It was not the sort of thing you could keep secret, that mighty bone announced its presence in all company. There was no such child.

Ernie began to hear disturbing rumours. The drinkers at The Bluebottle, Prawn and Oyster were working overtime, looking for an answer to this problem. It was a problem unlike any other, and thus required an innovative solution. There was a growing body of opinion that Ernie should be made to sire a brood of youngsters, in the hope that any one of them might preserve the miracle of his physiognomy. Where would they be without a Slapping Man or Woman? The sex was immaterial, the jaw was everything.

They'd all heard Ernie's boast, 'Slapping Men Are Born, Not Made!' Ernie wished he'd kept this stupid boast to himself. There was talk of establishing a communal fund and a special levy, whose sole purpose would be to support as many women and their offspring as Ernie could inseminate. Some women found this proposition quite attractive, as they would have an income for life. In their enthusiasm for this plan the most forward thinking of the clients at The Horn Room wondered aloud if the town might not even export such offspring.

Ernie wondered if the townsfolk were right. Did he have a duty to sire a brood in the hope that at least one prodigal jawbone might appear? Did he have the right to impose this heavy burden on the child, should he succeed?

Ernie's experience with sex had left him wary of the act. Having lost his virginity in a drunken haze by The Virgin Wall on the day his parents died, whenever he thought of sex he thought about his drowning parents. If he woke with an erection, he found himself plunged into a maudlin introspection concerning the demise of The Burner and Irene. Such thoughts always made him wilt at once; lost in such a strange confection of sex and death it was easier to rouse himself and leave his little bed, make tea, eat a boiled egg, then hurry off once more to the market, stretching and yawning as he stood on his little platform waiting for the working day to begin. The first slaps woke him up, and his usual morning reveries suffused him with such guilt that his devotion to his labours was renewed, each slap feeling like a blessing, convinced he was in need of some mortification for the crime he had committed when he stood inert and watched his parents die.

He was tempted to try and run away again, leaving the town to its worst excesses. Yet he suspected that this prospect had also been discussed at The Bluebottle, Prawn and Oyster. If he walked out onto the pier at three a.m. he was surprised to find he was not the only one who'd decided to stretch their legs and get some air. The only time he was alone was when he was in the shed. Even then he was never sure whether the rustling in the trees and bushes was caused by wind, rats, perhaps a stray cat, or by someone sneaking around the bushes to keep an eye on him.

It wasn't long before false claimants to Ernie's title began appearing. Women he'd never met bursting into tears outside The Bluebottle, Prawn and Oyster. How could he disown them? Had he been so drunk he'd forgotten they'd made love? Here was the child! Yet the offspring they thrust forward as Ernie's heirs clearly lacked the one thing needed to sustain their claims: their meagre mandibles had nothing in common with his own. Other women brought children with gigantic bottoms, trying to convince the informal tribunal that sat in The Bluebottle, Prawn and Oyster that this child was just as gifted as Ernie, even if the gift took a different shape.

'A slap is a slap! Look at those robust cheeks. And when you get tired of slapping, you can kick him. His buttocks can take it all. This child is more versatile than Ernie ever was! Forget The Slapping Man — meet Buttock Boy!'

But these claimants were unconvincing, and while they were amusing they did nothing to solve the problem which had now beset the town.

BREED!

Ernie was not consulted, yet a decision had been made. Handbills began appearing around the town: *WANTED, SLAPPING BABE. Fertile Women Needed For Humanitarian Quest. Remuneration Guaranteed. Interested? See Les at The Bluebottle, Prawn and Oyster.*

So many women were interested in the scheme that an air of relief began to spread around Ruination. With so many willing parties to the quest, surely it was just a matter of time before an heir was spawned. Though Ernie wasn't all that keen about a spawn fest with himself the seedy attraction. He hadn't realised that civic obligation could take such an onerous form.

Ernie became increasingly suspicious of anyone who tried to engage him in casual conversation. Even being wished 'Good morning' put him instantly on guard. So many chance encounters turned quickly to the question of his heir, and the foundation of his dynasty. Women winking at him while stroking their own well-defined jawbones, men wanting to buy him beer, only to start regaling him with details he didn't want to hear.

'She's the only woman who could do the job with certainty, and when she gets excited she gets so randy she'll scrape the skin off your pecker with her pubic hair …'

Ernie never stayed to hear the end of such tales. Some people said he was becoming the rudest man in town, you couldn't even stand the man a drink. It did nothing to lessen their desire to slap a bit of sense back into him.

To make things worse, rumours started spreading about Ernie's sexual preferences. He was known to love indulging in behaviours he hadn't even realised were part of the human repertoire. Sipping a quiet ale in The Perseverance, only to find some stranger slipping into the seat beside him.

'She hasn't washed her fan in months, from what I hear that's just your ticket!' Trying to escape, only to find himself collared by some other enterprising soul before he made it to the door.

'I've got the filly and the stud, they say your cock only gets hard when a strong man's stiffened your behind. Don't worry, he's not too big …'

Ernie was spending more time in the shed than he'd ever done in his life. Feeling he was under house arrest, even if it was self-imposed.

He still went to the market, though it took him longer to get there each day, and the closer he got the slower his steps became. It could take him half an hour to walk the last three blocks. Once there he was an easy mark, and it seemed that at least half his customers were interested in the scheme, they either knew the woman or were convinced they were the one to bring the tricky business off. It was not unusual for women to slap him, then fondle his privates as casually as if they'd been shaking him by the hand.

It did nothing to improve his opinion of the race in general, and the people of Salvation in particular. To his dismay even Jean was now an enthusiastic backer of the breeding program.

'You need to make a sacrifice, Ernie. This town's been good to you. You're not even being asked to raise the child, for God's sake, just give a bit of spawn to help revive an ailing town! I would have thought it was the least you could do.

'I wouldn't mind having a go at you myself, though there's no guarantee I'd conceive, nor raise a child with a jaw like yours. Come on, Ernie, we all have to do our bit.'

Ernie could understand the panic that possessed the town as it faced the prospect of life without The Slapping Man. He thought it logical that they wanted to establish a dynasty. He could countenance it in the abstract. It was only when he thought about the fact that he'd be expected to copulate with so many strangers that the plan lost its attraction.

To Ernie's amazement a date and venue had been announced for what some now termed The Spawning. Ernie wondered if he should just accept what to others had become obvious long ago — he'd have to sire an heir, if not a brood of Slapping Children, or be responsible for the death of Ruination.

THE SPAWNING

He had thought there would be, at most, a handful of women who'd turn up to present themselves as potential bearers of The Slapping Babe. To his amazement and terror there were hundreds, if not thousands, of candidates. It was out of the question that he might service such a mob. Perhaps if he did his best to fructify a few each day, that would make a thousand by year's end. Though he'd be so exhausted there be no slapping that year. He could already imagine the objections to this proposal. Was it possible to determine in advance which women had the best chance of spawning the requisite infant? Should he inseminate only those with large jaws? Why on earth had he agreed? Because it was better than being beaten to death.

Feeling frenzied and panicked, he ran out onto the wharf and immediately wished he hadn't. There was no way of escaping, unless he threw himself into the bay. He could choose to drown, or be fucked to death. It was always good to have a choice. The mob upon him now, the choice no longer his as they picked him up and carried him back to The House of Pearls. Ernie wished he could pass out rather than witness the dreadful scenes he imagined were to follow.

Telling himself he could at least die with a clear conscience. He'd done his best by the town. And what was his reward? To be pulled apart, while fully conscious, in front of an adoring crowd of well-wishers. People standing and cheering, applauding, shouting his name. It was a celebration, after all. Struggling against the many hands that held him, managing to get one foot free, kicking at random, making contact with a leg or arm before his limb was firmly tethered by the many clutching hands. Feeling his clothes being stripped off his body. If this was foreplay, he dreaded what was to come.

He could see a vast expanse of bellies, breasts and thighs, and felt seasick as he scanned so many faces, women who were eager to pin him to their bodies, determined to sire the creature necessary for communal survival. The great sea of would-be breeders did nothing for the fleshy needle in Ernie's groin.

'Come on, Ernie! Show us your stiffie!'

Wishing they had not started chanting, 'Big Jaw, Big Dick!' Castigating himself for ever making the sly remark, even if, unlike Skinny Rodger, his boast was based on fact. His organ had almost completely retracted inside his body. Ernie wished he could do the same, wanting to swallow himself and disappear.

'Come on, Ernie, we haven't got all week!'

Where to begin? And how? He began to wander as if he was browsing through the market, looking for a shirt, or handkerchief, trying not to look while looking, feeling himself lost in a sea of giddy flesh. Wandering like a lost child in a crowd, looking for some point of recognition or contact, something more than desperate grasping. He hadn't meant to start blubbering, and the sight of so many women advancing to comfort him made him weep the louder, there was a great press then of soft flesh and hipbones, of buttocks and elbows, with Ernie its sobbing centre. He found himself being embraced by several women at once, and his sobbing had become infectious, perhaps the desperation of the entire scene had finally become clear to all. It was a meat market, that was all, the women and Ernie nothing but fodder for the social carcass. The sobbing, heaving field of them, more like mourners than would-be lovers.

This communal sobbing tide was without a doubt one of the strangest sights ever seen in Salvation.

Ernie was suffocating, and growing light-headed from fear and weeping. He could see nothing but skin and hair, and was having trouble breathing. An elbow sticking in his ribs. Pressed and captured as he was between so many other sobbing bodies, he could not move. This odd chorus of lamentation that they made. He thought he was about to be crushed to death, and was relieved to find it was not so.

Perhaps it was the relief that proved to be his trigger. Ernie was appalled to find that his organ had begun to take up more room. A woman who was pushed against Ernie, her back to him, could feel this movement and decided to take matters in hand. Ernie was horrified. He could not see the face of his manipulator, and the buffeting of the wailing crowd around them provided all the movement necessary to animate a rudimentary coitus. Ernie did not find it pleasurable, or arousing; it seemed his body was capable of performing its mechanics without his consent, and without desire. Another woman realised what was happening, there was a wrestling of hands as Ernie's member was whipped out of a warm moist place and rudely thrust into another.

Ernie was so aghast at this new ordeal that he shrivelled and slipped out, only to be grasped by other hands who attempted to simultaneously revive and insert him, while others began to argue, or attempt combat, though this was difficult given the great press of bodies.

Someone called out, 'He's stiff and willing!' and this message quickly spread and became a new refrain, 'Stiff And Willing', which prompted a surging of bodies, as those who were too far to be able to lay a hand on Ernie struggled for proximity, while those who were being crushed attempted to push others away and make some room.

It was clearly going to be a harrowing and difficult afternoon. Ernie did his best to fend off the grosser assaults while attempting to acquiesce in other ways. To his relief he finally passed out, from a mixture of mortification and nervous exhaustion. Coming to inside The House of Pearls, Jean throwing water on his face to revive him. The crowd had dispersed, and Ernie was glad the thwarted breeding partners had not kicked him to death in their frustration.

PART SEVEN:

AN UNPEELED SAUSAGE

SOMETHING IN HIM BROKEN

Since his attempt to placate the communal desire and breed an heir, something had changed in Ernie. It was as if, after all those blows, his thick hide had finally been penetrated.

He felt like an unpeeled sausage, weeping at the sight of a butterfly being eaten alive by ants, or the memory of Harness Wilson and his trolley. He'd lost his composure. Where he'd been a model of implacability, now he began to weep spontaneously each time a hand was raised to slap him. It made people lose all desire to hit him, and he had to give their money back.

Each failed transaction made him grow more weepy, and there was a great feeling of anticlimax. Without meaning to he'd done himself out of a job, lost all prestige, and didn't need to worry about retirement. The demand for his services suddenly died, and he was rather wishing that he might do the same. There were skirmishes and fist fights outside the pub, and in the gardens. People jostled and grew angry as they fought over potatoes and mussels at the market. The incidence of friend-death, and domestic and random violence was on the rise.

Something had broken in him. Ernie couldn't stop trembling and shivering. He looked like he had a permanent fever, or was doing some crazy jiggledance, but he was just broken. Even walking up the small incline from the pier to The Bluebottle, Prawn and Oyster took such an effort he could devote half a morning to that achievement. When he tried to walk uphill it was not unusual for him to lose balance and find he'd just stepped backward, as if the past was now his preferred destination and his body could no longer propel itself forward.

His jaw was always full of animation, and the movement of the mandible made his lower lip wobble, so that he felt he was always about to weep. His shoes kept slipping off, and the difficulty of slipping them back on was so great he preferred to let them drag beside his feet, snagged on his toes, and didn't bother if his socks got wet when it was raining.

Ernie was appalled to think that he'd devoted his life to a worthless enterprise.

He dreamt one night he was a man whose body was all air. He could fly, and seep under doorways. The entire province of the town's secret life lay open to him. When he woke he was full of a dreadful agitation, and a certainty. That afternoon he paid a short visit to Les.

'The thing is done, I've just dropped our local history at the printer's. He's sending you the bill. That was our arrangement, was it not?'

Les blinked, and nodded in agreement.

It was a pity *The Encyclopaedia* was such a thick book. The printer made it clear he'd need some time to complete the task, and when Ernie relayed this news Les made a simple calculation and then announced, 'In that case we could launch it at The Shipwreck Feast.' Ernie didn't like to mention that the whole town might sink under the weight of those revelations.

RATBAGGERY AND RUMBUGGERY

Oddly enough something about Ernie's reduced estate brought Jean comfort. She felt easier around men when she knew she was more powerful.

Yet Jean was worried for Ernie, and decided to drop round unannounced one evening. Meaning to be friendly she was baffled to find she insulted him at once.

'By God you stink, man. Don't you ever wash?'

To Ernie's astonishment he agreed when Jean insisted she give his body a scrub. It made him feel like a child again, sitting in the bath, gladly giving over to the pleasures of being washed by a woman's hands.

Ernie was surprised to find that he and Jean became lovers. They didn't mean to sleep together, but found such solid comfort in their mutual company they hadn't wanted to sleep apart, and so crammed into Ernie's little bed. In the morning Jean felt the clumsy proddy poke of a wet nose against her bum; they were still both half asleep as she guided him inside her, the pair of them surprised by this development. Ernie felt like a small fish in a great ocean, and they stayed still for a long time. Jean began to laugh from deep down in her belly, it seemed so ridiculous yet so lovely. Ernie could feel the rise and fall of her belly with the contractions of her laughter, and the pair of them began to laugh so hard he slipped out, and felt a gladness he'd not known as she slipped him in again. They laughed and came together.

Jean whispering then, 'A bit of ratbaggery and rumbuggery is a good thing.'

It was only after Jean had left that Ernie realised what might have been obvious — he'd never made anyone breakfast before. It mattered not that he'd brought her nothing more than a cup of milky tea with sugar, a piece of buttered toast. As he thought about the care with which he'd cut the toast into triangles he felt a tremulousness, recognising now that he'd cut the toast with immense care, as if some fragile corner of the world depended on him doing it just so.

Jean was sitting on his bed. She could not remember when she'd last been subjected to such a simple act of kindness. By that one action, Ernie had made her feel not merely accepted, but wanted.

He'd confessed to her, 'I've always been terrified of sex. Ever since you had me by The Virgin Wall the day my parents died, sex and death have formed a terrible coalition.'

Jean was stunned. 'You haven't had sex since then?'

'No. Apart from my rather dismal attempts to sire an heir.'

Jean was too embarrassed to tell him that she had little recollection of their coitus by The Virgin Wall. The hour late, the booze too dominant to aid her memory.

Jean gave him a strange look then. Rising from the damp

bed, dressing silently, giving him a brief hug, leaving wordlessly. As she walked out the door he spoke to her back.

'You are so beautiful, Jean.'

She turned to face him. 'Don't mock me, Ernie, please don't mock me.'

Ernie had no idea how to reply. Feeling stupid, he held his tongue, and was relieved when Jean held him tightly, before easing away and walking home.

Jean spent the day cooking, scolding herself for not asking Ernie to join her in an evening meal. Yet each time she walked to the front door she hesitated, and turned back.

Ernie decided to skip his dinner and climbed into bed, enjoying the supple darkness, the moonlit shadows that spilled in through the windows. The smells of Jean's body on his sheets and pillow. The gladness he felt as he recalled Jean's solid presence, and the tenderness they found together. Wondering why he felt too cowardly to go to her.

Lost in his reveries he was startled by a soft knock at the door. For a moment he thought it was the wind scraping trees across the roof, or a rat scampering, until he heard the quiet knock again. Stumbling through the darkness, finding Jean on his doorstep, looking shy and apprehensive. They held each other in the doorway, then Ernie took her hand, they waded through the darkness, back to the little bed. They lay, and clung to one another, there seemed no need for words, instead they listened to the sounds of each other's breathing. They did not make love, yet something grew between them, which Ernie struggled to put into words, baffled as he was to find the pair of them enclosed by what seemed a fundamental intimacy.

BLOODED

Ernie's limited experience of sex had not prepared him for the pleasure he now found with Jean. Tracing a shy line down her flank with one finger, marvelling at the way she closed her eyes, smiled to herself, then looked at him in a way that was all-consuming.

Ernie felt quite unravelled by his desire for Jean. As if he'd stumbled over some aspect of himself he'd always been too scared to face. Astonished by the double-bodied furore they unleashed upon the bed, and the single-minded passion that became such a vehicle for delight. Even as something of this intensity made him utterly apprehensive.

The immensity of her physique enthralled him. Infused with an admiration for Jean's boldness as she cupped a breast in her hand and eased the nipple into his mouth. He hadn't meant to start gnawing the ripe bud of her tit and had worried he might hurt her, yet the harder he clamped his teeth around the nipple's base the more profound her sighs.

'You've really lost your virginity now, Ernie!'

The pleasure he took in her laughter then, despite the hardships they'd endured there was still some pulse of life that would not be extinguished, their mutual excitements so full-blooded and enticing, it seemed, in those briefest moments, that they'd found some restitution for the horrors and confusions of their lives.

Ernie was quite overcome by the willing flower of her cunt, the small jets of white cream that suddenly spurted as he nuzzled. The water flowing out of her was so abundant Jean worried there was a risk of dehydration, she'd never known herself to be so effusive. The high wafts of their fluids lingering for hours as the sheets slowly dried. The strong taste of her cunt surprised him, and his enjoyment of that meaty taste surprised him even more.

Jean gripped his arms so tightly she drew small points of blood out from the skin. She'd punctured him, yet Ernie seemed elated. Jean had blooded him. Bringing him into an aspect of the world he'd never thought to know. Jean insisted on cleaning the wound with alcohol. Ernie could not help beaming as she cleaned the skin, his smile making his lips plumper, his mouth gently open. Jean feeling a dread, afraid she'd lose her heart, if she'd not lost it already. Though something in the peace she felt made her want to face this dread, even embrace it.

'You and I, we're both alike.'

'What do you mean?'

'We're both celebrities. You with your famous jaw, me with my famous fanny. When people look at us they see one part of our anatomy, as if it has captured the essence of what intrigues others. Now here we are — The Slut and The Slapping Man.'

He could not believe the levity in her voice, she seemed so utterly uncaring. Yet something of Jean's courage infected him. Ernie was astounded to find that Jean had become his exemplar.

Wondering how she had found the strength to look back at her life, to stare it in the eye, and finally seem unflinching. Wishing that he might find something of what he could only call Jean's grace. It was not that she'd become immune to pain, rather she'd known so much of it she'd found some curious strength, an ability to swallow her pain whole and remain undaunted.

Ernie was scratching his jaw. Jean laughed again.

'I've had a lot of men. In fact, I rather think I've had too many…'

She stamped off to the toilet then, and made a point of farting loudly as she pissed.

When he thought about his microscopic experience and all the men she'd known and discarded, Ernie wasn't sure whether he felt giddy with envy or remorse. Feeling jealous, even angry, at the vastness of her experience compared to his naivety, sensing a humiliation. Wanting to clamber back inside his shell, his old ignorance, knowing it was an impossibility.

Ernie loved Jean's directness and lack of inhibition, even when it scared him. He felt she'd lived more fully than he had. Appalled by the ease with which she seized the vitality of her moments; she didn't think about the future, being utterly consumed by the present.

When Jean slipped her mouth around his moist corona Ernie sighed, Jean licked his stem and Ernie moaned, albeit timidly.

He was surprised to hear her say, 'There's a beast inside you wanting to get out. Let him out Ern, let him out.'

Jean was intent on arousing him utterly, and when Ernie began to groan, her desire to bring him to some state of blind pleasure only heightened. To Jean's content, Ernie's moans started to grow in volume. His pelvis had begun to rock involuntarily, Jean straddled him then, slipping her cunt around his cock and slowly swallowing him whole. Clenching his cock with her muscular organ, pinning his shoulders with her hands as Ernie flailed like a fish beneath her, teasing him as she slowly withdrew until just the tip of his cock was nestled within her, then driving the full force of her weight down, driving him deep inside her, the pair of them thrusting hard as if they might annihilate each other, some gay yet violent obliteration they both sought, as if they might erase the past with their ardour.

Ernie's voice had changed, something more bestial now released, staring at Jean eyes wide open, with a mix of disbelief and a vital commitment to the task at hand. The pair of them rocking and humping with abandon, and when Ernie arched and shot his bolt, Jean came with a whimper, their eyes locked on one another, she could feel his cock throbbing in her, her fanny twitching and clutching his stem.

'Oh Jesus, and to think I've just discovered sex!'

Jean kissed him behind the ear, licked his neck, felt herself grow giddyweary. Nodding off, and sleeping.

Ernie was shocked to think that he'd humped and grunted like an animal. It was a surprise to realise that he and that un-familiar beast were one. His essential physicality so unfamiliar.

When Jean woke, Ernie was staring at her, trembling.

'Are you all right, Ern?'

He nodded his head. He looked stunned.

'Will you hold me?'

Jean clutched him to her and held him so hard she heard his vertebrae crack. She loosed her grip a little, as Ernie began to smile. Something quite boyish that she caught then, a glimpse of some other essence. Glad when he spoke, in tones that nestled gently in her eardrum.

'You've unzipped me, woman.'

Stroking her neck, settling an easy hand upon a breast. Rearranging themselves for comfort they dozed peacefully then, with an intimacy that might have shocked them both had it not been so profound.

URCHINS

Jean and Ernie were sitting on the rocks near Knowledge Point, Jean dangling her feet in the water. Taking a small knife from a pocket, winkling limpets off the rocks, feeding Ernie the salty sweetmeats. They were a little tough yet tasty.

'Have you never eaten sea urchins?'

'Wouldn't the spines turn your mouth into a pincushion?'

'You eat the eggs, you fool. The males are black. The females have a crimson hue.'

Jean waded into the water, reached down and carefully plucked a female from her subaqueous perch. Knocking in the creature's side then splitting it open with her knife. Skewering the bright orange roe, offering it to Ernie at knife point. He sucked the salty slime of urchin eggs. Expecting to be disgusted, he was surprised how sweet this eggmeat was. Jean ate some roe then tossed the ruined animal back into the bay, slipped off her rock and foraged for another female. Ernie spoke.

'Do you know I was conceived here, on the pebble beach? My mother used to call the place Carnal Knowledge Point.'

Jean laughed as she split open the second urchin, then slurped the roe directly from the shell.

Ernie felt a little strange, making love with Jean in the very place his parents had made him. Wondering if this was not some strange perversion. He'd told Jean the tale of his conception, and felt somewhat confused when Jean led him to the beach and began to fondle him. His confusion only heightened by his responsiveness to her manipulations. Trying to dispel all thoughts of The Burner and Irene as he looked over Jean's shoulder at the waters of the bay.

Strange conflicts welling in him, the arousal competing with the feeling that he was committing incest, the confusion needling his arousal, unable to refrain from nuzzling at her neck, feeling Jean slowly entering him, or so it seemed as she stood on her toes and sunk onto his cock.

He got a shock when her blood started leaking out and dribbling down their thighs. The unexpected delight of this transgression made his cock grow harder, and he thrust more wildly, too aroused to know restraint. Jean was beating her fists against his chest, his back, biting his neck with no concern for bruising.

When Jean asked him to slap her arse Ernie didn't blink, and was astounded by the sudden pleasure as he heard his slap ring out and echo off the rocks. It brought their immediate revelry to an end as the pair of them heaved and shuddered, and when Jean finally caught her breath she could not stop laughing, nor could Ernie stop from joining her. They slowly sank onto the beach. It was uncomfortable on the pebbles. Jean took Ernie's hand and led him to the water. Wading in, scrubbing their thighs to wash the blood off.

Jean dived and swam out into the bay. Turning, treading water as she watched Ernie watching her.

'Not coming in?'

'I can't swim.'

Jean looked startled for a moment, before slowly breast-stroking back to shore. To Ernie's surprise Jean lifted him onto her back, his legs wrapped round her hips, and slowly breaststroked back out into the bay, Ernie clinging to her like a small monkey on its mother's back. Loving this new adventure, while feeling a glint of terror. He didn't mean to grip Jean's neck and shoulders so tightly.

'Don't choke me, man, or we'll both drown!'

Loosening his grip, feeling his trepidation mingling with delight. Jean swimming into the shallow water, slipping out from under him, holding Ernie in her arms so that he floated on his back.

He shivered, and heard Jean say, 'The body's just a meaty bag of water. Breathe deep and hold your air.'

Ernie had never floated, and felt a profound peace as Jean slowly walked around the cove, cradling him, while keeping an eye out for sea urchins on the rocky bed of the bay. Ernie closed his eyes, feeling the gentle rush of water against his skin as Jean propelled and lulled him. When he opened his eyes the sky seemed deeper and bluer, the clouds at once more dense and more translucent. Jean could see him smiling, and kissed him gently then. Ernie closed his eyes once more, his shy lips puckering, and wondered if he'd ever felt so safe, so free of burden. He could not recall a time when he'd felt so full of trust in another. She gently lowered him, helping him find his feet again, the pair of them hobbling from the rocks underfoot. Foraging for driftwood together amongst the rocks and dried seaweed, to build a fire.

As the flames slowly kindled Ernie said, 'You didn't think that I'd be such a goer, did you?' and Jean knew that if he'd ever been a novice, that time was well and truly over.

'Your beast has finally come to roost.'

Feeling a delight, and a culpability, that she had been the agent for his loss of innocence. Pondering an innocence that had once been her own.

Jean looked alarmed. It had turned out just as badly as she'd feared. She'd let herself go and had fallen in love with him. She was afraid of the sadness she knew could only follow, like a bill being delivered, after all that pleasure.

Ernie enquired after her welfare and was surprised when she said, 'I love you so fucking much it gives me the shits.'

AWAKE!

Something was changing in the quality of their lovemaking. A stillness at its centre from which they drew an essential nourishment and vigour.

One morning Ernie had been too tired to come, and to their mutual delight his ejaculation had choked before the imminent eruption. He stayed firm for longer than he believed humanly possible, and they enjoyed this novel, unorgasmic kind of love so much they started to perfect a new technique.

Ernie felt his eyes were growing bluer by the day. He'd stopped shaking involuntarily, as if he'd regained some vital quality of self-control. Feeling some days like a drum skin tightened by the sun. He could see that Jean was also blooming. Her skin seemed tauter, her breasts were not as droopy. Lying with and within each other, quiet as the shadows that slowly crept across the floor and joined them on the bed. A pulsing spring coiled in the midst of a quiet place, that's how their sex appeared to them right then. It seemed the pair of them were growing younger, even as they aged, and the days passed with a speed that seemed a cruelty.

Jean expected nothing more than enjoyment from their mingled pleasures, and was at first confused to feel something like a fire in her belly, though the source of heat was not her belly, nor her fanny, but some point between the two. A core of energy that seemed focused around her pubic bone, and that circulated around her legs and up her spine.

At times they felt a desperation, as if they'd discovered some vital aspect of their mutual company too late in life; they'd forget their quiet meditations as they flailed and thrashed and moaned most gaily on their bed. Not yet cadavered.

As they cavorted Ernie felt that with each extravagant gesture he was letting go of his inhibitions, sometimes as he slipped in and out of her he wondered if he was slipping in and out of consciousness. Relieved to find, after he'd come, that he was still of this earth. He knew, without needing to look, that he was more phallic in his nethers than he'd ever been before. When he rose from the bed this phallic strength stayed with him, and as he went about his day he wondered how he might best use this unexpected encore of vitality.

His fingernails had grown, and were more like claws than nails. His body hair was growing darker and more prolific. The tufts on his arms and body were more akin to fur than the lightly haired profusions he had known. He felt a little pointy-eared and goaty, to tell the truth, even his teeth felt sharper. Sinking his teeth into Jean's neck when they were copulating, glad to find he had such animation in him.

For the first time in his life he felt he was truly awake.

Realising only then he'd been immersed in a present so beguiling he'd managed to put all thoughts of Vronsky's tome out of mind. Now, when he thought about that alarming ledger, and Jean's prominent features so well displayed amongst its pages, he was filled with a terrible agitation. Staring at Jean snoring quietly in his bed, as he pondered the essence of betrayal.

There was a bitter taste in his mouth. He poured some water down his throat, staring out the window at the blackberry vines, listening to the sounds of thorns scratching the walls and roof.

He knew the time had come to tell Jean.

She was stunned as he outlined the parameters of the project, and to their mutual bewilderment, when Ernie finally blurted out that he'd already dropped it into the printer's, Jean appeared to laugh and cry at once, before she slapped him soundly on the face. Oddly enough this seemed to cheer both of them up. She'd bruised her hand on his jaw, yet embraced him with such enthusiasm that for a moment Ernie forgot what had triggered this outburst. Surprised to see her looking at him with something he could only call admiration.

'You stupid bastard, Ernie! I don't think if I want to know what this book says about me. I could guess. You say it's horribly inclusive? Sounds like the day of judgement will come early to Ruination. To tell the truth, I like the sound of it. They'll probably want to kill you.'

They made tea then, the pair of them confounded by this development. As she drank her tea Jean wasn't sure if she was more impressed by Ernie's folly or his bravery.

Ernie started feeling guilty about the defamations that would soon be spread about the living and the dead. He could only imagine the consequences when the document was finally unleashed upon the unsuspecting inhabitants of Ruination. He had a terrible recurring dream. The ancestors were sitting around a square wooden table, it was Ernie's trial, and at the end of the dream the ancestors always pointed at him and shouted 'Death!' in a terrible unanimity. Ernie was trying to fight off a dreadful agitation, yet never quite succeeding.

Without a doubt he would be Vronsky's scapegoat.

Ernie decided to hasten the end, no point avoiding what he knew was inevitable. He started drinking much more than he ever had. He and Jean gorging themselves on double creams, fatty cheeses, ripe camemberts that smelt like dirty socks, strings of fatty sausages sizzling in a pan. Oddly enough the diet seemed to agree with him.

Ernie's smell was getting stronger. Was it the garlic? He wore his smell like a protective sheath. Was it the fragrance of his own ambergris? He worried he might be turning into a walking fart, but people did not avoid him. Down at the market, as he strolled around, people jostled him in a friendly way, as if they were drawn to him. A dog had even tried to mount him, and he could see the funny side of that. The ringing in his ears had quietened, and he was glad of this small reprieve. On his worst days he still felt like an unpeeled sausage, bursting into tears at the sight of a three-legged dog who wet itself while pissing. Remembering the sight of Harness Wilson and his daughters. Couldn't decide who he cared for less, Harness or whatever power or mistake or god that could send a man into the world without his kneecaps.

THE SHIPWRECK BELL

One thing Ernie had never done, yet longed to do, was ring The Shipwreck Bell. It was only rung in the event of shipwreck or other maritime calamity, and within minutes a crew would be assembled by the bay, ready to assist the craft in distress. Even in such a reckless town this prohibition was observed, as all knew the benefits of hearing that bell ring if you were stranded on some boat that was being ground onto rocks inside The Birth Canal.

The only time this prohibition was relaxed was during The Shipwreck Feast, when one citizen took on the role of the Captain Cook of Salvation and rang the bell to mark the end of the six-day fast, thus announcing the dawning of The Shipwreck Feast. An annual pilgrimage of remorse to pay respects to the first dead of a stillborn town. This was always done at four a.m., which was reckoned to be the hour at which the *Good Hope* had come to grief. Its culmination was a gargantuan gorging on the beach as the townsfolk celebrated the ending of the fast and the simple fact that they were still of this world.

As a boy Ernie had often been tempted to ring that bell. He'd been amazed by his foolishness when he realised, some weeks after the death of his parents, that he should have rung the bell instead of standing aghast, watching his parents drown. Perhaps his father's last refrain had not been, 'Things Always Turn Out Badly.' Perhaps The Burner had been shouting, 'Ring the bloody bell!' It did nothing to improve Ernie's opinion of his own intellect, nor did it lessen his desire to ring that bell at least once in his life.

John Gobblelard had assumed the role of Captain Cook to be part of his birthright, and occupied that role each year from the time he'd first taken control of The Bluebottle, Prawn and Oyster. The few foolhardy souls who'd tried to wrest the role from John's hands had all decided to go swimming well before The Shipwreck Feast arrived. Ernie thought it a mere formality that Les would now fill the brother's ceremonial shoes.

The Captain Cook was permitted various liberties, though also undertook some heavy obligations. Among these was the need to organise a boat which sank within sight of land, in emulation of the *Good Hope*. The Captain Cook was also required to provide enough livestock to slaughter on the beach to ensure there'd be a good feed for all who came. Everyone brought some creature to this vast communal slaughter, but the Captain Cook had to provide at least two dozen good-sized beasts, as many of the townsfolk arrived with only one of their scrawniest chickens, or if they were truly desperate an insect or four or five periwinkles scavenged off the rocks. Hardly sufficient to sate the ravening craw of the starving town after six days of fasting and drinking.

THE SLAPPING MAN

The Captain Cook was expected to kill as many of those beasts as possible with his own hands. It was considered a special honour if your beast was chosen by the Captain Cook to be the first to have its blood let on the sands. While John Gobblelard always bestowed this honour on himself, he did his best to kill every beast presented to him. John so looked forward to this annual day of sacrifice that he found it hard to sleep for his excitement. When the seventh day arrived John was sure to stay up all night, boozing in his bedroom, or by the bay, and in this he was not alone. When four a.m. arrived John was always so wild-eyed with fatigue, booze and excitement that he rang The Shipwreck Bell like a madman. You'd swear he was trying to wake the spirits of the dead from their slumber — which, in fact, he was. That was one reason why the bell was rung — to tell those dead spirits that the living wished them well; here they were again, gathered by the bay with their offerings of calves and bulls and sheep and all kinds of living creatures, to appease those poor dead souls who had taken up residence in the ruined hulk of the *Good Hope* on the bottom of the bay.

The fact that Salvation's annual holiday coincided with wintry weather and foul tempests seemed in keeping with the fundamental spirit of the town. The market stayed closed for the entire week. There were few visitors from out of town, and for that week the people of Ruination felt they'd refound some vital aspect of their communal life, such as it was.

The Shipwreck Feast had the saddest fireworks imaginable. No small feat to achieve with consistency over the years. A single catherine wheel turning erratically on a boat whose immediate destiny was sinking. Perhaps a suicidal rocket shooting off into the night. There'd be a moment's elevation then — perhaps this year a rocket might explode in a cascade of showering sparks? This rarely happened, the rocket usually plummeting into the dark waters and drowning its sorrows.

Ernie didn't know whether he was delighted or appalled when Les asked, one night after closing time, if the town might pay its respects to Ernie and The Slapping Man. Would he assume the role of Captain Cook at the coming feast? A considerable civic honour was thus conferred. Ernie had mixed feelings about the slaughtering, yet he had that terrible thrilling urge to ring The Shipwreck Bell. Ernie nodded once, feeling his jaw move up and down like some great lantern. He could tell from the light in Les's eyes that his acceptance needed no words, and the two men drank a quiet ale together, the pair of them avoiding the glass eyes of John Gobbelard which stared at them from behind the bar.

GIANT RAT TRAP

Ernie could not believe how quickly the time had passed. Surely the globe was spinning more rapidly, in an attempt to hasten what could only be his inevitable doom? People had begun to observe the week-long fast. As the days of the fast progressed, their behaviour became more unruly. Ernie thought it a good indicator of what was to come.

Ernie had become possessed by a terrible idea. When *The Encyclopaedia of Betrayal* hit the streets of Ruination he knew there was only one way the town might stop short of self-destruction. The Slapping Man would need to be on hand. How else might the townsfolk vent their rage? He feared the inevitable consequences as the town slowly turned upon itself. He'd never intended to come out of retirement, yet there was no choice. He'd have to service the entire town.

Whenever he thought about it he became so anxious he closed his eyes, hoping to find some respite. Instead he saw a solid concrete wall being slowly struck with a massive hammer, until the wall was reduced to powder. Unwelcome vision of a future he felt certain was his own.

He only hoped that people would agree to his proposition, yet to be announced, that all who felt the need could slap him on the beach. Ernie decided to build a special rampart down by the bay for The Slapping Man's Finale. He was in no doubt he'd be called on to perform. Or would they prefer to tear him limb from limb?

Ernie's labours down by the bay aroused great curiosity. What was he constructing? And for what purpose? At The Bluebottle, Prawn and Oyster Les Gobblelard was running a kind of lottery. You could nominate whatever you thought was Ernie's prime intent. The winner, or winners, would collect the total stake, minus Les Gobblelard's fee of fifteen per cent for administrative expenses. The most popular bet was Gallows, though if that were true the stake would be shared among so many it would bring a poor return. Les was writing all the bets on a blackboard in The Horn Room. Aviary, Bog House and Barn For Burning were all popular. Giant Rat Trap was a favourite among those well acquainted with the family history. Memorial For The Drowned had its backers, though Gallows was the clear favourite, and by a long neck.

Ernie's refusal to discuss his project provoked disquiet, and made some people angry. They hoped he'd slip them a tip, that they might make a killing. He began to wonder if it had been a mistake to locate himself so close to The Bluebottle, Prawn and Oyster. Trying to ignore the threats to his person if he did not explain at once what he was doing. He'd expected to become a target of communal anger, but not so soon.

PART EIGHT:

HOW TO GIVE BIRTH TO AN ENCYCLOPAEDIA

SHARK-SKIN SUIT

On the eve of The Shipwreck Feast the six days of fasting seemed to reach some kind of peak. It was not unusual for brawls to begin, aided by excessive boozing. The smell of sausages hanging over the town like a fragrant fog, reminding them all of the transgressions of the ancestors. To say nothing of their own.

Ernie was wondering what to wear as the Captain Cook. John had always gone as Artemis Gobblelard, with a barrel of rum and the infamous Hellblade.

Ernie scratched his chin. And if he went as John? Struck by a curious notion he laughed then scratched his chin again, muttered, 'But you can't do that!' Laughing again, then nodding to himself. Yes, he'd make an entrance they'd remember when he stepped out as Captain Cook.

Ernie was surprised to find how easy it was to sneak in through the back door of The Bluebottle, Prawn and Oyster. Tiptoeing into The Horn Room. Pausing a moment to ask himself if he knew what he was doing, before deciding it might be better if he didn't.

Slipping into John's flayed hide, wearing the ghastly publican like an enormous glove puppet.

Tucked inside John's tanned pelt Ernie could not believe how free he felt. As if he might do anything he chose, no matter how stupid, or how transgressive. The blame would not be his, but the belated publican's.

Ernie was terrified by the ordeal that lay ahead, and needed a few drinks to bolster his courage. Helping himself to a beer in the ethereal quiet of The Horn Room, looking like John's ghost drinking quietly at the counter.

With the brother dead Les found the old pub scared him when he was alone after closing time. Wishing the pub could stay open all night, that he might have constant company. The eerie presence of John's hide was just a part of his unease. Sure he was hearing sounds he'd never heard before, footsteps in the corridor when he lay in bed with the light out. The brother's ghostly chuckle. Had he come to pay his respects? Looking in, as he so often had, with a friendly goodnight curse before he staggered down the hall and collapsed, fully clothed, in a haze of drink?

It took Les a moment to realise what was wrong when he walked into The Horn Room.

'The brother has gone missing! Or has somebody stolen the brother's bag? Someone has stolen the brother!'

Les had no idea what to do. Wishing the brother was still alive, that he might ask for advice. Had somebody really stolen John? Or had the brother decided to go walking? Les wanted to raise an alarm, yet found the whole thing so alarming it was all he could do to stand in the middle of the room, grappling with an agitation which now made his body tremble.

Les nearly died of fright when he saw the hunched and floppy yet animated form of his dead brother sneaking out the window. Had the brother come back to life? Les wanted to run and greet him, but was so terrified of the apparition that he turned and fled, trying not to scream too loudly, and knew that he was failing in this ambition.

Ernie could feel his blood pumping and rushing within the tight band of his skin. As if he was the stuffing in John's sausage. Or was Ernie wearing John like a giant condom?

Ernie had pulled the stuffing out of John's head and body, pocketing the eyes, before slipping into the hooded cape of John's flayed body. Because Ernie was so much shorter than John, the publican's legs dragged behind him when he moved. It made him look like a shark with a strange split tail. When Ernie slipped John's shark-tooth necklace around his head and jaw, with his great jawprow jutting out John's hide, the apparition was wholly sharky. This was a shark-skin suit the like of which they'd never seen. As if Ernie and John had fused into some strange new creature, The Sharkey Man, and when he stared and those teeth flashed brightly people fled, and that sprightly night shark began to chase them down the slope to The House of Pearls.

Each one was convinced they were the target of the animated, beastly phantom that now pursued them. Their guilts and fears become manifest as they ran, sure the sloppy sounds coming from their beer-filled bellies were the sounds of all their fears now ready to gush out. Becoming certain that they were responsible for John's death. His fatal goring by The Hooves of Heaven was surely an assisted suicide, and had they not all assisted? Who hadn't placed a bet? Who'd have thought a wager might yet become one face of culpability?

Those who could run no further were falling to their knees, bellowing their apologies to this phantom John who seemed to run and crawl simultaneously, his curious half-crouched gait.

Ernie found this unexpected potency made him want to laugh, and the half-strangled sounds that leaked out of his body did nothing to reasssure those who now grovelled before him, convinced their day of judgement had finally arrived.

Shrouded in John's full-length bodycape, Ernie could feel the wind blowing down into his body through his gaping mouth, inflating him; strange inspiration, he didn't know why he began to make a sound that was somewhere between a moan and a shout. The onlookers caught unawares by this, though the entire spectacle had left them dumbfounded. All utterly intent on this strange manifestation, none were moving, or talking, the clear air of anticipation as they waited for what-ever might happen next. Expecting what? Only that whatever might now occur would be unprecedented in the history of the town. A rising dread perhaps the only form of common sense right then.

Ernie felt as if some unfamiliar spirit had taken hold of him. Consumed by a role he'd not thought to perform, his stupid prank propelling him into unfamiliar waters. Perhaps at the moment he'd inhabited John's pelt he had stepped out of himself, and instead of reanimating the foul publican had stumbled into some more ancient and troubling realm. Ernie tried to begin the recitation of the list of the first dead of the town, yet found he could not make it past the first name, Anna Anczel. Could not even make it past the first syllable of the first name. A terrible cry he made now, as if the pent-up rage of all the town's frustrations began to find its voice through him. The rage of those who'd drowned after a long and dangerous voyage with land in sight. The rage of Harness Wilson, that he'd been born without kneecaps. The rage of Jean, that she'd given herself so freely yet been given nothing in return. The rage of a mute young Ernie as he watched his parents drown …

Something of this rage communicated itself to Ernie's onlookers, perhaps they simply recognised some aspect of their far-too-common destinies in the sounds issuing from the shark-skin suit, and gave their voices freely to this uncanny chorus, as if the voices of the living and the dead might join in the expression of a common rage, wracked by the pains and humiliations that beset Ruination's own.

A town where daily life had not become a horrid struggle but had always been one. A rage which expressed their anger that, at least for many, God had died, was dead and buried, yet as they moaned and wailed together there might have been an inkling of some curious resurrection. Was this some appalling new face of a shark god in their midst, or was this just the spectre of the inevitable jaws that would claim them in the end, no matter what they did to convince themselves that life might yet prove to be unending? Their sharkpriest moaning and shrieking, his awkward congregation shrieking with him, as they achieved a unanimity unheard of in the history of Salvation.

The shrieking joining with the wind and waves that seemed to shriek with them, surprised to find that they were somehow become part of the one landscape, the men and women and children and dogs and seabirds and winds and waters all part of a common song, no matter that the song was dismal.

The sound of his voice startled Ernie. Perhaps it was the way John's hide amplified his vocal tones, but his voice sounded deeper, with an authority he'd never heard issue from his larynx. Surprised yet calmed by this, as if a certainty he'd always known had finally claimed him. Surveying the mass of people in the dark, down by the bay. The booming wordless sounds of his own voice.

It took some time for this curdling chorus to peak and ebb and die; in time it did, though not before some had begun to bang their heads against rocks, or the stubborn ground. Those who'd picked up branches thinking to protect themselves from the sharky phantom were striking their foreheads, while others grabbed oars from boats and used the stout handles to batter themselves. Punishing themselves perhaps for the fact they'd ever been born in the blighted town. Many began to sob, collapsing to the ground as their bodies shook and small tears dribbled from their eyes.

It was time for Ernie's next task as Captain Cook. He had to light a lamp they'd salvaged off the *Good Hope*. Carried down to the bay off the pub verandah on this one day of the year. Les passed Ernie a burning taper, a warm glow spread as he lit the wick, and closed the lantern's gate.

Ernie could feel his body begin to shudder, if it was his body. Feeling both more and less than himself, neither knowing nor caring what would happen next. Somehow out of control, become the puppet for some other vital force so much greater than his puny self. Standing on the steps of The House of Pearls, some aspect of his demeanour stilling the sobbing crowd. Unless they'd sobbed themselves out, and wondered with him what would now happen.

Ernie felt an incredible jolt within him, a bolt of energy; he was Shark King, Shark Priest and King Sperm, he opened wide his jaw, the shark teeth seemed to glow in the dark, and the crowd fell silent.

Everyone had heard the stories about the equivalence of Ernie's jaw and male member, though no one was prepared for the sight of the great erection that now issued from the loins of the creature standing before them at The House of Pearls. An astonishment that provoked a dreadful silence as they witnessed this manifestation of a power they had no name for. Standing on the steps he looked like a giant hooded phallus which bore its own second erection between its legs. Looking straight up into the heavens, the shark-tooth necklace might have been mistaken at that moment for some gleaming crown of thorns, or a wreath of teeth garlanding this potent totem.

It was clear this vision was some crazed communion of the human and the animal, the living and the dead, animated by a

spirit of strange potency. They were spellbound, neither shrieking nor feeling mirthful, awestruck rather and void of
animation. How long did they stand there, transfixed by that
sharky pole?

Jean fell to her knees, her pose spread quickly through the
mob, they were all humbled by this. A phallic landshark so
impossible to comprehend or deny its immanence.

Perhaps he truly was enfolded by a godhead and had unwittingly become one face of the sublime? Who knows why,
when her knees grew too sore to remain kneeling, Jean chose to
stand and remove her clothes? Nor why others followed suit.
Why did they all? Standing erect before this erect unbidden god.
Or was it just the beer?

No one was moving, no one felt the cold. No one even
noticed that the winds had died long ago, the shrieking sounds
as it whistled through the trees and by the masts of boats all
dying with it. As if they were naught but mute corpses, stranded
by the waters. Standing, arms by their sides, unfeeling and
unknowing. Had they come face to face with some hitherto
unglimpsed aspect of a calm so profound it was beyond com-
prehension? Joined in a long and silent meditation whose
essential message might have been a kind of peace; as if, at that
moment, the townsfolk had joined with their dead in some
primary observance of a common mortality.

Ernie blinked. He felt he'd been away and come back. As he
blinked that massive organ began to quiver and shrink, then
disappear into the shadows of his shark-skin suit. Heard himself
laughing then, it was as liberating as a glass thrown against a wall
during a wedding feast, and he could hear that laughter bouncing back at him, a crazed embarrassment, perhaps, or recognition
of some vast absurdity they'd all been party to.

The laughter rose and broke and ebbed away with the
changing tide, and as it ebbed Ernie slowly descended from The
House of Pearls and made his way through the throng, which

parted to accommodate his slow progress. As he approached he noticed eyes were lowered, as if none dared look at him at such close range.

Once Ernie made it through the parting seas of this common crowd something changed in his demeanour; as he began to laugh and scream at once, and started running up the hill to The Bluebottle, Prawn and Oyster, no one stopped to ask for whys and wherefores, they merely followed their new leader in a joyful riotous progress up the hill. No one bothered dressing, as Ernie shouted, 'WE'RE NOT GOING HOME TILL THE KEGS ARE EMPTY! DRINK YOUR FILL! NO STINTING!'

Ernie ran into the pub, they followed suit, dashing after that agile creature, Ernie's shark-suit John. Arriving at The Horn Room to find the ghostly publican had thrown the taps open. Ernie was standing on a chair, but it looked as though John had reanimated the ghostly darkness of his domain. Nobody dared to turn a light on, it would have been a gross disrespect towards the dead man. Besides, they were all too keen to have a drink on the house.

'DON'T BE GLOOMY! DON'T BE SAD! DRINK YOUR FILL AND THEN BE HAD! WHAT'S THAT I HEAR? THE VIRGIN WALL IS SINGING!'

In no short time it was. This was a Shipwreck Eve of note. John had never thrown the bar open. Les was so overcome with terror and disbelief he dared not set foot inside the premises. Counting on his fingers as he tried to estimate the number of drinks being taken, the only way he could hold onto his wits.

ON THE BEACH

At four a.m. Ernie ran out of the pub, still wearing John's flayed hide, past The House of Pearls down to the shoreline until he got to The Shipwreck Bell. Grabbing the thick rope with both hands and giving it a tug. Surprised to find how heavy was the bell, how thick the rope. His first attempt produced no sound. Jumping then to grab the rope and use his weight to shift that heavy metal. Relieved when he heard the clapper strike the side of the bell. With his second pull he achieved a much more satisfying result, and kept at it then, jumping in John's skin, grabbing the rope and pulling as he dropped back to the ground.

Dazzled by the sound of The Shipwreck Bell, at close range it was deafening. Ernie kept ringing that bell as if he might yet save his parents if he rang it loud and long enough. Those not already gathered by the shore were streaming out of pubs and houses, stumbling briskly through the fog if they weren't capable of running, pouring down to the shore.

The boat was due to arrive, and no one wanted to miss it. It was considered the worst start to the year if you failed to witness the sinking of the boat. Yet the fog was so thick that if the boat was there it was impossible to know it. Should he wait for the fog to clear, or get ready for the slaughter?

Ernie could see people emerging out of the shadows and the fog, blowing trumpets made from the horns of cows and goats and bulls. Others were blowing conch shells, like an improvised orchestra of foghorns lowing and bellowing as they made their way down to the water. The cows grazing at Whisky Rocks were bellowing back in answer, which only inspired the hornblowers to greater efforts, cheeks puffing out, becoming red-faced as they expelled their noisy air through the bones of dead animals. As the strident noises carried through the fog the dogs began to bark and yowl. Knowing the time to begin the communal sacrifice had come.

Ernie could not get the sound of John's voice out of his head.

'They need the release of that hot animal blood spilling from the neck, Ernie. What can take the place of blood? Who can underrate the need we have to make a sacrifice? How else might we redeem ourselves?'

John's words had betrayed a depth of feeling and subtlety Ernie had not expected from the ungainly publican. He'd never forgotten John's remarks, though wished he could as he contemplated the inevitable. Now he had to wield that knife himself. It seemed easier to kill a fish, letting it die slowly as it flapped and floundered in the bottom of a boat. Wishing the coming task did not make him feel so queasy.

It was a bad time of year to be a chook who'd stopped laying, or the scrawniest piglet in a litter. The most well-off led fat cows, goats or sheep, or tethered whole broods of hens by the neck and dragged them down to the beach. Ernie had bought two dozen calves as his own contribution to the coming feast.

The assembled beasts on the shoreline were as scraggly an offering as had ever been made on the shores of Ruination. Flea-bitten bovines, goats with hipbones protruding from tough hides. Ernie did his best to bolster his courage, and repeated John's phrases under his breath like a prayer. 'What can take the place of blood? How else might we redeem ourselves?' Trying to block out the reservations he harboured about the grisly business. Trying to convince himself this was no time for excessive reason, but rather a day on which excessive unreason was the key to action.

Knowing that he was under an obligation to kill as many of the animals as he was able did nothing to improve his equanimity. John Gobblelard had made it a point of honour to administer what he called 'the fatal kiss' to every beast that was proffered to him. Ernie knew that such a feast of killing was beyond him, and knew as well that he'd have to cut the throat and spill the gizzards of at least one of those bleating, braying creatures.

Les was handing him a knife. Ernie knew without looking it was the trusty Hellblade, handed down from Gunter Gobblelard to John to Les, rumoured to have been used by Artemis Gobblelard himself at the first of what had become their annual day of remembrance. Ernie didn't know why but he couldn't look Les in the eye.

So many faces peering at him, hoping Ernie would lead their offering to the shoreline to be the first sacrifice. He could sense the dismay when he refused to unburden them of the proferred animal.

Ernie chose a small rabbit for his first offering. It was not quite as impressive a gesture as one of the rams or stallions John had despatched in previous years. It was Jean's rabbit, and the smile she gave Ernie when he took it from her made him forget momentarily that he now had to kill the creature. Stroking the soft fur as he and Jean nodded to each other.

Ernie managed to cut the rabbit's throat, and having done so felt such a confused blend of guilt and relief he forgot this was the beginning, not the end, of his ceremonial duties.

He'd never realised how stubborn the life force was, nor how much force he'd need to cut the throat, nor how much time could elapse between those fatal knife strokes and the stilling of the beast, the shudders and moans, the spouts of blood, the smells ... Ernie had forgotten about the gizzards, the heart and lungs and liver, did not know which was which.

Les stared at him, before deciding that Ernie had done the minimum and that he might now intervene before the man rendered the day's food inedible. Ernie was relieved when Les grabbed the knife out of his hand and shouldered him out of the way. Intrigued to see Les reach a hand inside the rabbit's carcass, then carefully remove some internal organ.

'You have to get the bladder out unbroken or the flesh is ruined!'

Ernie nodding with incomprehension. Glad Les knew what he was doing, as if he'd finally become his father's son.

Les stripped and cleaned the carcass, then handed the rabbit back to Jean who held it by the ears. She'd have to take it to the bleeding racks, and then it would be tossed onto one of the many beds of coals that had smouldered on the beach for the best part of a week.

Les started on the next startled creature, a small lamb, and as he cut the throat a glint of determination seemed to straighten his spine and give his knees the strength he needed to hold the beast. Kissing it on the head just as his brother John had done, and every Gobblelard worth the name who'd ever butchered living flesh. Les was surprised to find that single kiss held the potency of a prayer.

Les now worked with such intensity and concentration it seemed he'd entered into some sort of ecstatic killing frenzy. It lasted until he'd slaughtered over twenty animals, there was already the makings of a giant feed. Les collapsed then and started sobbing on the beach. It acted as some kind of signal, as if the key formalities had been concluded. People began to slaughter their own animals; small groups of friends and families were dotted all around the beach and rocks, letting the blood of their chosen sacrifice, and preparing the carcasses for The Shipwreck Feast. The first charred flesh on the coal beds filled the air with heady aromas; after the long fast the smells made some feel instantly delirious with hunger. Everyone knew the hazards of gorging after such abstinence, though it was hard not to overeat, and quite usual to see poor souls collapsing, making themselves regurgitate that they might gorge again. These were the real traditionalists.

Ernie watched as a flock of sheep was driven through the fog, bleating and scampering, shepherded onto the beach, where their throats were cut. The blood of the sheep draining into the sand or running in dark streams into the bay, whose waters now grew pink around the edges. The sharks would pick that scent up soon enough, and there'd be dorsal fins gliding through the water, barely visible through the fog. It was, without a doubt, the very worst day of the year to wade into the bay and go swimming.

It was only then that Ernie realised he'd been so absorbed by this conquest of killing and filling he'd forgotten all about the sinking boat, and didn't give a toss. He just hoped the damn thing had sunk.

HOW TO GIVE BIRTH TO AN ENCYCLOPAEDIA

Ernie had hoped to launch Vronsky's local history at dawn, it seemed auspicious, but had not realised how long it would take to slaughter, butcher and roast the animals for the feast. The sun had risen over the bay and people had only just begun to eat. The slaughter had quelled Ernie's appetite. The dread he felt as he thought about the riot that would erupt when the contents of the encyclopaedia had been digested was a further hindrance to his ability to gorge.

After the feast people were sprawled around the shoreline, doing their best to avoid the puddles of vomit soaking into the sand.

They were at their weakest then, they were defenceless. That's when Ernie drove the spike in. He was a canny little bastard, or else the gods were on his side.

HOW TO GIVE BIRTH TO AN ENCYCLOPAEDIA

They were ready for a bit of history, but had no idea they were about to witness the birth of an encyclopaedia. Nor could they have guessed just how many things would change in its wake. By midday the first copies had been ferried to the beach, and Ernie was impressed by the furious concentration that ensued. He'd never suspected the inhabitants of Ruination might be such devoted readers. Les Gobblelard was somewhat startled to see the title.

'*The Encyclopaedia of Betrayal?* What sort of history's that?'

Ernie didn't like to tell Les just what a definitive account it was. He suspected it would only confirm the distaste the population had always harboured for the past, and was wondering why he'd ever gotten involved with such an unprecedented stupidity. Ernie had taken the precaution of announcing that The Slapping Man would be on hand for all who felt the need, and was already standing on the rostrum he had built.

The table of contents was enough to prompt a general state of agitation. Vronsky had laid the whole thing out like a perverse alphabet of Ruination. A for Adultery, B for Buggery, C for Catastrophes, D for Dooms and Downfalls, and so on. The final entry was Zymosis, an alarmingly full account of the spread of infectious diseases in Ruination. It indicated the extent to which venereal disease had not only infiltrated the entire population but may have been the force driving the town.

Les Gobblelard was staggered to discover what a bastard progeny his philanthropy had spawned. No one complained that it was full of lies. No one was misrepresented, unless being depicted with excessive accuracy is another form of deception. When people had digested enough of the contents, had at least devoured the essential slanders of themselves and their families, they wanted to murder Vronsky, and cursed the fact that he was already dead. Then there was Ernie.

There was one reality that was, however, slowly dawning: it was obvious that *The Encyclopaedia of Betrayal* had been faithful to some curious democratic spirit. No one was spared. It was hard to put on airs and graces when your worst secrets had been made public. Yet everyone was in that boat. All covered in the common mud of their poor infamy. People started laughing at each other, and then were silenced by the laughter that came echoing back. It was a moment without precedent in the history of the town, and there was a curious sense of confusion. It slowly became clear that no one had the first idea what they should do.

Oddly enough, for many people the greatest sense of betrayal and discomfort came not from the revelation of some great infamy. That they could cope with, it even helped exalt their status. What caused most discomfort was the disclosure of some most intimate detail — the need to shave their pubic hair and the manner in which they achieved it, the fact that they'd never been able to stop masturbating on a daily basis — small, defining things that seemed to show them in the truest light of all. Their bathroom secrets, or those of kitchen and bedroom.

They began to see a new rightness in the town's emblem of The Bluebottle, Prawn and Oyster. The bluebottle is transparent. The prawn has a thin shell which is easily ripped away. The oyster, once prised from its shell, is a naked self par excellence, a tremulous pulse of mush, which is how they felt when their failings and infamies were so exposed to public view. Feeling that they were suddenly living in the open, and were utterly defenceless. None of them could point a finger now they knew the worst about each other. Who could take the high moral ground when it was clear they were all in the swamp together?

Ernie was flabbergasted to witness this unexpected hiatus. No one had laid a hand on him. Many were still poring over copies of the encyclopaedia; some wept, others took one look at the title and ran away to hide.

In view of the prevailing confusion, Ernie felt it best to

accommodate a minor change of plan. He cleared his throat and made a small announcement:

'At eleven o'clock tomorrow The Slapping Man will be on hand for all who feel the need to make use of his services.'

Then Ernie briskly walked away. To his amazement nobody tried to stop him.

The arrival of Vronsky's tome on the beach seemed to have stalled their appetites. Their drinking and eating more circumspect now, as if they suddenly had much more to digest than they'd initially apprehended. The slow fires burning all day, and through the night. Delving ever deeper into the entrails of the town. It was more than food for thought. It was a gross cultural slander and communal defamation. It was surely retribution fodder.

There are those who, when faced with calamity, are unable to speak. There are also those who are unable to remain silent. Finally Vronsky stood revealed as one of the latter. Having chewed his lips for years he'd felt the need to make a full confession. Not of his own dismay and calumny, but what one might term their collective cowardice, or villainy. Nor did they suspect that he'd armed himself with such a potent armoury of intelligence. Had the man forgotten nothing in his lifetime? Sitting quiet in the pubs, keeping to himself, rubbing his ears after a hard day's work, and all the while those ears were flapping as he lay doggo, taking them in.

Vronsky's testament cast them all in a bad light, with this small glint of hope: now the worst was known, might they yet have the chance to begin again, freed of the burden of suspecting that any of them might be innocent?

Ernie had landed what became known as The Great Slap, and in that one blow some said he had delivered the town. After a lifetime spent fielding their blows, they had to admit The Slapping Man had copped them a beauty. Despite their misgivings there was a certain admiration. He'd shown himself to be a true child of Ruination at the end. A right bastard of a son.

A SLAPPING FEAST

Ernie was dismayed next morning when he saw the queue. The entire town had turned out. It was not unexpected, though he was sure he'd overestimated his ability to provide this essential service. The entire clan of Hans Magnus had arrived, more than fifty of them standing in a clump. Magna Magnus, his widow, stood resplendent at the head of the queue. *The Encyclopaedia of Betrayal* had outlined the preferred form of sexual expression of Hans Magnus. Rubbing himself between his wife's breasts until he covered her neck in what he called a 'string of pearls'. The House of Pearls would never be the same.

Ernie told himself that he was only Vronsky's scapegoat, and knew that he was lying. He'd given the thing a life. What did he expect? Les was standing in the queue, counting on his fingers, lower lip trembling. Ernie thought Les was trying to calculate just how many slaps he'd need to land to appease the honour of himself, his late brother and the entire Gobblelard clan. The queue extended past the beach and disappeared out of sight beyond The Bluebottle, Prawn and Oyster. The Human Pickle and The Man Who Never Laughs were standing side by side. Ernie could not remember when he'd last seen such a congregation, if ever. Fingering his jaw nervously, waiting to hear the eleven chimes of the town hall clock.

He never got to hear those chimes. A mighty roar spread among the crowd, accompanied by the sound of many hands clapping. The din was such it obscured the sound of the clock, though Ernie was in no doubt the time had come.

People began rubbing their hands together, getting warmed up. The more enterprising ones were doing complicated finger exercises, stretching the joints and limbering their muscles. The chaotic rhythm of the crowd settled into a steady slow hand clap, as people started calling, 'Slapping Man! Slapping Man!'

There was nothing for it. He stepped onto his rostrum, took a single bow, and then announced, 'May The Slapping Now Begin!' To his surprise he saw a figure surging through the crowd. The crowd parting to accommodate her passage. She was possessed of such a righteous fury it seemed she had asserted some kind of moral precedence, as if she might single-handedly achieve their communal retribution.

Jean had been determined to stay away from what she thought was a lamentable gesture on Ernie's behalf. When she read the full account of her own activities in *The Encyclopaedia of Betrayal* her point of view had quickly altered. It included a list of every man she'd bedded. She hadn't known they'd all confessed to Vronsky, bleating about their guilts and their desire to bed her again. Ernie had never seen her so angry. Nor had he ever felt so terrified.

Jean put Ernie over her knee, ripped his pants down, and began to spank The Slapping Man's bare arse. There were roars of approval, and squeals of delight. Each time she struck him the roars and shouts grew louder. Ernie wishing his backside had some of the toughness of his jaw. He could see, between winces, The Man Who Never Laughs looking stunned, shellshocked. Perhaps the exhaustion and the booze had brought him undone.

When he felt her mighty slap he didn't expect to hear laughter break out of the crowd, like a gust of wind. He could feel his legs trembling uncontrollably before he felt the second slap. It was as if his terror at that moment encapsulated the varied terrors of the town, and Jean's fury caught their need for revenge. They had all suffered at the hands of Vronsky's perverse history. Perhaps the week of fasting and drinking had played its part, the laughter began to escalate, and despite the shock of the blows, Ernie felt some small relief.

To his amazement he could see The Man Who Never Laughs begin to quake, and then the astonishing sound of the man's laughter. The Man Who Never Laughs was laughing uncontrollably, his diaphragm discovering an unknown liberty after years of being rigidly controlled. The Man Who Never Laughs was rocking, with a shocked and pained expression on his face, his abdomen seized by a sudden mobility. His laughter booming out above the rest of the crowd. It seemed to fuel the curious humour that was now spreading on the beach. Jean kept on slapping, and with each slap Ernie grew more terrified. The more terrified Ernie looked, the more ridiculous he appeared. Ernie didn't know what to do, beyond trying to shield himself from the blows. His confusion only heightened the odd effect their curious display had upon the crowd. Ernie could see groups of friends and strangers clutching at each other, or holding their sides, gripped by the convulsions of their laughter. Some people had begun to hyperventilate.

Impossible to state with certainty who was the first to

topple to the ground, as entire groups lost their footing, grasped at neighbours, and dragged each other down. The sight of people laughing as they fell, clutching their sides with a laughter they could not choke, spread the hilarity along the beach. It seemed the entire mob had fallen victim to some terrible spasm, the communal diaphragm seized in a curious epidemic of spasticity. The Man Who Never Laughs had turned purple, and gasped for air.

Ernie was flummoxed. He'd not foreseen this possibility, and had no idea whether he had failed in his intentions or succeeded beyond his expectations. He began to grow concerned for the welfare of those sprawled and gasping on the sand and the greater his consternation, the greater the waves of laughter and fitting. The orderly line of people queueing had long since disappeared as those at the rear pushed forward to get a better view of the unfolding scenes of mayhem, only to find themselves caught in the unruly communal tide. There was a terrible crush around the little podium Ernie had built, and the conflict between uncontrollable laughter and the fear of being crushed to death did nothing to ease the growing hysteria.

Ernie began to panic, convinced he was about to witness a communal calamity. He could see The Man Who Never Laughs convulsing in the sand. Ernie escaped from Jean's lap then, pushed through the crowd and slapped him in the face. Jean followed Ernie's lead, and together they made their way through the convulsing crowd, slapping people back to their senses.

In no time at all another mania gripped the crowd. Jean and The Human Pickle had combined forces, taking it in turns to slap The Man Who Never Laughs. He'd become The Man Who Could Not Stop Laughing, though he was not alone. Total strangers slapped each other, regained their breath and senses briefly, only to lose them again as they observed the chronic pantomime that had engulfed them all. Laughing again, and being slapped back to their senses, then slapping others who were at risk of unusual death from convulsive laughter. Some of the slaps were so hard they were answered with closed fists, this only triggered fresh waves of hilarity at the sight of so many scuffles and fist fights.

Jean was swinging a handbag around her head, then whacking it into Les Gobblelard, who was cowering on the ground trying to shield his face and head. Jean didn't mean to start kicking him, but couldn't help herself, and found a new and frightening liberation in the process. Feeling at last some vindication for Les's contribution to the death of Beau.

Les was begging her to stop, and the more he cringed and pleaded the greater exaltation Jean felt and the harder she hit him. Some wicked aspect of her humour had been unleashed, and she might have beaten poor Les to death had she not spied near at hand one of the men who used to call her Footie, and forgotten about Les as she set upon her new quarry. Similar scenes were being enacted all around the beach. It was a re-enactment of an aspect of the first shipwreck like no other, truly embracing the desperation of the shipwrecked company of the *Good Hope*.

It was a monstrous thing. Ernie was glad he was blessed with such a strong jawbone, though it was no help when people kicked or punched him in the stomach. Dodging some blows, copping others, as he ducked and weaved. The Pincushion Man had Ernie in a headlock and was about to punch him in the face. Ernie squirmed, and rammed his jaw into the thin man's kidney, broke his grip, then landed a lovely kick on his Pincushion arse.

The Man Who Never Laughs was staring at them, tears dripping down his cheeks as he clutched his sides. He seemed to be in an hilarity of pain, and he had the surprised look on his face of a man who has realised that he may be about to die. Yet still he could not stop laughing, his body locked into its dreadful spasm, and his plight only triggered further waves of hysterical laughter in some people. Ernie was still trying to dispense corrective slaps to those who were utterly submerged and panicked by their uncontrollable laughter, while around them the violence seemed to ebb and flow. The whole thing was preposterous, yet oddly liberating. Ernie's intended act of penance and benevolence had turned into a wholesale riot.

After perhaps half an hour of this mayhem, a communal exhaustion seemed to overtake the mob. No one had the strength to stand, there were odd flutters of spastic laughter from those who still had the strength for it. The Man Who Could Not Stop Laughing was gurgling face down in the sand, it was enough to send those nearest to him off into titters. It seemed, though, that the thing had run its course.

Ernie was relieved by this hiatus. He felt it was up to him to provide some leadership, he certainly felt responsible for the mob's unruly outbreak. He'd let their dreaded history out of its box, and invited them all to come and take a swipe. He'd hoped to find some small atonement in the deed, instead he'd perpetrated another villainy. He didn't have the strength to laugh, nor did he dare to, fearing that he might trigger a new and fatal outbreak of this violent laughing epidemic. He made his way back to his little rostrum. He didn't know what else to do, and so he surveyed the ruined crowd like a general who has led his troops into a terrible defeat. Or was it a victory?

Looking around him he felt a confused certainty. He'd always felt so separate from the mob, he'd always been He Who Is Slapped. In the midst of the mayhem he'd let himself go and launched a couple of excellent slaps himself. It didn't only thrill him, somehow it made him humble. His hand was hurting, yet he didn't mind that pain. He was surprised to feel that he was just one of the mob.

Looking at the faces on the beach, with no idea what might happen next. He felt a certain peace, and he felt uneasy, and could see just by looking at those faces that he was not alone.

People felt ashamed and bewildered by what they'd seen and done, and yet there'd been a profound satisfaction and release. As if all their pent-up rage had been released in a manner they could never have achieved or known if they'd simply whacked The Slapping Man. This short episode of communal frenzy had been worth a year of letting fly at The Slapping Man.

People realised that for all the bruises, lacerations and bodily harm, they'd actually enjoyed themselves. It was a difficult thing to countenance, yet seemed in keeping with some essential spirit of the town. Or was it a glimmer of a new humanity? There was a curious thought in the back of the communal mind. Something that only later could be articulated. Though as people started staggering off the beach ready for a drink, or were carried home by friends, there were already signs of things to come in those first whispers. Might it not be that they really only needed that one good stoush a year? Purging themselves of villainy and anger, finding the strength to make it through another year. There were answers to the questions which had just begun to form, though none would have dared guess what a fundamental change they'd wreak upon the features of the town. Without realising it they had made The Slapping Man redundant. Who would have thought that The Slapping Man could finally rest in peace, superseded by The Slapping Feast? Or that The Shipwreck Feast would suffer the same fate?

Who knows why Ernie decided to go swimming at the end of that long, strange afternoon. Perhaps he merely intended to wash the dust off his hide. Perhaps his fatigue momentarily overcame his common sense. Had he forgotten how much blood had already seeped into those waters? He waded in up to his waist, enjoying the surge of water around his hips. Was he taken by a shark? Did he slip on a rock? Did The Octopus decide that Ernie's time had finally come? It's true that Ernie seemed to slip, before disappearing beneath the water's surface. Did he hear the desperate ringing of The Shipwreck Bell?

A SLAPPING FEAST

At first the townsfolk thought it was some drunkard's prank. By the time they got a boat out there was no sign of the one they'd called The Slapping Man. What could they do but head back to the pub, and mourn? Returning dazed and emptied, haggard as they drank on through the night at The Horn Room, paying their respects to Ernie and The Slapping Man. Knowing they'd seen the last of a man of unique talent and dedication.

'There's never been a Slapping Man before. I doubt we'll live to see the like again. A great man has been among us.'

Les muttering his quiet words behind the bar, as the drinkers nodded heads in mute approval. So cowed, the wonder was that no one started lowing.

YOU WHINGEY BUGGERS!

A great fog was rolling over the town, and there were those who said The Octopus was so disgusted it couldn't bear to look at them, that the fog wasn't fog at all but The Octopus's ink mingling with the moisture in the air to create a fog of a density never seen before.

The marketplace was empty.

Jean wept for three days, never sure whether she was weeping more for Ernie or herself. Les succumbed to tears as well, as he thought of his poor dead mother eating pumpkin seeds, and his punctured brother. To say nothing of his suicidal father.

After three days Jean couldn't stand the sound of Les's crying any more. She shouted at him, 'Cheer Up!' Looking at the maudlin drinkers staring at John Gobblelard's flayed body, the whole lot of them gone all weepy. Wondering had Jean lost her mind as she stood on the bar shouting.

'Cheer up, you whingey buggers! Cheer up, for God's sake, it's not that bad! Get out, the lot of you, we're closed for renovations.'

Sweeping the teary drunkards out the door as if they were the leftover butts and dregs of some binge.

That bloody rhino's head was going. So was the groper's. The whole maudlin bestiary of beasts killed by John Gobblelard was going, to say nothing of the flayed carcass of the late publican. Though Les looked troubled by this last pronouncement. As an interim measure he finally agreed to lock the brother in a cupboard.

As people stumbled outside they had trouble seeing. Their eyes were watering and blinky. For a moment they couldn't fathom what had happened, and only slowly realised that the inky fog was lifting, and they had sunshine in their eyes. The bay was an uncanny golden green.

Jean stood on the threshhold of the pub, surprised to find herself giving thanks to whatever powers had formed her world. Glad if nothing else that she had known Ernie. Finding a rightness in her capacity for grace, villainy, restraint, abandon, despair, grief, even hope. No longer demanding of herself an impossible perfection or wickedness. Her personal darkness and her light were both parts of her small totality. Telling herself she was equal to anything that life might hurl at her.

Deciding to take herself down to the bay. Wading in the shallows, feeling mournful as she thought of Ernie, their brief idyll sundered. Despite the cold she threw herself into the water. Stunned at that moment to realise she really was a woman of water, part of some elemental lifeforce and lifethrob.

Perhaps it was possible, after all, that the face of the divine was as open-handed and permissive as she'd dared imagine.

Feeling she'd found some place within herself, a place she could reside, with all its comforts and discomforts.

Appalled and yet delighted to think she might have finally come to terms with her nature, even if she'd had to utterly embrace her grief to achieve it.

Finding her own sense of a possible sacred, the bay might be her church, all she'd ever needed, or would need. Seeing her swimming as a kind of moving prayer, she swam with bold deep strokes out into the wide mouth of the bay.

CREATURES OF RIDICULE

If one speaks of The Slapping Man now it is not without misgivings. Was he the best or worst among them? Had he not betrayed them all? Or were they liberated, even as he forced upon them the burden of a terrible responsibility — forcing the truth down their throats, not caring whether they might choke as they tried to swallow it.

It's difficult to countenance the intestines of history, especially when they've been devoured. Yet The Slapping Man helped them finally digest the terrible truth of their beginnings, to say nothing of their middles and their ends. They did not feel so mired by the horrid history of the town. It was, after all, their own.

Odd that a man they spent their whole lives slapping was the one who finally knocked a bit of sense back into them.

Les looked as if he'd been relieved of a burden, having had the faults of himself and his family so publicly aired. He decided to change his name. He was sick of being a Gobblelard, and called himself Les Eatfish. He liked the sound of it, though every time someone called his name it made him hungry, and he was putting on a lot of weight. He decided to change his name again, calling himself Periwinkle. He liked that even better, and could eat a lot of periwinkles without getting any fatter.

Periwinkle was surprised one day to find a single bone lying on the shore at Knowledge Point. The sea creatures had done a good job. Ernie's jaw, as clean as a wishbone. Wrapping it in his shirt he carried it like a precious relic and put it on the counter of The Horn Room. After much discussion he decided to do the right thing, putting Ernie's mighty jaw in its own glass case in the back bar of The Bluebottle, Prawn and Oyster.

Every other bastard swears they've got a clavicle, or fibula, or bit of sternum. The town still full of frauds and liars.

Periwinkle decided that each year *The Encyclopaedia of Betrayal* would be updated, using one half of one per cent of his weekly takings. People who felt they'd not been infamous enough in the first edition began stealing, or committing adultery. It was unfortunate that people who'd lived exemplary lives felt compelled to commit some gross offence, just to ensure they'd find their place in that mighty ledger. They all wanted their little place in history.

The transformation of The Shipwreck Feast into Slapman's Wake has been perhaps the most remarkable of the many transformations that have occurred in Salvation. A day when their worst aspects are celebrated. The new edition of the encyclopaedia always helps to fuel a necessary rage. Some people take precautions, padding themselves and wearing helmets. When the Captain Cook announces, 'May the slapping now begin', the whole town ducks, and one vast communal blow announces the beginning of ceremonies.

CREATURES OF RIDICULE

It's become a big attraction, and people come from other towns for a week of fasting and drinking, and then that great communal stoush. Who would have believed that Salvation's ruination would beget Ruination's salvation? People print their own bootleg additions to the encyclopaedia, listing all their worst attributes, and circulate them around the town. It seems there's no such thing as a secret life these days. It's a terrible infatuation, and once a person's ill-repute is public knowledge there is no going back. Their good name is squandered, their villainy revealed. There is one compensation: they've become a member of that preposterous commonwealth, a creature of Ridicule, no less. Some claim this is the new name of the town.

FAREWELL TO SALVATION

To their surprise something of Ernie's odd legacy lifted the local's spirits.

The town seemed more confident in its identity. Almost a cocky tone in the voice when people said, 'Welcome to Ruination.'

A giant replica of Ernie's jaw was erected near The House of Pearls. Built with the jackpot of The Man Who Never Laughs. When people arrive by boat it is the first thing they see.

There'd been so many oddities in Ruination. Yet The Slapping Man was unique. It was only later that other places tried to claim him as their own, as stories of his exploits spread, spawning broods of imitators. Though they'd always know the truth. The Slapping Man was a native son of Ruination, growing out of the muddy soil of the local psyche. No other town could have produced such a prodigy. No other town would have felt compelled to make such free use of his service. In any other place The Slapping Man might have enjoyed a brief renown before slipping into obscurity. They had all helped to make him what he was. They were enthusiastic slappers.

He was as unique to Ruination as The Octopus, that fatal, single-minded, many-tentacled current. No other place could boast a current like it. And it wasn't just The Octopus. Where else but Salvation were found such diverse species as The Man Who Never Laughs, or The Humans Pincushion and Pickle? To say nothing of a bayside pub of charm and beauty with a Virgin Wall possessing magical properties of deflowerment and dereliction?

They no longer felt the need to claim they were better than other places. If they were no better, it came as a shocking comfort to realise that they were no worse. It did nothing to improve their estimation of the world at large, and yet they felt a wee bit better about themselves. Even if they all agreed the world must be a wicked place.

Periwinkle finally decided to get rid of John's flayed body. Even if he was dead, it was never too late to go swimming. Periwinkle took him out to the end of the pier and gave him to The Octopus. For some reason The Octopus seemed reluctant to have him. Poor John's body kept getting spat out of the bay and washed back onto the beach. His body tossed back in, staying out of sight for several weeks, only to be regurgitated once again. Some people swore the fatal current was playing a game with Periwinkle, but if that was true they'd have to say The Octopus was winning.

After several months of this losing game Periwinkle decided to do the decent thing and had the brother put back in his rightful place, looking down over the till in the back bar. His periods of immersion and drying in the sun had left John rather salted and somewhat barnacled. It only made him seem more at home in his preferred locale. Jean decided to put the fish back in. Even that bloody groper's head. She nailed the rhino's head over the women's toilet.

The exploits of The Slapping Man grew, post mortem, into yet another aspect of his identity. Those who'd never utilised his services became experts, confessing their addiction and their need, the sleepless nights as they wrestled with their desire to go and slap him, while feeling that to do so would be to perpetrate some calumny. And as they bragged and boasted to some group of drunken strangers, they cursed themselves for missing out on what was, without doubt, the defining moment in the town's short life. Why had they been so stupid and not realised they'd been face to face with history when The Slapping Man was alive? Why had they not seized their chance? Growing more sullen the more they drank and boasted, until they lost control. Turning on some poor soul as they swaggered drunkenly, saying, 'Do you know how it really felt to be The Slapping Man?' At the inevitable shaking of heads and mumbled No's they'd slap the faces of those who listened, before saying deadpan, 'It felt like that, exactly, with this one difference: The Slapping Man was not able to feel a thing!'

Stumbling out into the night, weaving down to the bay, collapsing drunk against a tree. Wondering, in their stupor, if it were true The Slapping Man was numb and felt nothing his whole life. Or had he felt more of the town's living pulse than any other, and it had been the slappers who'd been dead to the life that thrilled and throbbed around them?

ACKNOWLEDGEMENTS

The *Slapping Man* grew from work begun in 1988, alongside *The Breadmaker's Carnival*. Now it's 2003, and many people have assisted the writer in the completion of this work.

A stray remark of the late Frank Ponton's around 1977 lingered until in 1988 it sprouted as 'Ernie's Dream', *The Slapping Man's* midden. Frank was a theatre director and head of the Communications Department, Mitchell College of Advanced Education, from 1972 to 1974. In 1977 I made my first foray as a street clown with Michael Shirley in Bathurst, and was set upon by a small mob of local kids — something of this preposterous spectacle has also stuck to *The Slapping Man*, so thank you Michael!

A chance encounter with *Brewer's Dictionary of Phrase and*

Fable in 1996–97 provided an important spark (cf Buckhorse). Thank you Greg McCart.

'Those who have not sinned will know only the minor of what we feel' is, I believe, a phrase or paraphrase of Rasputin. Source unknown.

The Man Who Never Laughs owes something to François Rabelais. Milan Kundera's *The Art of the Novel* (Faber & Faber) contains a discussion of Rabelais and his invented word 'agélaste', a man who never laughs — cf Part Seven.

A discussion of the physiology of 'laughing epidemics' can be found in F. Gonzalez Crussi's *Three Forms Of Sudden Death* (Picador).

Crowds and Power by Elias Canetti (Peregrine) remains a source of astonishment, puzzlement and dismay.

Many thanks to the Eleanor Dark Foundation for a New Writer's Fellowship to Varuna in 1997, and a Writer's Fellowship in 2000. Particular thanks are due to Peter Bishop, Inez Brewer and Sheila.

Many thanks to Wendy Guest, Paul Sommer, George Quinn, Christine Rijks, Janet Fulop, Gogo della Luna, Jocelyn Harewood and Jeannine Fowler for critical responses to the work-in-progress.

This project has been assisted by the Commonwealth Government through the Australia Council, its arts funding and advisory body. Residencies at the Tyrone Guthrie Centre, Ireland, and the B R Whiting Library in Rome were vital to the work's propulsion.

Thanks also to the Australian Ireland Fund, past and present staff of the Australian Embassy to the Republic of Ireland, especially David Keyes, Tom Sinkovits, Ambassador Bob Halverson, Michael Roche; staff of the Australian Embassy to Italy, especially Clelia March Doeve; Lorrie Whiting; Mike Cooper and Maria Galante; Gachi, Elfi Perkhofer, Roberta Begnoni and Besito de Coco; Eduardo Lamora; Professor

ACKNOWLEDGEMENTS

Bernard Hickie, members of the Berkeley Circle in Lecce; Giovanni, Rita and Paula Corallo; Rosaria; Professor Anthony; Professor Guiseppe Serpilo; Luciana Balbitu and the Balbitu family; the Red Lion mob; Roberto; Angelo; Angelica Turno; Giancarlo and Laura; Professor Maureen Lynch Pèrcopo, Dotteressa Luisa Pèrcopo and staff at Cagliari University; Giorgio and Giulia Donati; Jacob Olesen, Anna Maria and the boys; Compagnia Donati-Olesen; Nicoletta Boris and Otto, Boris and Luce; Stefano Buscaglione, Marina Senese, Sebastiano, Caterina and Margherita; Patrizio Lloyd and family; Il Lanternone and Lupo; Franco, Raimonda, Pietro and all at Valebona; Filippo; Ingo and The People Upstairs; Bern and Wil at Daffy's in Limerick; Nuala Shine; David and Molly and The Shoebox; Staff of Bewley's Theatre, Dublin; Kavisha Mazzella, Rusty Stewart, Carmel and Francesco Davies; Betty France, Robert, Oscar and Luigi; David Walker, Jason Twomey and Blind Man Driving; Wendy and Hair Off Bellair; Carolyn Atherton, Jac and Dave and Alex and Amelia; Keith and Lettuce Deliver; Sara Jefferson and Kensington Natural Therapies; Atlas and Tokai; The Rockin' Dr Robyn Rowland, Norm and The Buzz Boys; The Peanut Man; Listowel Writers' Week; Billy Keane; Stephen Newman and Mike in Limerick; Peter Baxter and Jane Fitzpatrick; Templebar Properties; Mike Maloney and Prison Arts Foundation, Belfast; the 'DOC'S' at Maghaberry Prison; staff of Tyrone Guthrie Centre, Annaghmakerrig; Gráinne Millar; the Irish Writers' Centre; Peter Sirr; Seamus Hosey; Rónán Ó'Snodaigh; Marian Finan Hewett; Rita at Dœn Laoghaire; Zannie Flanagan; Paula Jenkin and the 'cheese maidens' at Woodside Cheesewrights; Simon and Thunderbird Catering; Sarah Stegley, Marieke Brugman and Howqua Dale Gourmet Retreat; Joy Durston and Claude Forell; Vito; Denise; Peter Orchard, Jacqui and Nick; Vilia Dukas and Leigh; The Edible Carnival Band in Melbourne and The Edible Scratch in Dublin; Kerry and Porter's Bookstore, Kensington; Craig Watters and the crew of the Volcano; Australian Society of Authors, especially José Borghino and Rob Pullan; John West, curator of Australian Shark Attack File, Taronga Zoo; Louise Byrne; Terry and Leah; Gaby Naher and Jill Hickson.

Peter Leovic for years of good advice; Helen and Jordan; Elias Ellis; Anna Tranter; Anne Rattey; Trish Solomon; Paul Laszlo and Ann Palumbo; Gabrielle Carey; Deborah Harbin; Dawn Gardiner and family; James Royal; Barbara Biggs, Heather Walkerden and Erika; Enric Monforte, Dr Susan Ballyn and staff of Barcelona University; Ip Michael and Vagn Lundbie.

And of course my family, whose constant support has made all the difference — especially Phil, Hilarie, the Rijks mob — Christine, Col, June, Adam, Philippa and Annabel — Ingrid Bell, Graeme and Lindsay Orr, and my sister and family in Perth.

Thanks to all at Allen & Unwin, in particular Annette Barlow, Jemma Birrell, Christa Munns, Julia Stiles, Sophie Cunningham, Tabitha King, Ali Lavau and the reps who did such a great job last time!

To the many others who've helped the writer and who are not mentioned, thanks to you all!

In closing I'd like to acknowledge my endebtedness to Frank Ponton, Dorothy Hewett, Owen Weingott and Jacques Lecoq. They shared a love of theatre and language, and expressed it with exuberance, drive and wisdom. Each, in their way, has been a source of inspiration. They were forces of nature and remain, for me, vital presences. May their spirits travel well.